PRAISE FOR *BREAKERS*

'*Breakers* is as brutal as it is tender, as emotionally compelling as it is nerve-shredding and action-packed. Set to be one of the stand-out crime novels of the year' Chris Brookmyre

'This may be Doug Johnstone's best book yet. An unsparing yet sympathetic depiction of Edinburgh's ignored underclass, with terrific characterisation. Tense, pacey, filmic' Ian Rankin

'*Breakers* is absolutely what great crime fiction should be – a cracking story, great characters, but it's also *about* something and really addresses the "whys" of crime' Mark Billingham

'Doug Johnstone is for me the perfect free-range writer, respectful of conventions but never bound by them, never hemmed-in. Each book is a different world, each book something new in this world' James Sallis

'*Breakers* again shows that Doug Johnstone is a noir heavyweight and a master of gritty realism. This may be his finest novel yet' Willy Vlautin

'*Breakers* is bloody brilliant. Gut punch after gut punch after gut punch and you can't put it down. But it's the final, huge punch to the heart that blows you away. Pages you can't stop turning, characters that linger long after you've finished the book. This is premier-league crime writing' Martyn Waites

'Doug's books are what the phrase "no filler, all thriller" was invented for. His no-nonsense style is tight and taut but still carries emotional depth. A tough, gritty and effective ride into the dark side of Edinburgh' Douglas Skelton

'I absolutely loved *Breakers* ... Doug does characters so well, and this cast are perfectly drawn. The tale is both horrifying and uplifting, and one of those books I looked forward to picking up each time I had a moment to read...' James Oswald

'Pacey, harrowing and occasionally brutal, it's a stunning thriller about poisonous families and one decent kid's desperate attempt to do the right thing. It had me in tears at the end. I couldn't recommend it more' Paddy Magrane

'I thought *Fault Lines* was good, but *Breakers* is off-the-scale amazing! Stayed up almost all night to finish it. Absolutely brilliant' Louise Voss

'Oh. My. God. This was sooo good. Read it in two days. Gripping, dark, fast, but still somehow full of heart' Louise Beech

'A tightly plotted and unflinching story ... *Breakers* is only a short book but it punches well above its small page count for both character and story depth, giving the reader a deep and profoundly human story' The Tattooed Book Geek

'I had my heart in my mouth at several points, particularly near the end of the book when danger was never far away. But above all, it's a darkly brilliant thriller filled with tension and humanity' Portobello Book Blog

'Gritty, brutal, shocking and heartbreaking ... I struggled to put it down' Off-the-Shelf Books

'Doug Johnstone writes gritty, grimy crime fiction like no one else. It's a raw, visceral visit to Edinburgh, with top-notch writing and dialogue that spits out at you from the page' The Book Trail

'Harrowing, heartbreaking and brilliant' Goodreads reviewer

'I'm speechless, emotional and just in awe of Doug Johnstone's *Breakers*. I feel completely catatonic from the dark, despairing plot. Pure brilliance! This will definitely be one of my books of the year' The Reading Closet

'The main characters leap off the page and into your head and remain there. It's hard to put this book down once you start' Amazon reviewer

'A fantastic read, heartbreaking, brutal, compelling' The Book Review Café

'It's as psychologically rich as it is harrowing. I've come to expect nothing less from Doug Johnstone, one of the genre's premiere writers' Megan Abbott

'Doug Johnstone has crafted a superb, highly original psychological chiller ... a masterclass in suspense' Steve Cavanagh

'Once again Doug Johnstone shows why he's at the forefront of Scottish crime fiction's new guard' Eva Dolan

'Creates a world so convincing you find yourself forgetting it is a work of fiction. Richly characterised, beautifully crafted, this is a book that you truly inhabit. A true must-read' Emma Kavanagh

'Sexy, fearless and addictive ... Doug Johnstone just gets better and better' Helen FitzGerald

'Johnstone weaves his compelling and original tale with great skill and elegance from the gripping beginning to a tense and explosive end' Amanda Jennings

'I'm a massive fan of Doug Johnstone's books ... From its chilling opening to its explosive ending, this is a thriller not to be missed. Superb!' Luca Veste

'Doug Johnstone manages the rare feat of bringing something truly original to the crime genre. Blending powerful imagination and plotting, this is the work of a writer at the top of his game' Stuart Neville

'Brilliant premise, fascinating setting, great characters and a story that plays with every single emotion. Doug Johnstone is an excellent writer who tries new things with every book, and always succeeds' SJI Holliday

'With its brilliant sense of place and uneasy atmosphere throughout, this had me hooked from the first page' Cass Green

'I was completely swept away by this story with its wonderful setting, short, fast-paced chapters and thoroughly satisfying ending' Caroline Mitchell

ABOUT THE AUTHOR

Doug Johnstone is the author of nine previous novels, most recently *Fault Lines* (2018), with several of his books becoming bestsellers and award winners. He's taught creative writing and been writer in residence at various institutions, and has been an arts journalist for twenty years. Doug is a songwriter and musician, with five albums released in various bands and three solo EPs, and he currently plays drums for the Fun Lovin' Crime Writers, a band of crime writers. He's also player-manager of the Scotland Writers Football Club. He lives in Edinburgh.

Follow him on Twitter *@doug_johnstone*.

Breakers

Doug Johnstone

**ORENDA
BOOKS**

For Tricia, Aidan and Amber

Orenda Books
16 Carson Road
West Dulwich
London SE21 8HU
www.orendabooks.co.uk

First published in the United Kingdom by Orenda Books, 2019
Copyright © Doug Johnstone, 2019

A catalogue record for this book is available from the British Library.

ISBN 978-1-912374-67-0
eISBN 978-1-912374-68-7

Typeset in Garamond by MacGuru Ltd
Printed and bound by CPI Group (UK) Ltd, Croydon CR0 4YY

For sales and distribution, please contact: *info@orendabooks.co.uk*

1

Tyler stared at his little sister as she watched television, the light from the screen flickering across her face. Some cartoon about a boy who discovers a magic ring and turns into a superhero girl, so there was some cool gender stuff in it. Bean chewed the edge of her lip then smiled, and he saw the space at the front where her baby tooth had come out. He'd scrambled together two quid from the tooth fairy once he found out from her what the going rate was in the playground. He was surprised she still believed in that, given everything else that was going on.

'Right, Bean, time for bed,' he said.

She shook her head, still looking at the television.

He reached for the remote and the screen died, just soft light from the corner lamp remaining.

'It's way past bedtime,' he said. 'And I need to go out soon.'

Bean turned round. 'Where's Mum?'

'In bed.'

'Is she drunk?'

Tyler sighed. 'She's tired.'

'She's drunk.'

Let her think Angela was drunk, the truth was worse.

Bean played with Panda's ear. Tyler had lifted the toy from a house in Merchiston on a job years ago. He'd felt bad for a moment, but the kid had a hundred soft toys lined up on her bed, and Bean had nothing. He wondered if the other girl cried when she realised Panda was gone.

'Can we go on the roof?' Bean said.

'No, come on.'

'Please.'

'It's school tomorrow.'

She gave him a look, chin down, eyes up, like a Manga character. 'Pleeeeease.'

Tyler looked at his watch. What difference did it make in the scheme of things? He looked around the tiny living room, two ragged sofas, scratchy carpet tiles, bar heater in the corner. The only expensive thing was the Sony LCD widescreen he'd taken from a mansion in Cluny Gardens that backed onto Blackford Pond. They wouldn't normally bother with televisions, they were a pain to carry, but he wanted it for Bean.

'Just for a minute,' he said.

She smiled and hugged him.

'I mean it,' he said, 'I have to go out. Barry's coming round.'

Bean frowned and Tyler regretted mentioning their half-brother. He held out his hand and she took it, her hand clammy in his as he led her down the hall.

He lifted the keys from the wooden crate that served as a table at the front door. He picked up the hook-and-stick that he'd improvised from a curtain rail, and a blanket bundled on the floor. Bean was in her jammies and onesie and it would be cool up top, any breath of wind turning into a gale this high up. It swept down from Liberton Brae, over the hospital and the flat expanse behind Craigmillar Castle, and with most of the other tower blocks knocked down, theirs took the brunt of it.

He put the door on the snib and headed along the corridor, away from the lift and the other flat, where Barry and Kelly lived. Barry had intimidated a Syrian family into leaving months ago, and now the Wallaces had the floor to themselves like a downmarket penthouse apartment.

Tyler used the hook to open the hatch in the roof and pull down the aluminium ladder. He climbed up with the blanket over his shoulder and the keys in his hand and undid the padlock on the steel door at the top. This was a service-access door, but he'd jimmied the original lock and replaced it with his own years ago, and the maintenance guys never came up here.

He looked down at Bean. 'Up you come, but use both hands.'

She placed Panda on the floor and climbed the ladder. He helped her at the top then pushed the heavy door open and felt the cold air on his face. He switched on the torch on his phone and they walked across the scabby tarred roof to the western edge where there were two folded garden chairs. He unfolded one and sat, and Bean clambered into his lap as he spread the blanket over them both. He switched the torch off and the darkness swallowed them.

They were fifteen floors up at the top of Greendykes House. Across from them was the identical Wauchope House – they were the only two tower blocks left in the area. They were surrounded by waste ground and a huge building site where Barratt were creating Green-acres, hundreds of apartments and homes. That's what it said on the large sign with the happy, smiling family on it. For now it was just diggers and rubble surrounded by razor wire and patrolled by private security. Presumably in case someone felt like stealing a digger, some cables or piping. Tyler thought about the logistics of lifting something so large, but he was used to smaller items.

He thought about what it would be like, having hundreds of new neighbours once Greenacres was built. Couldn't be any worse than the shithole it was before, burnt-out houses and tumbledown shops, drug dens and gang hangouts. The streets used for racing hot-wired cars and boosted scramblers.

Past the floodlit, fenced-off area was more scrubland, thick grass and broken concrete until you got to the futuristic spread of the hospital at Little France. Grassy tussocks and clumps of hedge spread uphill to Craigmillar Castle, the ragged turrets just poking through the trees at the top of the slope. Both Tyler and Bean's schools were hiding beyond the trees, fenced off and watched by CCTV.

The space between here and there was a big fly-tipping site, a tangle of rubber tubing, soggy mattresses, a couple of car doors, a shattered windscreen, piles of bin bags full of Christ knows what, some broken fencing once used to keep someone out of somewhere. He could see it all in the security spotlight overspill from the building site. He glanced at Wauchope House, the twin of the tower block they were on. He never understood why they didn't tear down these last two dinosaurs with the rest of the place. Hadn't just carpet bombed the whole of Niddrie, Craigmillar and Greendykes and be done with it. Beyond Wauchope was a spread of new homes, cheap and thrown together, but still better than what they replaced. At the back of Greendykes House was Hunter Park then more developments, all of Edinburgh's brown-belt land being reclaimed for commuting professionals.

'Tell me again,' Bean said, snuggling into him. A strand of her dark ponytail had come loose. He'd given her a bath earlier and she smelled of strawberry shampoo.

'It was a dark and stormy night,' he said, putting on a dramatic voice.

Bean giggled as he tickled her ribs.

'A fateful night,' he said, 'when the world's greatest superhero, Bean Girl, was born, a force for good battling the dark, evil powers of Niddrieville.'

'Go on,' Bean said.

'Angela was just a normal woman from a normal family, when she was visited by space aliens who told her she was to have a beautiful baby daughter with special powers, a girl who could fly, smash tall buildings and leap over mountains, who could shoot lasers from her eyeballs.'

Bean stared at the hospital in the distance and widened her eyes, made cute little laser-fire noises, *tchew-tchew*, *tchew-tchew*.

Tyler kept talking, making up stuff whenever it came to him, giving Bean Girl immense powers, making her triumph over evil. The truth about her birth was less impressive. Angela's waters had broken when she was off her head on heroin and vodka. Barry and Kelly weren't around and weren't answering their phones, so ten-year-old Tyler had to try to sober Angela up before heading to the hospital, so they wouldn't take the baby away when it came. He called an ambulance but they'd had a spate of attacks in the area and refused to come. There was no money for a taxi so they walked across the fields, slow in the dark, and presented themselves at the maternity ward with no paper-work. Two hours later Bethany was born, four and a half pounds and six weeks early, no doubt from the booze and drugs. Tyler was the first person to hold her, his mum out for the count. Both he and Bean were small for their ages, something they shared, a bond stronger than anything either of them had with Angela.

He felt Bean sagging on his lap, her arms becoming heavy as she tired. He stared at the hospital where she was born, it was like a glowing spaceship in the night.

He heard footsteps on the ladder behind them, then the clatter of the steel door as it swung open.

'Thought I'd find you girls here.'

Barry strode over and was silhouetted against the security lights below on the building site. Tyler couldn't see his face, just the muscle-bound shape of him, the hardman stance, fists clenched. He was a source of darkness, a lack of light.

'She should be in bed,' he said.

'Like you care.'

Barry took a step forward and Tyler felt Bean flinch in his arms. Barry stared at her for a moment then turned to Tyler.

'Come on, bitch,' he said. 'We've got work to do.'

2

It took just ten minutes behind the wheel to get from the most deprived scheme in Edinburgh to millionaires' homes. From Niddrie they cruised through Craigmillar on the main road, past Peffermill and the biscuit factory, the smell of burnt oats coming to Tyler in the back of the car. Round Cameron Toll and they were into the affluent Southside. He wondered if people around here even knew that Niddrie and Greendykes existed. Edinburgh was so small that everyone was cheek by jowl, investment bankers round the corner from families like the Wallaces. Most of these people were ignorant of the fact they were being stalked and targeted. This was their hunting ground, from Mayfield through Newington and Marchmont, down to The Grange, Morningside and Merchiston. Every once in a while they would explore a little further, into the New Town and Stockbridge. It kept the heat off if they'd had a close shave. Sometimes it made sense to leave the Southside fields fallow for a while, give homeowners time to relax and lower their guards again.

They turned up Mayfield Road, left into Relugas, then into the smaller streets. They stayed off the main thoroughfares and stuck to residential areas, less passing traffic and more chance of going unnoticed.

Barry was driving, Forth One playing a stream of charmless pop on the radio. Tyler's half-sister Kelly was chopping out coke lines on the car's manual, pulled out of the glove compartment and placed on her knees. They were in Barry's metallic-grey Skoda·Octavia, boosted a year ago from outside a place in Sciennes when they found the keys in a bowl next to the front door of the house. It'd been fitted with new plates by Barry's mate Wee Sam at his garage. An Octavia was perfect, a nothing kind of vehicle, not flashy or tacky, and every second car on the road these days was grey.

Tyler watched Kelly. She was twenty but looked older, tall and broad, peroxide hair. Wide nose, wide hips, wide shoulders, everything about her was wide. Her bright hair wouldn't make any difference for the job, they always had their hoods up in case of CCTV. Like Tyler and Barry, she was wearing a nondescript hoodie and joggers, Primark's finest, no logos or patterns.

They were in Lauder Road now. Some colossal houses here but the road was wide and exposed. Barry slowed the car but not too much, he didn't want to be conspicuous. There were 20 mph limits all over the city now which helped them, allowed them to go slow and check the area without seeming suspicious.

Kelly bumped a large line of coke then passed it to Barry, holding the rolled-up note for him so he didn't have to take his hands off the wheel. He kept his eyes on the road and snorted, shook his head and flexed his jaw.

Kelly reached over and placed her finger under his nose, wiped up some grains there. She held the finger out to Barry, who leaned forward, sucked it and grinned.

Tyler looked out of the window, checking for houses with no alarms and lights off like he'd been taught. Preferably detached in case the neighbours heard something, but it was amazing how seldom that happened. People don't like to get involved in someone else's business, especially if that business could get them hurt.

'Some fucking gaffs, these,' Barry said, jittery now from the buzz. They never offered Tyler any, mostly because they wanted it for themselves, but also because they knew his stance. He'd seen what drugs did to their mum.

Barry turned right into the narrower, winding Dalrymple Crescent. Quite a few candidates here. It wasn't a school holiday, that was their busiest time, when homes were empty for weeks. But rich people had social lives, they'd be out at dinner or a party, the theatre or cinema. It didn't take long, this thing, in and out in minutes.

Tyler hated that he knew all this. He didn't want to be here but he had no choice. Barry and Kelly needed someone small to squeeze into top-hung fanlight windows if the doors were deadbolted. He could fit and he couldn't say no. Barry was already making noises about bringing Bean along instead and Tyler couldn't allow that.

Barry came to the end of the road and turned right into Findhorn Place, then down to the bottom and right again. They went round the block, Kelly doing another line, then Barry too. Back in Dalrymple Crescent. Barry had spotted a place. Tyler had too, he just hadn't mentioned it. When they passed the second time, he took it in more fully. Semi-detached, but no lights on in either house, low horizontal fence at the front. No alarm box, security lighting or cameras, a handful of mature trees in the front providing cover and suggesting a decent shed full of garden tools.

It was perfect.

They went round the block one more time, Tyler feeling a trill in his stomach, a flutter in his chest. He thought of Bean, tucked up in bed back at the flat, snuggling into Panda, bedside light on. He thought of his mum crashed out in her bedroom and hoped Bean didn't wake with a bad dream, like she'd been doing recently.

They drove past 13 Dalrymple Crescent one last time.

'That one,' Barry said, then pulled in thirty yards along the road.

3

The trick was confidence. You can get away with anything if you act like you know what you're doing. That's how the elite did it, the politicians, army officers, Oxbridge guys running banks and companies, just act as if you're entitled to the world and people go along with it. Tyler had heard about a scam two guys from school ran on a slice of waste ground between tenements off King Stables Road. They stole hi-vis jackets and charged a fiver a go for parking. Ran it every day for weeks over the summer, right in the centre of Edinburgh, and made thousands. Never got caught.

Barry and Kelly were buzzing up ahead. Tyler rolled his neck and tried to stay loose behind them. Barry went straight up to the front door and rang the doorbell. They were already pretty sure no one was home, but just in case. One time they'd done this, got no answer, then gone round the back. Saw a middle-aged couple hard at it, fucking each other's brains out on the kitchen floor.

Barry didn't look through any of the front windows, too suspicious. Instead he led the way round the side of the house, down the dark passageway, past recycling boxes and into the back garden. Tried the back door, locked. The windows likewise. A quick look under plant pots and bins for a spare key. Nothing.

They turned their attention to the garden, walked towards the shed at the bottom. Barry twitched as he went, Kelly wiping her nose on her sleeve. Tyler looked around. Neat lawn, cherry-blossom and crab-apple trees along the left-hand wall, sheltering them from the neighbours' upstairs windows. Perfect. On the other side were some rose beds in front of a six-foot stone wall with shards of broken glass cemented along the top. What use was that if you could just walk round from the front? People didn't think about security.

The shed had a small padlock on it but the wood was old. Barry lifted his boot and kicked it, and the metal plate peeled away from the plank beneath. One more kick and it was splintered, the door sagging open to meet them.

Barry put on leather gloves and went into the shed, then signalled for Tyler to close the door behind him. Tyler put on his own gloves and saw the light from Barry's torch slip through the cracks between the wooden panels. A minute later Barry came out carrying a pair of secateurs with long telescopic handles. Everyone had these for pruning trees, perfect for jimmying a back door.

Barry pushed past Kelly to the back of the house. Wedged the secateurs' blade between door and jamb at the level of the lock. He heaved it forwards and back, bending and tearing the uPVC around the lock, making a gap. He kept going a few times, the door creaking with each exertion.

Tyler heard something and looked around. He put a hand on Barry's arm. Barry flinched and almost punched him. Tyler tugged at his earlobe and all three of them listened. The sound of a car far away, wind rustling in the cherry blossoms. Then a hiss.

Tyler turned to face the sound. A black cat high on the wall between this garden and next door, staring down at them. It had four white paws like it had stepped in paint, and they glowed in the gloom. Weren't black cats meant to be lucky? Tyler put his hand out and made a beckoning sound between his tongue and teeth, but Kelly took a step towards it and lunged, making it leap down into the other garden.

Barry removed the secateurs and handed them to Tyler, then threw his shoulder against the door. It shook but stayed solid. Again, same result. Barry tutted under his breath and tried again. The door bent in the middle but only a little. A decent deadbolt, most likely with five bolts into the frame up and down the door. Probably hooked too. It wouldn't give. Modern doors like this were becoming more common, but around here you still sometimes got the old plastic ones with a single bolt, or even original wooden doors that you could almost blow open.

Barry turned to the kitchen window. It was one large pane with two smaller hinged fanlights along the top. He took the secateurs from Tyler and thrust them into the point below the window lock. Pushed the handles and it popped first time. No one ever reinforced fanlights, they were always a weak point. Half the time they weren't even locked.

Barry dropped the secateurs as Kelly lifted a black wheelie bin over, careful not to drag it and make a sound. Barry helped Tyler onto the bin then held it steady with both hands. Tyler pushed the small window open as far as it would go then gripped the open ledge and pulled himself through the gap headfirst. He was midway, his weight balanced half inside the kitchen, half outside. Kelly reached out and gave the soles of his trainers a shove and he slid forward, hands out. He was skinny but his hips stuck in the window frame. Kelly gave another shove. He was over the kitchen sink, his hands near the draining board, and he wriggled his jeans against the lip of the open window, squeezing one hip sideways then the other. He slipped the last few inches, braced his hands against the draining board, swivelled his legs sideways through the gap and flopped onto his hands and knees next to the sink.

He paused for a second assessing his body, listening for noise inside the house. He'd done this dozens of times but his heart still throbbed in his ribcage, the pulse like a message in his ears. He scooted onto his bum then jumped down into the kitchen. He was lithe and flexible but he still wished he had a cat's body, the ability to slip gracefully through the world. He looked around. Marble worktops, brushed chrome hob and oven, long oak breakfast bar. They'd spent their money on that rather than security.

He went to the back door. Sometimes they left the key in the door, but not this time. He had a quick look round, found a spare set on a shelf next to some hardback cookbooks, faces he recognised from television.

He put the key in the lock. It was stiff because of the damage Barry had done from outside but it turned with a jiggle.

He opened the door.

'Good work,' Barry said, coming inside, Kelly trailing after.

He raised his eyebrows at Tyler and tilted his head, meaning upstairs.

'The usual,' he said.

Tyler ran upstairs. It was good to be away from the other two. He did a quick tour of the rooms, three bedrooms, a bathroom and an office. No one home. Always best to check, you never knew if someone had gone to bed early, taken something, slept through the doorbell.

The décor was old-fashioned, a retired couple maybe, kids grown up and left home. That was common, not many younger people could afford places like this.

Tyler stood in the hall for a moment, collecting himself. Soaking up the atmosphere, imagining the people, the lives they lived here. What was it like to be them? Worked in a bank or office all their lives, kids at university now, time to enjoy the garden.

In the master bedroom he went into the linen closet, pulled out a couple of pillowcases. There was a dresser with a mirror, a few jewellery boxes and trinkets. He swept it all into a pillowcase. Tried the drawers, more jewellery, mostly costume but some nice silver and gold. You could accumulate a lot of stuff over a lifetime.

He had a quick look through a chest of drawers, in case valuable stuff was hidden underneath pants or socks, but nothing. He checked bedside tables. Scottish crime novels on her side, books about military history on his. A half-empty packet of Viagra in his drawer.

He did the office next. Shelves lined with hardback books, classics mostly. A laptop and an iPad on the solid desk. He scooped them into the pillowcase. Checked through the desk drawers and lifted out power supplies and charging cables, bundled them up. He looked around. A bottle of expensive whisky, two crystal glasses, a water jug. An old record player and some shelves of vinyl, classical and jazz. Nothing portable.

In the bathroom he lifted two bottles from the cupboard, temazepam and morphine. Barry would want them. He looked at the toiletries and thought if they needed anything at home. Threw the Colgate and Radox in the pillowcase.

The other two bedrooms were mostly empty. Tyler had been right, grown-up kids had moved away. In the back bedroom he found an old Nintendo DS and games, pocketed them. Spotted the charger and took that too. Sometimes you got PlayStations or Xboxes, but not here. In the other bedroom he found an old Polaroid camera with two packets of unused film. He couldn't sell it but he took it anyway. Maybe Bean would like it.

He was done and downstairs in a few minutes.

When he walked into the living room Barry had his cock out and was pissing on a sofa, Kelly watching and smiling.

'Fuck's sake,' Tyler said.

This wasn't the first time, Barry had been pushing things recently.

'Anything good?' Barry said, zipping up.

The smell of piss snagged at Tyler's nostrils. He stared at Barry for a moment before answering. 'Laptop and iPad, some necklaces and rings.'

Barry had a DVD player, another laptop and some other stuff in a tote bag. Kelly waved some money she'd found in a drawer and a pair of expensive headphones.

Tyler looked around. More bookshelves, they were big readers. A couple of original paintings on the wall, abstract things, pastel shapes that didn't make sense. Dark leather sofas, pictures of the kids on the mantelpiece, a phrenology head on display. Classy people living quiet lives. He wondered how they would take this.

'Come on,' Barry said.

They went back through to the kitchen.

Barry stopped at a bowl in the middle of the breakfast bar and rummaged through it. Loose change, golf balls, a calculator, stained corks from wine bottles.

'Fuck, no car key.'

Barry looked around the kitchen and Tyler followed his gaze. A set of flashy knives in a block, copper pans hanging up, a huge fridge-freezer. He thought about what they had to eat at home.

Barry took one of the knives from the block and dropped it in the middle of the floor with a clatter that was shocking. A warning to the owners. He went out the back door. Kelly smiled at Tyler and followed. Tyler took a last look round and left the house.

4

Barry and Kelly were yammering up front, buzzing from the job. They were talking over each other, Rihanna's new single throbbing away on the radio. Barry was doing well over thirty, his caution of earlier evaporated. Tyler had the adrenaline rush too, but it felt like a betrayal. He was ashamed of what he'd done but the endorphins pulsed through his bloodstream, making him feel as if he'd achieved something, like a caveman escaping the jaws of a sabre-toothed tiger. He learned about it in biology at school, fight or flight, but knowing the physical reason didn't make it easier to accept.

They drove north through Newington then left into Sciennes and Marchmont. Not many pickings here, too many student flats, the uni just over the Meadows. There were also too many people in the streets, students walking home from pubs and clubs in the Old Town. Barry steered them through Whitehouse and skipped round the edge of The Grange into Morningside. It was the famously posh part of the city, where all the old-school money lived, as opposed to the brash New Town hedge funders.

Barry was too high from the first job and the coke to focus on the houses they drove past. Tyler spotted two candidates that Barry missed, but he didn't say anything. It was the owners' lucky night. Kelly couldn't spot a good mark at the best of times. Thick as shit in a bottle, Barry said, even to her face, like it was a compliment. She just smiled and stroked his arm like she was brainwashed. As if on cue, she laughed at something Barry said, flicked her hair off her shoulder, eyes shining from the coke bumps.

They wound into Craiglockhart, then north to Merchiston, then sat at the lights at Holy Corner for ages, Lorde's new single playing on the radio. Tyler liked her, she had something interesting about her, not like the other crap Forth played. He didn't like the charts generally, preferred electronica and chill out. He found some stuff on Spotify one day, trying playlists for meditation, looking for something to help his mind settle. He wanted to stick his earbuds in now, listen to his own stuff on his phone, but Barry always slapped them off his head if he tried that on a job. Awareness of your surroundings, Barry said, that was key. How that squared with a coked-addled brain and a jaw that never shut up, fuck knows.

The time idling at the crossroads seemed to quieten them down in front. They went across into Churchill, along Chamberlain Road and right into Churchill Gardens. Too open, too busy, even at this time of night. A couple of lefts and they were into Greenhill Place, a terrace along one side, bigger detached houses on the right. They went to the end, turned right, round the block. A funeral directors on one corner. Tyler imagined what they might find there. But businesses were always better protected, alarm systems linked to the police, CCTV, money in a locked safe.

Barry turned right into St Margaret's Road and slowed. Tyler spotted it before he sensed anything from Barry. A standalone Victorian upstairs-downstairs, bay windows, trimmed hedge and narrow gravel driveway. Ivy crawling up the wall around the front door. Dark, no car in the driveway or street, no sign of an alarm. The windows at the front looked old sash and case, probably the same round the back.

Barry went round the block to be sure, making a purring noise under his breath. Kelly got the coke out and sorted a couple more lines on her lap. Barry slowed the car as they came back into St Margaret's Road and eyeballed number four again, then he pulled up between streetlights and under an overhanging chestnut tree. They both did a line in front, Barry making a gargling sound, Kelly sniffing into her throat. They were both fucked when they needed to be sharp.

'Look lively,' Barry said, climbing out of the car.

✳

Getting in was easier than last time. A conservatory extension had been added round the back, but it was old so the lock mechanism wasn't up to much. The sliding doors prised away from the support without much grumble, no need for Tyler's monkey climb this time. He wished he could stay in the car but that wasn't how it worked, Barry wanted them all involved. Tyler reckoned it made him feel more secure, knowing his brother and sister were in the shit with him if a job went tits up.

They split up like before, Tyler taking the stairs two at a time, Barry and Kelly spreading out from the kitchen, one to the living room, the other towards the office. So much space in these big houses, Tyler wondered how you got used to it. He pictured the flat he shared with Mum and Bean. At least it was just the three of them since Barry and Kelly had taken over the place next door. Before that it had been unbearable, everyone under each other's feet the whole time. And getting Bean away from those two was a relief. She wasn't safe around them.

He found a pillowcase in the cupboard at the top of the stairs, stood for a moment and breathed. Sniffed the air. He wondered if you could smell wealth. Maybe this was what it smelt like, sandalwood and floor polish. All the floors were stripped hardwood, an expensive runner along the length of the hall. No carpet meant more creaks and squeaks, but that didn't matter, in fact it helped. If the owners were in the house, it was harder for them to sneak up on him.

Main bedroom. He played his phone torch over it. He should get one of those head torches that strap around your skull so he could keep his hands free, the ones that hillwalkers and runners use. He'd suggested it to Barry, who just laughed and called him a poof.

The king-sized bed had purple satin sheets, tacky as hell, out of keeping with the décor in the rest of the place. The bay-windowed room was big enough for two dressers with mirrors, his and hers, sleek Scandinavian lines. Tyler went to the woman's first. Lots of gold and platinum, bracelets and anklets, brooches and rings. He swept it all into the pillowcase then went through the drawers. More of the same. These guys weren't shy about spending money.

Over to the man's side. Three flashy watches on the top that he lifted, more rings, heavy, probably solid gold. There was more in the drawers too. Who needed seven designer watches? Some people were stupid with money. If Tyler had that kind of cash he'd take Bean on holiday somewhere sunny with an empty beach, a wee shack selling fried chicken and cold drinks. Space and time, that's what money should buy you, not Cartier and TAG Heuer.

In the bottom drawer of the dresser were six brand-new iPhones still in their boxes. Tyler frowned as he placed them into the pillowcase. Didn't make sense. Either this guy was crazy rich or he was up to something.

He switched the torch off for a moment and looked out of the window. Just a quiet street, the soft sodium glare from the light down the road. There wasn't a Neighbourhood Watch sign anywhere on the block, but those were mostly bullshit anyway. It was hard to coordinate coherent security between neighbours in a city like Edinburgh, where people didn't talk to each other. Even harder in a rich area, where a lot of people were only here half the time.

Something caught his eye. A fox padding along the road, tail flat, head bobbing, its fur sleek in the yellow light. It stopped to sniff at a hedge, lifted its head to look around, seemed to stop and stare at him. Did foxes have good eyesight? Could he see Tyler standing in the window? The fox sloped off, flitted down the street and out of sight, and Tyler thought about fight or flight.

He turned and switched the torch back on. There was an iPad on the bedside table with a pair of Gucci reading glasses lying on top. Into the pillowcase. He opened the top drawer and found a silver money clip full of twenties. Christ. He riffled them, guessed there was maybe five hundred here. Barry would be ecstatic. Hard cash was so much easier than all the fencing and haggling. Tyler removed a glove, slipped five twenties out of the clip, folded them and placed them inside his briefs against the elastic. Once on a job three months ago, Barry had made him turn his pockets out afterwards. They'd been empty that night, but the threat was clear. Tyler put the money clip in the pillowcase and recced the rest of the room. He came up with some more trinkets of jewellery, cheaper than the earlier stuff.

Back into the hallway and he could hear Barry and Kelly downstairs, rummaging and snooping, a cabinet door opening and closing, the clank of something metal. The sounds of people's lives being turned upside down.

In the next bedroom he hit the jackpot. A teenage boy, a gamer, with an Xbox One and a PlayStation 4, loads of games, controllers and headsets, other add-ons. He went to the hall cupboard and pulled out a duvet cover, went back and filled the thing. He looked around. A Hibs poster on one wall, the cup-winning team standing around the trophy, a picture of Kim Kardashian with her bum sticking out on the wall opposite. Some glossy motorbike and car magazines piled up next to the bed, standard spread of joggers, trainers and hoodies across the floor. It could've been Tyler's room, if Tyler lived in a million-pound house with money to burn. He looked about for any signs of the boy's identity but didn't see anything. Girls tended to have more of that stuff than boys. Their names in fairy lights above the bed, printed-off selfies with BFFs stuck to mood boards or mirrors, names on diaries. Tyler preferred when they did houses with girls, he could lift something small to give to Bean as a present. It was also more calming being in that female space compared to the shoot-em-ups and hotrods, the wrestling and rugby of boys' rooms.

He walked to the next bedroom but it was just a guest room, simply furnished, bed and a desk, nothing worth taking. He got on his knees and checked under the bed. Nothing. He realised he hadn't checked under the bed in the main bedroom, so he went back and crouched down, played the torch beam under it.

He sat on his haunches staring for a long time.

Eventually he reached in and pulled it out. He'd never seen a sawn-off shotgun before. He'd fired plenty of airguns in his time, aiming at Coke cans on waste ground near home, but this was a different league. He put the torch down and lifted the gun in both hands, felt the heft of it. There was a part on the underside of the barrel that slid backwards and forwards in his right hand. Pump-action. It made him think of *Call of Duty*.

He didn't know how to check if it was loaded. His gloved finger stroked the trigger. He stood up with the shotgun in his hand and looked at himself in the dresser mirror. Pointed the barrels at the mirror and made a face. He swung the gun round to see it in profile, posed like a soldier, then back again, sniper style, his eye lined up along the sight. He dropped to one knee then spun round, imagining Barry bursting through the bedroom door, getting a blast in the face.

He heard a noise. Outside. Wheels on gravel, engine cutting out. Clunk and blip of a car door being closed and locked.

He scurried to the window. There was a car parked in the driveway and he caught a glimpse of someone stepping towards the front of the house, a woman in leggings and trainers.

Shit.

He listened. He could hear Barry and Kelly downstairs, still clearing out the living room. They couldn't have heard the car.

He saw himself in the mirror. He was still holding the shotgun.

'Fuck.'

He scrambled across the room, threw it under the bed, picked up his phone and switched the torch off. He shoved it in his pocket and picked up the duvet cover and pillowcase full of stuff.

He was at the top of the stairs when he heard the scratch of a key in the front door, then it opened and the hall light came on.

The noise from the living room stopped.

Tyler stood at the top of the stairs. The staircase doubled back on itself so he couldn't see the front door from here.

His heart banged at his chest and his fingers tingled. He started taking soft steps down the stairs. Made it as far as the landing.

'What the fuck?'

A woman's voice, high pitched but rough, not what you'd expect in this neighbourhood.

'What the fuck are you doing?'

He came down a few more steps, could see her trainers as she stood in the living room doorway. They were pink and sky blue, expensive Skechers. Her leggings were dark blue, tight, hugging her slim legs. She walked into the living room and Tyler lost sight of her feet.

'Don't move,' Barry said.

Tyler took some more steps, hesitated.

'Don't threaten me,' the woman said. 'This is my home. You have no idea who you're dealing with.'

'Put your phone down,' Barry said.

Tyler took two more steps.

'If you have any sense,' the woman said, 'you'll get out of my house immediately. And leave my fucking stuff. How dare you?'

'Put the phone down,' Barry said. 'I won't say it again.'

Tyler recognised something in his voice and felt his skin prickle. His stomach was a rock weighing him down. He took another step and could see into the living room. With the main light on it all seemed too bright. The woman stood just inside the door, phone in her hand. Barry was taking slow steps towards her, glancing at Tyler over the woman's shoulder. Kelly was off to the side, still as a statue.

Tyler took another step and the Xbox in the duvet cover clunked on the stair behind him.

The woman turned and stared at Tyler, the phone pressed to her ear.

She was wearing a dark Adidas tracksuit top zipped up, jet-black hair tied in a high ponytail like she'd come from the gym. She was mid-forties maybe, lean and fit, high cheekbones, fire in her eyes.

As she looked at Tyler, Barry rushed her. Tyler's eyes widened as he saw his brother move, and the woman began to turn back, following his gaze, when Barry rammed into her, his hands low at her waist. She stumbled into the doorway, shoulder bouncing off the frame, mouth open but no sound coming out. She dropped her phone and car key, threw a confused look at Tyler then put a hand to her back. She brought it to her face and it was dark with blood. She reached for the door jamb but missed and collapsed into the hall, her head thudding on the floorboards like a basketball.

Behind her, Barry stood with a long kitchen knife in his hand, the first few inches soaked in blood. Kelly stared at Barry, the knife, the woman on the floor.

'Fuck's sake,' Barry said. He dropped the knife, the clatter of it ringing in the house. 'Let's get out of here.'

He turned and picked up a canvas bag full of stuff and stepped around the woman. Tyler could see her face. She was breathing, staring at the skirting board.

Barry picked up the car key the woman had dropped and threw it to Kelly.

'You take it,' he said. 'Usual place.'

He sauntered to the front door like he hadn't just stabbed someone.

'Come on,' he said to Tyler. 'And don't forget your stuff.'

Tyler picked up the pillowcase and duvet cover and came down the rest of the stairs. Barry was already outside, Kelly behind him, staring at the Audi logo on the car key in her hand.

Tyler stopped at the doorway and looked back.

The woman hadn't moved, was still lying with her torso in the hall and her legs in the living room. He could see the wet patch at the small of her back, the ragged tear where the knife had slipped through the Lycra. She was trying to speak but nothing came out. Her eyes darted to Tyler's face, then, with a muscle pulse at her temple, back to the floor. The fingers on her right hand began to twitch, like she was trying to indicate something, then the hand fell.

Tyler picked up her phone from where she'd dropped it and left the house, switching the light off and closing the door behind him.

5

Tyler was in the front seat, Barry tailing Kelly in the Audi up ahead, both of them at thirty, slowing for speed bumps and stopping for lights. Tyler wanted to scream. He felt the woman staring at him from the floor, eyes empty. While Barry drove, Tyler got out the woman's phone. It wasn't locked. He went to settings, disabled the geolocation function, then switched it off. They were at Cameron Toll, so that would be the last traceable location until it went on again. They headed out to Craigmillar, went past the turn-off for Niddrie, they were heading to Wee Sam's in Pinkie round the back of Musselburgh.

'That's a beauty,' Barry said, nodding at the car in front. 'That'll get us a fair few quid.'

'Fucking hell, Barry.'

Barry's hands tightened on the wheel. His teeth were clenched and he swallowed hard. He drove in silence until they stopped at a red light at the Fort. He put the car out of gear, pulled on the handbrake and grabbed Tyler by the throat, thrusting him back against the seatbelt support and choking him. Tyler scrabbled at Barry's hand with his fingers, tried to prise his neck free, but couldn't get any purchase. His windpipe was blocked and he wheezed, tried to suck in air.

'Nothing happened back at the house,' Barry said softly. 'Do you understand?'

Tyler tried to speak but just spluttered.

Barry leaned across the space between them, still gripping Tyler's throat. 'Do you?'

Tyler was dizzy, sparks flashing in the corners of his vision. He tried to swallow but couldn't. His nose made a noise, a gag reflex in his throat. He nodded as much as he could with Barry's fingers digging under the joint of his jaw.

A car horn sounded behind them. Barry loosened his grip but still held on. Tyler sucked in air. Barry turned to look behind them. A guy in a Toyota was pointing past them at the lights, which had turned green. Kelly was already away through the junction.

Barry stared at the man in the car behind for a long beat, then let go of Tyler's neck. Tyler gasped and brought his hands up, touching the skin there, as Barry put the car in gear and drove off. He held a hand up to the guy behind, a gesture of apology, and accelerated to catch up with Kelly. He stared in the rear-view mirror at the car behind.

'Fucking cunt,' he said under his breath.

Tyler blinked long and slow, tried to get rid of the spots dancing across his eyes. He stared ahead at the Audi's number plate, MH 100. A private plate on a top-of-the-range Audi, the posh house, the woman on the floor. A drawer full of iPhones and designer watches, a sawn-off shotgun under the bed. None of this was good.

*

The Skoda sat outside a row of low concrete garages, doors closed but light seeping out from under the corrugated iron. Faded blue-and-red lettering across the doors that Tyler couldn't read. There were no streetlights, and Tyler noticed the moon for the first time tonight, blurry behind strips of cloud. The smell of engine oil lingered in the air. Kelly stepped out from one of the doors, grinning as she walked. Barry turned to Tyler.

'Shift.'

Tyler got out of the passenger seat and climbed into the back as Kelly sat in the seat in front.

'Fifteen hundred,' she said, waving a roll of twenties.

Barry smiled. 'Fucking A.'

They circled back through Musselburgh and Fisherrow then west past Newcraighall. Tyler looked at the clock on the dashboard.

Thirty-five minutes since they left the house in St Margaret's Road. He pictured the look on her face, the darkness of the blood, much darker than he expected, darker than fake Halloween stuff. He imagined this was an elaborate scam, Barry and Kelly setting him up, ready to turn round any minute and shout 'gotcha!', reveal the hidden cameras. You thought we killed someone but it was all a joke, she was in on the whole thing.

How else to explain their behaviour in front? Kelly was chopping out lines on her knee, Barry humming along to some blues guy on the radio singing about going to church. As if anyone did that anymore. Kelly looked up from the coke and smiled at Barry, reached out and stroked the back of his neck.

Tyler looked out of the window. Past the Wisp turnoff and the Jack Kane Centre then they were on home turf, turning along Greendykes Road. They pulled up outside Greendykes House and Tyler thought of Bean at the top, asleep and dreaming.

They sat in the shadow of the tower, engine idling.

'We're heading out,' Barry said. That meant the casino on Ocean Way in Leith, where they could drink until six in the morning and piss as much of the money away as possible.

Barry nodded at the stolen stuff next to Tyler on the backseat. 'Did you get any cash?'

Tyler remembered the money clip. He delved into the pillowcase and handed it over, thinking about the notes he'd hidden in his pants.

Barry looked at the clip and whistled. 'Cunt was loaded, eh?'

Tyler shrugged.

'Take the rest upstairs,' Barry said. 'We'll sort it tomorrow and get it over to Fluff.'

Tyler sat there for a moment.

'Chop-chop, prick, off you trot.'

Tyler got out and dragged the bags with him.

Barry called after him. 'Sleep tight, bitch.'

Tyler closed the door and watched as Barry revved the engine and shot away with a squeal of tyres.

He looked up at Greendykes House, dizzy at the height of it so close. He imagined being able to fly to the top, soaring on thermals and swooping onto the roof.

He took the woman's phone out of his pocket. With geolocation off, the phone was only traceable when it was on, Tyler knew all about it from the phones they boosted on jobs.

He stashed the stolen gear behind the bins and began walking away from the tower block, through the park at the back and across the football pitches for ten minutes until he was at the back of the ice-cream factory at The Wisp. There was no CCTV. He switched the phone on and dialled 999.

'Ambulance, please.'

He waited. Wondered if it was too late.

'Yes, there's a woman with a life-threatening knife injury. She's at number four St Margaret's Road. Number four, OK?'

He ended the call and switched the phone off, then trudged back towards home.

6

He heard the sound of the television as he opened the front door. His first thought was Bean but when he went into the living room it was his mum alone in the darkness with the light of the screen shimmering across her face. She was watching a dumb shopping channel selling jumpers with pictures of wolves on them.

He dropped the stuff from the break-ins, picked up the remote to turn the volume down.

'You'll wake Bean, Mum.'

Angela was lying on the sofa, head at an angle. Her eyes were drooped but still open, a joint smouldering between the fingers of her right hand. There was a bottle of vodka on the floor next to her with an inch left in it, alongside a spoon with a used cotton filter, lighter and needle. She still had the belt loose around her upper arm.

'Fuck's sake,' Tyler said, picking up the heroin gear. 'You can't leave this lying around.'

Angela turned her head like a sloth from the screen to him.

'Don't throw that out.' Her voice was ragged. 'It's my last needle.'

Her hair was greasy, blonde at the ends, flecks of grey through the darker stuff at her scalp. She was short and emaciated, limbs like twigs, arms pocked with puncture marks. She wore a stringy off-the-shoulder top with *Pineapple!* across it, no bra underneath, leggings covered in joint ash and other stains.

Tyler imagined grabbing her and shaking, screaming in her face to get her shit together.

She turned back to the TV, lifted her hand to her mouth and took a drag of the joint.

'Look at this shit,' she said, waving a finger at the screen. A woman wearing too much make-up was talking about a bed throw with a family of bears on it.

Tyler took the syringe and the rest to Angela's bedroom, placed it in the drawer next to her bed, then went back to the living room. He got a blanket from the chair by the window and opened it out, laid it over her. He tucked the corner away from her joint hand, found an old tea mug and placed it on the ground as an ashtray. She let out a breath in acknowledgement.

He reached into his pants and took out the money, peeled a twenty off and replaced the rest.

'Here,' he said, holding the note out to her.

She turned, saw the money, smiled and took it.

'Sweet boy,' she said. 'Come here.'

He sat down on the sofa but not close enough to hug. She tucked the money into her leggings and touched his hand on the blanket. Her skin was damp with sweat.

'Mum,' he said, staring at the screen.

'I know,' she said. The faintest squeeze of his hand, like a ghost. 'I'm trying.'

He closed his eyes and pictured the woman from the house, lying on the floor and staring up at him. When he opened his eyes, Angela was blinking at the screen again.

He went through to Bean's room. She was lying across the bed, feet dangling over the edge, covers on the floor. She clutched Panda tight in both arms, the toy pressed into her chest. Her nightlight was on, throwing a blue shadow across her face.

Tyler eased her round the right way, pulled the covers over and tucked her in. She was a restless sleeper, would likely kick them off in five minutes anyway, but it was good to feel you were doing something. Her mouth was slack and her breath caught in her throat a little as she snuggled into her teddy. Tyler stared at her for a long time then left, pulling the door almost closed.

He went out of the flat, along the corridor and pulled down the ladder for the roof. Climbed up and took gulping breaths of cold air as he opened the door at the top, then walked to the western edge and looked down. Forty-six metres to the ground. High enough.

He gazed out. So strange to be the only two buildings left standing, like a pair of lookouts keeping watch for trouble. He looked at the lights of the hospital campus. He wondered if she was there already, rushed to A&E in the back of an ambulance, past the football injuries and domestic abuse, the turned ankles and allergic inflammations. Already being cared for. Or maybe they hadn't believed him, thought it was a crank call and hadn't bothered. He had no idea what their protocol was.

'Tyler?'

It was Bean behind him, by the access door, holding Panda.

He went over. 'What are you doing up?'

'I had a bad dream,' she said, lines on her forehead. 'Barry's dogs were after us. They chased you away, I couldn't find you.'

He picked her up and stroked her hair.

'It's just a silly dream.' He carried her back down the ladder, smiling for her benefit.

'But it seemed so real,' she said.

He could feel the tension in her body, but it was easing.

He kept his voice level. 'Don't worry, nothing will ever chase me away from you.'

7

He was already awake when the alarm rang. He stared at his phone for a few seconds then switched the sound off. Bean stretched out next to him and threw her arm over his chest. He lifted it off.

He'd got her back to bed and straight to sleep after being up on the roof, but then she woke again at half four, came padding through to tell him about another bad dream. A dark, shadowy monster ripping Tyler to pieces in front of her. Always the same, evil forces separating the two of them. Didn't take a genius to work out where it came from. Tyler had lifted the covers and she got in beside him, Panda too, and after a couple of minutes she went back to sleep as he stroked her head. He was too hot with her body next to his, flipped his covers off, his mind thrumming, chewing everything over. He stayed that way as the sky lightened outside, and now it was time to get up.

'Wake up,' he said, rubbing Bean's nose. 'Time to get ready for school.'

She opened her eyes and smiled. 'You're here.'

'Where else would I be?'

He got up, pulled black trousers on and opened the curtains. It was a clear morning, the sun already halfway up the sky to the east. He was glad his bedroom was at the back of the flat, it meant he couldn't see the hospital from here.

He'd looked up the number for A&E on his phone as he lay in bed earlier, his thumb over the call button. But how would that work? He didn't have her name. And the only way he could describe her incriminated himself.

Bean got up, rubbing her eye, dragging Panda by the ear.

Tyler smiled. 'Your uniform's laid out in your room.'

'Can you help me with the tights?'

He made a show of a dramatic sigh. 'Go on, then, but you're a big seven-year-old, you should be doing that yourself.'

He hated doing her tights. Whatever he did they weren't comfortable, weren't quite right, and she always did a silly dance hoisting them up then picking them out of her bum crack.

He threw the rest of his clothes on then helped her, and they wandered to the living room and kitchenette. Angela wasn't there, so she'd somehow managed to get to bed. Tyler was glad. Seeing her like that wasn't good for Bean, no matter how much bullshit he fed her about Mum being unwell. She was a smart kid, she knew what was going on. Living round here, you grew up quick or got left behind. Addicted and abusive parents were all over this neighbourhood, three generations of the wasted and the institutionalised fuck-ups, left, right and centre. More than half the kids in Bean's class only had one parent, and half of them were flagged as being at risk.

Tyler thought about the woman on the floor, about her kid. Her son's room was full of teenage stuff. How much easier life was for them because they had money. He tried to imagine that woman shooting up in front of her son, like Angela had done in front of him for years. He'd tried to help her so many times. But at some point people had to take responsibility for themselves, right? He had no time to waste on his mum anymore, he had to make sure Bean was protected, that she got to and from school OK. And that she was kept away from the two next door as much as possible.

He got Aldi own-brand Shreddies out of the cupboard, sniffed the milk from the fridge. Found a clean bowl and wiped off a spoon at the sink, stuck them on the breakfast bar. Bean had put cartoons on the television and he let her watch as she crunched and slurped. He made toast for himself, picking the flecks of mould from the crust and flicking them in the bin. He got his and Bean's schoolbags together. She got free school meals, so that was something. He remembered the money in his pants and touched the edge of the notes. Safest place for it. If Barry found out he was skimming, he'd get another beating.

On TV now was a show where a cartoon boy lived in a real family's house. They were Northern Irish for some reason. He always got them into scrapes, but by the end of the ten-minute programme it was all good again, the happy and loving mum, dad and sister giving him a big hug. Tyler was glad Bean had stuff like this in her life, it gave her something to aim for when she grew up instead of the shitshow going on around her.

'Can we go see Snook and the babies?' Bean said, a dribble of milk on her chin.

Tyler made a face and looked at his watch. 'If you're quick brushing your teeth.'

She bounced down from the stool and out to the bathroom.

He put her bowl and spoon in the sink, rinsed them and stuck them on the draining board, did the same with his butter knife. He grabbed some food for Snook from a cupboard and shoved it in his schoolbag.

He turned and stared at the pillowcase, duvet cover and the rest of the stash still piled in the corner of the room. Bean hadn't asked about it. He remembered the Polaroid camera from the first job last night and pulled it out.

'Ready,' Bean said from the doorway. Her uniform was scruffy, black leggings thin at the knees and he knew there was a small hole in the crotch that you couldn't see except when she did cartwheels. The jumper with the school crest on it was stolen from the school's second-hand sale, a hand-me-down.

'Come here,' Tyler said. 'Turn round.'

He took her hair-tie out, ran his fingers through a few times, tied it back up, neater.

'Look at this,' he said, showing her the Polaroid.

'What is it?' She turned it around in her hands, fingers running over the buttons.

'A camera.'

'Like on your phone?'

'Not quite, look.' He opened a packet of film and loaded it. Pointed it at her.

'Say cheese.'

She pouted and did a peace sign with her fingers. The camera flashed and whirred then spat out the picture. She took it from him.

'There's nothing on it,' she said, staring at the white square.

'Wait.'

Her face emerged slowly and she raised her eyebrows.

'Wow,' she said. 'Can I take it to school?'

'Sure, but don't waste the film, it's not like digital. Once they're used up, that's it. Make each picture count.'

'Let's do a selfie,' she said.

He shook his head but leaned in next to her, turned the camera and pressed. Flash and whir. He held the picture until it emerged, two smiling faces, a sliver of time captured forever. He handed it to her but she shook her head.

'You have that one,' she said. 'So you don't forget me while I'm at school.'

He stared at the picture as she stuffed the camera into her bag.

'Let's go,' she said. 'I want to see the little ones.'

Tyler put the picture in his pocket and switched the television off, then picked up both schoolbags and ushered her out the door, all the while thinking about the woman's hand rising then falling to the varnished hardwood floor.

✳

They headed round the building site and came to an isolated derelict house, Bean holding Tyler's hand and singing the theme tune from that last show on TV. When all the other houses were knocked down, this one was left standing for some reason, but the owners eventually moved out and it was now a slab of concrete frontage and crumbling roof in the middle of scrubland.

They walked round the back where the board over one of the windows was loose. Tyler looked around out of habit. Just the new-build houses of Sandilands Close on the horizon, the hospital, then offices further south. Someone walking a dog halfway up Craigmillar Hill. He was always worried this place would get taken over by junkies. He prised the board away from the window frame, peered in and heard a whimpering sound. He lifted Bean through the gap, careful not to catch her uniform on the broken glass of the window frame. He climbed in after her and waited a moment for his eyes to acclimatise.

'Snook.' Bean ran over to the mongrel on the mattress. She was part collie and part something else, black-and-white fur, one of her ears ripped, her right eye blotchy red. Her tail thumped on the edge of the mattress as Bean ruffled her ears and got licks to the face. Snuffling around Snook's teats were three drowsy puppies.

They'd come across her in the process of giving birth on the way home from school a week ago. She was laying in some bushes by the side of the road, moaning and keening to herself. Bean had asked what was happening and Tyler tried to explain. He got her to comfort the dog and she stuck to the task, whispering a stream of mushy gobbledygook, stroking her ears and nose, nuzzling her like they were part of the same pack. When the first puppy began to emerge Bean stared with wide eyes. Her hand stopped on the dog's snout. Snook whimpered and began licking Bean's hand, and she went back to stroking her, talking in her ear, but this time she kept her eyes on the other end, raising her eyebrows as the first puppy slithered out and a second one crowned. Tyler placed the first one near its mum's face and Snook moved her head away from Bean and began licking the pup.

Ten minutes later she had three in total, furry little things making sucking noises and wriggling around. It began to rain. Tyler took his jacket off and bundled the puppies into it, tying up the sleeves and handing it to Bean.

'Be careful.'

He'd lifted Snook in his arms and they jogged down the hill. Tyler was going to take them back to the flat but then thought of Barry. God knows what he'd do to three newborn pups and an exhausted mother. The way he treated his own dogs was bad enough.

So Tyler stopped outside the house they were now in, found a way in round the back and deposited Snook and the pups inside. On subsequent visits they'd brought everything the dogs needed, an old mattress from the street as a bed, plastic ice cream containers for food and water dishes. Tyler liked how simple it was. Food, shelter and a mum who looked after you, that's all you needed to stay alive.

He looked at Bean playing with the puppies now. He had no long-term plan here, no clue what to do when they got older. They couldn't stay here forever, but for now it was enough. It was good to feel as if things were contained, under control.

He emptied dog food into the bowl and filled the water bowl from the tap in the bathroom. For some reason, the water hadn't ever been turned off. When he came back Snook was picking at the food, the puppies fussing as she nudged them out of her way.

Tyler looked at his watch.

'Time to go.'

'Aw.'

'We can pop in after school.'

'When can we take them for a walk?'

'The puppies are too small, I told you. And we can't take their mummy from them.'

Bean thought about that. This mother-and-babies thing was throwing up all sorts of stuff in her mind, and Tyler didn't like that. He just wanted to get her to school on time, then home, then same again tomorrow and the next day.

'Say goodbye,' he said.

Bean gripped Snook's neck then lifted each puppy in turn and snuggled them. Tyler rolled his eyes. Bean took the Polaroid out of her bag, pointed it at the dogs and it flashed. She grinned at Tyler then the picture, then stuffed it all back in her bag.

'See you after school,' Bean said to the dogs. 'Stay safe.'

✳

Craigmillar Primary was a new orange-brick building surrounded by security cameras and a spiky fence. It had been closed as part of the PFI scandal a year before, after a wall in a similar school across town fell down, but they found nothing wrong with it and reopened. It was a lot better than the crumbling shithole Tyler attended a few years ago, and a hundred times nicer than the Castlemound High dump next door that he went to now.

Bean let go of his hand as they came through the gates and ran to Isla and Aisha, who were showing each other the JoJo bows in their hair. Bean had been after one for ages but they were nine quid a pop. Maybe he should get her one from the money he'd skimmed last night, but he never knew how long he would go between paydays, so he always felt guilty buying luxuries over food and electricity. And now he had to buy dog food into the bargain.

Bean was Bethany to her pals, she was only called Bean at home. Tyler couldn't remember how it started but he hoped it wasn't Barry's idea, nothing good ever came from him. Maybe it was because she was so small, six inches shorter than Isla and Aisha.

The bell went and Bean and her friends meandered over to the line. Tyler hung back with the mums. A few of them weren't that much older than him, which meant they'd had their kids when they were still at school. Tyler watched to see if Bean would look over when Miss Kelvin called them in, but she was gabbing with Aisha, engrossed in her own world.

He walked away, avoiding eye contact with Miss Kelvin and the mums, then he went out of the gate and turned left, the opposite way from the high school. He walked down Niddrie Farm Grove past the red-and-white terraces then the doctor's surgery and came out at the bus stop. He waited a few minutes then jumped on a number thirty, pressing his fake pass against the ticket gizmo. He'd taken it from a house months ago, stuck his own face over the owner's. Martin Lawrence. It had never been cancelled so it still worked, Lothian Buses' systems obviously weren't airtight. People think security systems are in place to protect them, but nine times out of ten they don't work. They need authorities to be joined up, communicating with each other, and who has the time for that? Everyone is under the cosh, everyone's job is up for review, budgets slashed, working more hours for less money. People don't give a shit about a teenage boy riding the bus for free on someone else's pass. They don't care about an Xbox that's covered by insurance, or a car that gets fenced. They get a replacement, it's shinier than the one that was nicked, more features, better satnav, Bluetooth for your iPhone, heated driver's seat.

He plugged in his earbuds and played Boards of Canada. Everyone in his year listened to hip-hop or metal. He got enough angry shit at home. He loved Boards of Canada, what the future would sound like projected from the past. He'd Googled and found out they were two East Lothian brothers who never did interviews or played live, which he liked.

He stared out of the upstairs window as wobbly synths and drunken drums fought with each other. He had the same feeling as last night, the quick transformation from the grey pebbledash of Niddrie and Craigmillar to the bigger houses of Prestonfield and Newington.

He took the woman's phone out of his pocket and stared at it for a while, then switched it on. The screen showed that she had six missed calls, one from the emergency services last night, the rest from 'Derek'. A husband or boyfriend wondering where she was. Or a son. He switched it off and put it away. If they were already tracking the phone, they'd get a ping from the mast at Prestonfield.

He jumped off at Dalkeith Road and walked amongst the massive houses of Blacket Avenue. He cut onto Grange Loan then up Dalrymple Crescent, last night's first job. He took deep breaths but didn't alter his stride. A teenage kid walking down a street listening to music, that's all. He glanced at number thirteen as he passed. No sign of life, nothing to show they'd been in there. He thought about the Polaroid camera, in Bean's schoolbag right now. He kept walking, swallowing hard, blinking. When he closed his eyes he felt his lack of sleep but also his adrenaline levels topping up by being back here.

He bumped along Dick Place and Blackford Road, more million-pound homes, the pavement shadowed by tree canopies reaching over high walls and thick hedges. He imagined people inside, sitting in their summerhouses, picking a dress from a walk-in wardrobe, playing a racing game on a home entertainment system.

His heart caught in his throat as he walked up Whitehouse Loan and reached St Margaret's Road. He turned in without hesitation. You never knew if CCTV was watching, and loitering was suspicious. As long as you looked like you had a purpose you could do anything. He glanced at the houses as he went past, and it was only now that he noticed the numbers went up one side – one, two, three – then down the other. It was a tiny street with only eight houses. He went over in his mind why they hadn't chosen the others. A recent alarm system on one, not enough tree cover on the next, cars in the driveway and a streetlight outside the third.

Then he was already passing number four. He took the edge out of his stride, not enough to notice but enough for him to concentrate, eyes wide, soaking it up. He saw the stone driveway posts, the climbing plant along the sidewall, the neat garage next to the house, the white front door, closed. He imagined going up to that door and ringing the bell, making up some bullshit that he was doing a marketing survey, or trying to sell windows. He imagined the woman answering the door, tea towel in her hands or a glass of juice, smiling at him, saying no thanks but with a friendly look in her eyes. She didn't recognise him from last night, in fact last night hadn't happened at all. She got in from the gym, had a shower, made a sandwich, maybe drank a glass of red wine, then off to bed with a book, waiting for her husband to come back from the office night out he'd been dreading.

Then he remembered the shotgun under the bed, the pile of phones, the money clip. The look on her face as she lay soaked in blood.

He was already round the corner by now, near the end of Greenhill Place. He leaned over and puked behind an electrical exchange box on the corner, wiped his mouth and walked on.

He continued in a daze, like he wasn't in charge of his movements. He found himself on Strathearn Place then Greenhill Gardens, Church Hill then Clinton Road, the houses getting bigger all the time. He went along, checking the security of the buildings. It was broad daylight but he felt invisible, like a ghost walking through rich people's lives. The delivery boy, the Uber driver, the cleaner, the handyman, the gardener. Not a part of this world, so they ignored you until they needed you.

There were houses here with turrets and towers, crenellated outlines that looked like castles. He felt the urge to stop being an observer and take action. He recognised the feeling, he got it every time after the night jobs. His antennae tingled. There was a house he could use. No alarm, old windows and doors, lots of cover. He walked up the driveway, crunching footsteps like gunshots. He reached the front door, ornate etched glass panels in solid oak. Rang the bell, his heart choking his throat. He swallowed hard, cricked his neck. Waited. Rang the bell again. Cocked his head and listened. Light rustling of leaves in the birch trees. He took two steps back and looked up. Victorian, at least five bedrooms, the stonework recently cleaned and repointed. Some attic rooms with small windows were tucked away on the second floor. He turned and looked at the garden. He was fifteen yards from the road already, a tall stone wall and some sycamore obscuring the view from the street.

He walked round the side of the house and tried the rear door of the adjoining garage. Open. He went through the garage, past shelves of paint and fertiliser, and tried the connecting door to the house. Locked. He went back outside. Above the garage was a landing window, small but big enough to get through. He went back into the garage, brought out a ladder and propped it against the wall. Clambered up and onto the garage roof, tried the window. Unlocked. He flipped it open, breathed and jumped, gripping the ledge and yanking himself up onto his elbows. He scrabbled with his trainers against the stone, pulled himself up and over, hands bracing on the inside ledge, and slithered through the gap and onto the floor like a newborn foal.

He crouched for a full minute and listened to his own breathing and nothing else.

He was in.

8

He wandered from room to room getting a feel for the place. This was a home in hibernation, not empty but not in everyday use either. In all the bedrooms, things were tidied away in drawers and cupboards, no bedside books or glasses of water, no piles of clothes on the floor of a teenage boy's room, a thin layer of dust over it all. Neutral bed covers that hadn't been slept in, tasteful lamps and dark wood fittings. But there were signs of life – a bookshelf full of Harry Potter, some boys' own adventure stuff, young James Bond.

It was the same in the main bedroom. It hadn't been used in a while, but there were clothes hanging up in the wardrobe, an array of women's heels in the cupboard shelving. The bathroom had a few bottles around the deep bath but there were no soapy splodges, no damp towels, the tiling bone dry. It was almost like a show home, the odd piece of personal stuff here and there, positioned to give it fake character. Or like an Airbnb place waiting for some rich family to stay at festival time while they took in overpriced theatre and comedy.

The attic rooms were the same. Small iron fireplaces, dust bunnies under the beds, the view from the higher windows out onto the garden. Through the foliage he could see a BT van in the street, workmen standing around a hole in the road. He watched for a moment then went down two flights of stairs, his hand sliding down the banister, not caring about fingerprints. No one looked for prints if they didn't know their house had been broken into.

The ground floor had some personal stuff. A collection of classical music on vinyl stacked next to a Linn turntable. He flicked through the records, arranged in alphabetical order, and pulled one out. Erik Satie. He took it out of the sleeve and placed it on the turntable. Switched the machine on with a pop and hum, then placed the needle on the record. The room filled with the warm wash of it. Slow piano, melancholic, lots of space. He felt his breathing and heart slow as he wandered the room. There were framed family pictures on the mantelpiece. Mum, Dad and two sons. The dad looked military, square shoulders, upper class, officer material. The woman was beautiful in a skeletal way, sharp features and empty eyes. She was smiling but it didn't feel warm. The two boys were stocky teenagers, one a little older than Tyler, and they were trying to be like Daddy, chests puffed, chins sticking out, the same air of entitlement.

Tyler went to the front door and picked up the mail from behind the door. Bills and junk. Judging by the number of letters, no one had been in the house for weeks. But they were still getting bills sent here, so it was the family home. Fotheringham, Jason and Charlotte.

He replaced the mail and went to the kitchen. Black slate on the floor, chrome fittings, a long breakfast bar in some white stone or other. He went to the fridge, almost empty. They weren't planning on rustling up a snack anytime soon. The freezer had homemade stuff in Tupperware – lasagne, chicken cacciatore, venison stew. Ben & Jerry's cookie-dough ice cream and a bottle of Grey Goose. In the cupboards he found biscuits and crisps, tins of tuna and kidney beans. He took a Kit-Kat and unwrapped it, then heard a crash of breaking glass.

He stopped chewing the chocolate biscuit and listened.

The ambient piano music was still playing in the other room.

He walked towards the kitchen doorway and looked into the hall but couldn't see anything out of place.

Another crash. More glass and a thump from the living room.

'Fucksticks.'

He looked up the stairs. He had a clear run from here, could be up the steps in half a dozen bounds, out the landing window, nobody any the wiser.

But something about that voice.

He stared at the living-room doorway as piano notes drifted out. Someone grunted.

He walked to the doorway with the Kit-Kat still in his hand.

A window was smashed, chunks of glass sprayed over the rug, a smooth stone from the garden sitting in the middle. The window was unlocked and pushed up and a girl in a red school blazer was clambering in, holding the palm of one hand in the other.

'Fuck.'

She was slim and bony, a few inches taller than him, about the same age. She wore a white blouse under the blazer, a navy skirt to her knees and navy tights, flat black shoes. Her strawberry-blonde hair was tied in a ponytail. As she righted herself, Tyler noticed her features, pointy nose and green eyes, strong cheekbones and jawline, small mouth.

She turned. Her eyes showed surprise, went from his face to the Kit-Kat, then up and down his uniform.

'Who the hell are you?' she said.

'I was just thinking the same thing.'

'This isn't your house.'

Tyler thought about the Fotheringham family photos. 'Ditto.'

'You're trespassing.'

'Right back at you.'

She sighed. 'This could go on all day.'

She looked at her hand and Tyler saw it was dripping blood onto the rug, the same red as her blazer.

'Whoever you are, do you know where I can find a bandage?' she said.

Tyler turned. 'This way.'

9

He turned on the cold water at the kitchen sink and looked over his shoulder. She'd followed him, leaving drops of blood on the floor. She came close, her eyes narrow, staring at him.

'Hold it under the water,' he said.

She did it and winced, keeping her eyes on him. He watched the pink water swirling down the drain. He wondered where he would keep a first-aid kit in a house this big. He walked to the utility room at the side of the kitchen, washing machine and tumble dryer in there, winter jackets and boots stowed. He found a zip bag with a cross on it in the second drawer, full of plasters and antiseptic, stuff for insect bites, a roll of bandages and scissors. He brought it back through, dumped it on the draining board and held out a tea towel.

'Let me see.'

She lifted her hand. There was an inch-long gash across the heel of her hand, long but not deep, blood blossoming along it as they watched. A little lower and it would've been on the wrist, across the vein.

He was aware of her watching him, felt his cheeks flush.

'Can I?' he said.

She held out her hand to him and he patted it with the tea towel. It felt weird, like a religious ritual.

'I think it's dry now,' she said eventually, and he blushed.

He dropped the towel, tipped some antiseptic onto a cotton pad and took her wrist. He'd dealt with enough stuff with Bean to know what he was doing.

'This'll sting.' He dabbed.

'Jesus wept.' She flinched and pulled her hand away. He was left touching her fingers with his for a moment, then she offered her hand again. He dabbed at it as she sucked her teeth and breathed heavily.

'Think it needs stitches?' she said.

He shook his head. 'It's not deep.'

He measured out some bandage, cut it to size, and placed the start in the crook of her thumb. 'Hold that.'

She pressed her finger on it. He wrapped it round the back and over the cut, around the wrist and up, testing tightness as he went. He found a small safety pin and pinned it.

She lifted her hand, flexed her fingers and made a fist. 'I look like a boxer.' She made a couple of jabs, feinted one way then raised an uppercut with her other hand.

'How are you going to explain it?'

She looked at him. 'Who do I need to explain it to?'

Tyler shrugged.

She smiled. 'I'll just say I was self-harming, everyone at school is at it.'

She pointed at the badge on her blazer, a thick red cross surrounded by leaves, some Latin across the top. 'Inveresk.'

The posh boarding school in Musselburgh. He'd never met a pupil from there before, they kept separate from the regular kids in town to avoid trouble. The school had high stone walls and lots of security to keep the locals out.

Tyler read the inscription on her badge. *Spartam nactus es, hanc exorna.*

She rolled her eyes. 'It's some ancient guff about Sparta. It literally makes no sense, like "Sparta is yours, embellish it". These days they say it means "develop your talents". All very motivational.'

He tried to think of his own school motto, but he wasn't sure they even had one.

'What's your name?' she said.

'Tyler.'

'I can work with that.' She held out her damaged hand to shake. He took it but didn't squeeze, felt the contrast between her soft skin and the rough bandage.

'I'm Flick,' she said. 'Since you're never going to ask. It's Felicity, but no one calls me that except my parents, and I never see them.'

Tyler shook hands until it felt awkward.

'Nice to meet you, Flick.'

She dropped his hand and looked around theatrically.

'So, why are you in my ex-boyfriend's house on a Tuesday morning?'

He began putting the stuff back in the first-aid kit then zipped it up and put it back in the drawer in the utility room.

'Strong, silent type, eh?'

He came back in and leaned against the sink. 'You're the one who broke in.'

'So did you.'

'You don't know that.'

'I bet I can find evidence.'

Tyler thought of the open upstairs hall window, the ladder propped against the garage wall outside. 'Not tons of glass on the living-room rug and blood everywhere.'

Her mouth was puckered, like this was a game.

'You're not one of Will's friends.'

'Who says?'

She made a show of examining him. 'Because you couldn't be more different from that arrogant sack of shit.'

Tyler should be gone, he should've bolted when he heard the glass from the living room. But he was still here enjoying looking at Flick's face and the curve of her hip, and he could smell her too, something citrus.

She touched the end of her ponytail. 'So you're a thief?'

Tyler put his hands out. 'Do you see me robbing anyone?'

'Maybe I caught you in the act.'

'Yeah, you sneaked up and caught me red-handed, with all your smashing of windows and bleeding.'

'OK, smart arse.'

Her accent was posh Edinburgh, the kind of voice you heard from newsreaders or daytime TV hosts. He'd never met anyone who sounded like that in real life. Her voice had a confidence that came from never having to worry about buying food or paying the leccy, those things weren't on her radar. He made a mental note to look up the fees for Inveresk.

She nodded through to the living room. 'What's with the music?'

It was only when she mentioned it that he realised the album was still on, spacey music floating through.

'It's relaxing.'

'You broke into someone's house to listen to piano music.'

'I told you, I didn't break in.'

'Whatever.'

He stepped away from her and picked up the tea towel. 'We should probably clean up the mess you made.'

She frowned. 'Why?'

'So they don't know we were here.'

'What if I want them to know?'

He shook his head. 'That's just stupid. You want to be arrested?'

She gave this some consideration. 'What do you have in mind?'

'We can't hide the broken window, so we leave the glass and stone, close the window, remove any traces of blood, that's the main thing. Then maybe it just looks like some idiot chucked a rock at the window. They don't have CCTV, so that's not a problem.'

He ran the towel under the tap and squeezed it out then wetted a cloth in the sink and handed it to her.

'Come on.' He began retracing their steps, checking the floor, kneeling to wipe where he saw blood. The slate and the marble were no problem but the rug in the living room was harder. But it was dark and patterned, they might get away with it.

She knelt next to him and dabbed at a spot.

'Careful,' he said. 'There's glass by your knee. The last thing we need is more blood.'

She sat back on her haunches and examined him. Looked around the room then went back to the floor. 'Why are you helping me?'

'Why not?' He scoped the room. 'That'll probably do.'

'Won't they call the police?' Flick said. 'Get forensics out?'

'Shouldn't you have thought about that before you threw a stone through their window and climbed in?'

'I wasn't thinking.'

He got up, closed the window and locked it. Rubbed at a drop of blood on the wooden frame until it came away.

She stood up. 'Don't you want to know why I'm here?'

He put his hands out, inviting her to speak.

She walked over to the mantelpiece, stared at the family photo and pointed at the younger of the two brothers. 'This prick treated me like shit. He promised things. It was all lies. He was screwing Tabby the whole time, probably others. I want revenge.'

Tyler went over and took the cloth from her then they walked to the kitchen. He rinsed the cloth out and placed it on the draining board, then wrung out the tea towel and shoved it in his pocket.

'Can't really leave this,' he said. 'Too obvious.'

'You've done this before, haven't you?' Flick said.

She was standing close enough that he could smell her perfume again, lemons and flowers.

'Why, if you're not taking anything?'

He thought about the woman on the floor in her own blood, Barry stepping past her, the shotgun under the bed. He thought about Bean on the roof, his mum crashed out on the sofa, the dog in the abandoned building.

'What exactly are *you* doing here?' he said. '"Revenge" is pretty vague.'

She waved her bandaged hand around. 'I don't know, mess some shit up. Take something. Set fire to his room.'

'Get done for arson? Great idea.'

'Well, what do you suggest?'

He wasn't sure if she was really after ideas or not. Her smile suggested she wasn't sure either.

'Anything you do just shows he got to you,' Tyler said. 'Plus it's almost guaranteed to get you in trouble. If you let him know you were here, and he's the dick you say he is, then he'll get the cops on you.'

'So?'

'So act like he's nothing. Forget him and move on.'

Flick chewed at her lip, thinking it over. 'You're kind of wise for a small guy.'

Tyler guessed they were the same year at school but he didn't say anything.

Flick was smiling now. 'Can I at least pee on his bed?'

'Some guys might get off on that.'

She made a face. 'Actually he might, knowing him.'

In the living room the music finished with a scratch and clunk. The silence felt like it exposed them to each other. They walked through and Tyler lifted the record with his fingertips, put it back in its sleeve, then returned it to its place on the shelf. He looked at the glass and the stone on the rug, at the broken window, then he heard a noise that made him freeze. Footsteps on the gravel outside, louder as the person walked towards the house. Flick threw him a look, but he just shook his head. The steps got louder then they stopped and the bell rang. Tyler grabbed Flick and pressed her against the mantelpiece. They stood in silence. He heard a shuffle of feet on the step outside, then the flop of letters coming through the letterbox, dropping onto the mat. If the postie took a step to the side and looked in, he'd see them. Even if he just turned this way he'd spot the broken window. Tyler moved his foot and cringed as it knocked against the fireplace grate, a scrape of metal on stone. Flick raised her eyebrows. Tyler stared at the window, waiting to see a face. A few more seconds, silence in the room and outside. Then the scrunch of footsteps retreating down the driveway.

Tyler thought about the ladder leaning against the garage, out of sight from the front of the house.

'We should go,' Flick said. 'Any idea how to get out of here?'

Tyler smiled.

10

Tyler resisted looking back at the house as they strode down the drive. Act like you belong, as if this is all yours. The wind bristled the silver birch, sparrows fluttered around the pond to their right, a cat watched the birds from the edge of a rhododendron bush.

He could feel the energy between them, the thrill of transgressing together. Flick seemed electrified by it. He never felt like this on the nightcrawls with Barry and Kelly, never felt like part of something, as he did now.

They reached the bottom of the drive and Tyler made to turn right towards the bus stop but Flick touched his arm and nodded the other way.

'I'll give you a lift.'

'You have a car?'

'Yeah.'

'And a licence?'

'Provisional. Technically I'm not allowed to drive without a fully licensed passenger, but who's to know?'

The BT workers were standing around their van and the hole in the road, doing nothing. There were hardly any cars parked in the street, since all the houses had driveways. The nearest was a bright-red Volkswagen Beetle Cabriolet, standing out like a throbbing thumb amongst the grey road and stone walls.

'Please don't say that's it,' Tyler said.

'Beautiful, isn't it?'

She headed towards it getting her key out. The workmen across the road stopped talking and watched as she walked by. She was something to watch. He should turn and walk the other way.

'Come on,' she called behind her.

He followed her to the car and got in. The inside smelled of leather and new plastic. She started the car and the engine purred, then she pulled away.

'If they suspect anything at the house, you're not exactly being anonymous.'

'So what?'

'Those workmen will remember you.'

'They don't know me.'

Tyler shook his head. 'A pretty girl in a red blazer driving a flashy car. You'll be easy to track down.'

'You think I'm pretty.'

'That's what you got from that?'

She smiled and moved through the gears. She was driving fast, over-steering, revving the engine. She pressed play on an iPod between them and the new Paramore record came on.

'It's like you want to get caught,' he said.

'What do you mean?'

'Just drive like a normal person.'

She didn't slow down. 'Where can I drop you?'

They were at Cameron Toll already.

'Anywhere.'

She frowned as they pulled away from a pedestrian crossing with the engine at a high whine. 'Are you ashamed of where you're from?'

He didn't speak. She stole glances at him as she negotiated the roundabout and headed east.

'I'm sorry,' she said eventually. 'That was uncalled for.'

'It's OK.'

'Please just tell me to shut up.'

'Shut up.'

She laughed and he liked the sound of it. He looked out of the window as perky guitar music filled the space between them. As they passed Peffermill he looked at his watch.

'You could drop me at school,' he said. 'I should probably go to class.'

'Where is that?'

'Not far. Off to the right in a bit.'

'Craigmillar?'

'Niddrie.'

Those two names carried such weight, so much reputation. The hardest and most deprived parts of the city, up there with the worst in the country, bywords for poverty, crime, drugs and the rest. Every cliché of social deprivation and he was the embodiment of it. He felt dirty in this clean car, like he was soiling Flick's pristine life with his presence. He imagined what he looked like to her and felt queasy.

They drove in silence until he pointed to the turn-off, past the medical centre and Aldi. She rattled over speed bumps and round corners, braking outside the school gates. A couple of younger lads bunking off school stood and gawped at the car.

She flipped her phone out of her pocket, unlocked the screen and handed it to him. 'Stick your number in.'

He looked at her but didn't take it. Remembered the touch of her skin, the bubbles of blood along the cut on her hand. The sound of her voice from the other room, swearing. He breathed in her scent, mingled with the smell of the car.

'Don't make a girl beg,' she said. He saw something in her eyes, a flicker under the bravado, maybe it was a front to cover something deeper. Maybe she wasn't as confident as she made out. 'Don't you want to see me again?'

She put on a coy look and the vulnerability in her eyes was gone, back to confident Flick.

He took the phone and typed his name and number. He used his real surname, why not? She wasn't going to grass on him about the house, she would put herself in the shit too. And he did want to see her again. He handed the phone back and she looked at it.

'Tyler Wallace,' she said, as if weighing up the worth of his name. 'If you've given me a fake number I'll hunt you down and kill you.'

She laughed too hard. He thought for a second she was going to press dial to check his phone rang in his pocket.

'I'll call you, Tyler Wallace.'

'I hope you do.'

He got out and closed the door. She revved away with a squeal of tyres and it felt like the whole thing had been a dream.

11

He got no grief for missing most of the morning. His lack of attendance was noted but turn-up rates were so low around here that anyone appearing for class was a triumph. They couldn't punish him, he was old enough to leave anytime he wanted. The school roll plummeted as soon as kids turned sixteen, most of the boys leaving for apprenticeships or the army, or just to doss about. The armed forces were smart, they had regular recruitment drives around the poorest parts of the city, signed up plenty of fodder for the latest war in the Middle East. The girls all became trainee hairdressers or got temp jobs in nail bars and tanning salons. Stereotypes, sure, but when your horizons start narrowing on the day you're born, when you don't see anyone around you doing anything else, you go along with that crap. No one from here became an academic or a surgeon or a solicitor, those careers cost money.

The school also knew they couldn't give Tyler a detention because he had to pick up Bean. They knew all about his home life, social workers made sure of that. He and Bean were on the register, but there were hundreds in the same boat around here, far too many to tackle, and no one had the time or resources to help, swamped with paperwork and firefighting emergencies. It worked against Tyler that he kept himself and Bean going, that he did a decent job of raising the two of them, so they weren't deemed a crisis.

He imagined sitting in Will's house with Flick, Bean doing cartwheels in the garden while he sipped on a nice middle-class drink, a G&T or Prosecco or some shit like that. Chin, chin. Bean stopping to scoop cookie-dough ice cream into her mouth in between leaps and stretches.

It was afternoon interval when he found out.

He was walking out of English, searching 'Felicity' and 'Inveresk' on his phone, when Connell grabbed him.

'Did you hear?'

Connell was thick as pigshit but had a good heart. He was tall and broad, probably weighed twice what Tyler did, but he didn't have an aggressive bone in his body. His ears and cheeks were permanently red like he'd just come in from a snowball fight, and his school tie was always a mess.

Tyler looked at him. 'I don't know, did I?'

Connell leaned in and lowered his voice. 'Some morons broke into Ryan Holt's house last night, took a bunch of shit, stabbed his mum.'

Tyler put his phone away. His heart was a stone and he felt sick, sweat sticky under his arms. 'What?'

Connell's eyes were wide. 'I know, right? The Holts.'

'Shit.'

'I wouldn't want to be in their shoes right now. When Deke Holt catches them, they're gonna get destroyed. Fucking tortured and shit. They're gonna wish they were dead.'

The Holts were Niddrie legends, the biggest crime family going back for decades. They used to run with the Young Niddrie Terror gang back in the eighties and had grown in power and reputation ever since. Deke was the head of the family, had gone semi-legit, ploughing drug money into property, but he'd done time back in the day for violent offences. His son Ryan was still kicking his heels in their year at school. Folk stayed out of his way because of his connections and because he had that thing in his eye, he wouldn't stop if he got started. Tyler knew the Holt men by sight, but not Ryan's mum.

'Where was this?' he said, trying to keep his voice level. His fists were damp with sweat in his pockets.

'Somewhere up in Bruntsfield, I think.'

'They don't live around here anymore?'

Connell looked at Tyler like his brain was loose. 'Would you, if you had the money to leave?'

'So why's Ryan still at Castlemound?'

Connell shrugged. 'His gang's here. It keeps him in touch with all the other bams.'

Tyler thought about the sawn-off shotgun under the bed, remembered pointing it at himself in the mirror, the weight of it in his hands. He thought of the woman, the knife dropped by her side. He thought of the bag of stuff, the Holts' stuff, still sitting in the living room back at his flat.

He closed his eyes and tried to remember the piano music from Will's house, tried to picture Flick standing in the middle of the room. But all he could see was Ryan Holt's mum on the floor, swimming in blood.

He swallowed. 'Is his mum OK?'

He wasn't religious but he was praying hard to every god there was.

'She's in hospital,' Connell said. 'Critical but stable, whatever that means.'

'Shit.'

Connell looked at him. 'Are you OK? You look a bit ill.'

Tyler forced out a laugh that sounded wrong. 'Didn't sleep last night, that's all.'

Connell shook his head. 'I wouldn't want to be those cunts. They can't have known it was the Holts' place. Why the hell would you rob them? There's going to be some serious payback when Deke finds who did it.'

'How would he find them?'

Connell frowned at the question. 'They took her car for a start. He'll put the word out and track it down. And they robbed loads of stuff from the house. That'll start turning up. He's probably got his boys putting the word out already. Folk will talk, they're all scared shit-less of Deke.'

Tyler licked his lips, trying to work moisture into his mouth.

'Are you sure you're OK?' Connell said.

12

Something lifted from him when he saw Bean's face. She ran across the playground to him, offering up a tub of gooey slime, the latest craze, green and gloopy.

Miss Kelvin smiled from the open door of her classroom and came out. They had an understanding, Tyler picked Bean up from school but sometimes he didn't make it on time, depending if he had a study period last thing. If he didn't, Bean hung around with her teacher, helping tidy up, playing by herself if Miss Kelvin had paperwork. They had an after-school club, but Tyler couldn't pay. When he'd brought it up with Angela, she laughed. Miss Kelvin wasn't supposed to do this, but she'd heard all about their home life from Bean. It helped that Bean wasn't a pain in the arse.

'Hello, Tyler,' Miss Kelvin said.

She was young, just out of teacher training – maybe why she cut Tyler some slack. A more experienced teacher might just have set them adrift. The management made noises about inclusivity and helping out families in poverty but the truth was the school could barely fork out for essential supplies, let alone anything else.

'Hi, Miss Kelvin.'

Bean was squidging her slime and grinning.

'Go get your bag and coat,' Tyler said.

She gave him a quick hug and darted back into the classroom.

'Make sure you've got everything,' he called after her.

He turned to the teacher. 'Was she OK today?'

'Of course, as always.' She was the same height as Tyler, her black hair in a short bob. 'You know parents' evening is coming up.'

Tyler pursed his lips.

'There's a letter about it in her bag.' Miss Kelvin studied him as he shuffled his feet. 'How's your mum?'

He scratched his head. He realised what a cliché he was, the incommunicative teenager, but he couldn't think what to say.

'Is there a chance we'll see her at parents' evening?'

'I can ask.'

'That would be great.'

There was a clatter from inside, Bean dropping her water bottle in the hurry to get her stuff together.

'She had a lot of fun today with her new camera,' Miss Kelvin said.

Tyler thought about how to answer. 'It was a present.'

'She talks about you all the time. She's besotted with you.'

'She's a good kid.'

Miss Kelvin watched as Bean stumbled out of the classroom to join them. 'You're a good brother to her, Tyler.'

He looked at Bean. 'Sorted?'

'Yeah.'

'Come on, then.'

He put his hand out and Bean took it. 'What do you say to Miss Kelvin?'

'Thank you, Miss Kelvin.' Delivered sing-song, like a joke.

'You're very welcome, Bethany.' She turned to Tyler. 'Look after yourself.'

They walked away, Tyler feeling Bean squeeze his hand as they went.

✳

'Snook!' Bean ran over as soon as Tyler lowered her through the window. The dog was on her feet snuffling around her litter, pups falling over each other in comedy fashion. Snook's tail thumped at the sound of Bean's voice and she began licking the girl's hands and face.

'Good girl,' Bean said as the pups came to see what all the fuss was about.

They were cute but they would grow up quick, need feeding and walking. He wondered how Bean would cope with that. They couldn't keep four dogs, and there was no guarantee they wouldn't just wander off. Snook was semi-wild, one of plenty who ran around the waste ground south of the castle, scavenging for scraps. Tyler imagined what that was like, the freedom to roam, a whole world to explore. But the flip side was living on the edge of hunger and violence all the time, fights with other animals, cruelty from humans. He didn't know if the trade-off was worth it.

He refilled the water bowl and put it down next to the mattress. Snook had taken to crapping in the other corner of the room but the puppies still left a skittery mess around here. He tried to clean up as best he could using old newspaper. They needed to be toilet trained but he had no idea about that. And weren't puppies supposed to get jabs of some kind?

Bean was in the middle of a bundle of fur, giggling and laughing, lying down on the mattress and letting the pups tumble over her. He resisted the temptation to tell her not to get her uniform dirty, just stood watching her, smiling at her happiness. After a while the pups seemed to tire.

'Think we should head home,' he said.

'Aw.'

'The puppies look sleepy. And I'm hungry. Let's get a snack.'

There was an elaborate farewell between Bean and the dogs then they went along the road, the rumble from the building site accompanying them. Diggers hauled chunks of earth out of the ground, cranes swung large pipes through the air and placed them into ditches, lots of guys in hi-vis telling each other what to do.

As they crossed the road to Greendykes House a woman got out of a Ford parked outside. She stretched and looked around, taking in the view, then pretended to spot Tyler and Bean, as if this was a coincidence.

Detective Inspector Pearce. She was short and stocky, shoulder-length curly hair, white blouse and black skirt. She'd interviewed him a couple of times at the station on Duddingston Road West, once just a rounding-up of the usual suspects, the other time a serious fight at school between two girls in his class. Pearce had grown up in Niddrie and liked to let you know it, and while that gained some respect, the decision to join the force threw it out the window. She'd visited their flat before too, chats with Barry and Kelly, but she'd never managed to nail any Wallaces yet.

She smiled as Tyler and Bean approached. 'Tyler.'

He lifted his chin in acknowledgement.

She kept the smile painted on. 'Can I come up for a wee chat?'

Tyler thought of the bags of stolen stuff in the living room.

'Not without a warrant.'

'You know your rights.'

'That's a state education for you.'

'I hear from your school that you're pretty bright.'

Tyler handed Bean his house keys. He didn't want her listening in, but wasn't sure what waited for her upstairs. Likewise with Pearce. He couldn't invite her up but being seen talking to her out here wasn't good for his health either.

'Let yourself in,' he said to Bean. 'There's crisps in the kitchen cupboard next to the kettle. I'll be up in minute.'

She was reluctant to go, eyeing up Pearce, but Tyler let go of her hand and waved her away, watched her go inside.

'They grow up fast,' Pearce said.

'What do you want?'

'I'm here to help.'

'Of course.'

'Community policing, keeping you safe.'

Tyler made to walk away. 'If you're not going to get to the point.'

Pearce stood across his path. 'Busy last night?'

Tyler stepped back. 'No.'

'What were you up to?'

'Stayed in, watched telly.'

'Can anyone confirm that?'

Tyler shook his head. 'Bean was asleep. Mum was crashed out.'

There was something on Pearce's face, something he didn't like. Sympathy. It was the same look he got from everyone when they found out what his home life was like. Teachers, social workers, police, all with good intentions, showering him with condescending applause for coping. Fuck that.

'Have you heard?' Pearce said.

Tyler gave her a blank look.

Pearce sighed. 'A woman was almost killed in a burglary last night. On St Margaret's Road. Know it?'

'No.'

'Just down from Bruntsfield Links. Nice part of town.'

Tyler glanced up at the tower block, wondered how many pairs of eyes were on them, whether Barry or Kelly were at the window.

Pearce looked at the unmarked police car. Tyler saw a second officer in the passenger seat. They always went in pairs, but why hadn't he got out of the car with Pearce? Made this unofficial, no corroboration, so anything he said was between the two of them. The car was a grey Ford Focus, chosen to blend in, the same tactic Barry used for the robberies. But you could still spot a cop car from a mile away. For a start it had two aerials. The cops flattened down the second one, they knew it was obvious, but you could still see it. And there was something strange with the number plates too – they had a different supplier so the 'S' was oddly square, like a backward 'Z', and the 'R's were weird too.

Pearce turned back to him. 'Her name was Monica Holt, ring any bells?'

MH 100 on the Audi.

'No.' Despite himself, he pictured the look on her face as he left the house.

'Deke Holt's wife.'

'Right.'

'I know you know all about the Holts.'

'If you say so.'

He wondered if she was awake in hospital. If she would be able to pick him out of a line-up. She'd seen more of Barry and Kelly, but he had locked eyes with her as she lay on the floor.

'She's in a bad way,' Pearce said, as if reading his thoughts. 'But she'll pull through. Still unconscious but she'll wake up, and I'm sure she'll be able to help us with our inquiries.'

It seemed unlikely Monica Holt would talk, Deke would want to handle it himself. But Tyler couldn't be sure, this was different from the usual turf bullshit that flared up every now and then. This was trespassing in a man's home, attacking his wife. They were in a situation now that Tyler knew nothing about, all bets were off.

'I hope she gets better soon,' Tyler said, and he meant it.

Pearce stared at him. She knew, of course, but she couldn't prove anything. Or maybe she didn't know, maybe she was more stupid than she seemed. But she wouldn't be here if she hadn't already heard something about the Wallaces being out last night.

'Look, you're a good kid.' She gazed up at the block towering over them, then at the building site. 'You do really well with that wee sister of yours, considering the situation at home.'

He scuffed his trainer on the ground.

'I know you're not a bad person, Tyler, everyone tells me that. But you're mixed up in something serious now. This is not like lifting a laptop from Costa, this is the big league. This is breaking and entering, armed robbery, attempted murder.' She sighed. 'And the Holts. Really? Did Barry pick this fight deliberately? If so, he's suicidal. If it was an accident, well that's unlucky up to a point. But the knife?'

She leaned in, her voice softer.

'I know Barry is a maniac, you know Barry is a maniac. In the past maybe he could protect you. But he can't protect you from this, do you understand? He's going to lose one way or the other. Either the Holts get him or we do. Are you going to go down with him?'

'I don't know what you're talking about.'

'Think about what will happen to Bethany.'

There was kindness in her eyes, but a hardness too. She was about the same age as Tyler's mum, maybe they went to school together. He wondered what she thought of Angela, if that came into play. Everything came into play in a place like this, the ghosts of people's childhoods haunted your every step in a community this interconnected.

'Think about what'll happen to your little sister if you're not around. Who'll get her to school? Who will make her tea and get her into the bath? Who'll stop her making the same mistakes as her mum?'

'I need to go.' Tyler looked around. A couple of old women at the bus stop, a kid on a BMX doing wheelies along the pavement. Flat grey cloud overhead, the smell of damp earth from the building site.

'This is your chance to say something,' Pearce said.

'I don't know about any of this.'

'We're just starting the investigation and I'm already here. We haven't even got CCTV from the street yet.'

Tyler thought about walking down that street this morning with his hood up.

Pearce shook her head. 'And forensics. Normally we wouldn't waste manpower on a burglary, but attempted murder is different.'

Tyler thought about the gloves he'd worn, tried to picture Barry's hands, Kelly's.

'And people talk,' Pearce said. 'If they don't talk to us, they'll talk to Deke Holt, you know that. The clock is ticking.'

'I have to go look after Bean,' Tyler said.

Pearce held his gaze for a moment then stepped back.

'Fine, just one more thing. Castlemound told me you missed a few classes this morning. Where were you?'

'Walking around.'

'Whereabouts?'

Tyler waved behind him. 'Just getting some air.'

Pearce raised her eyebrows. 'So if we check CCTV for this morning, we won't see you anywhere near St Margaret's Road?'

'Of course not.'

He thought about standing in the living room of Will's house, bandaging Flick's hand at the kitchen sink, racing away in her car. Closed his eyes for a moment and felt tired.

Pearce reached out and touched his arm and he jumped in surprise.

'I know you feel bad,' she said. 'I know you wouldn't do something like this. But I know you were there and soon I'll have proof. If you help me I can protect you, I can make sure you and Bethany stay together, that you're looked after. But if you let this escalate there's nothing I can do.'

She reached into her pocket and took out a card, handed it to him. Detective Inspector Gail Pearce, Police Scotland logo, mobile number. He looked at it for a second then buried it in his pocket.

'Call me,' she said, heading towards the car. 'Soon.'

She got in, started the engine and circled out of the car park. He watched the car drive away, feeling the fifteen storeys of the tower block looming over him.

13

He came out of the lift and walked towards the flat but he knew he wouldn't make it. His body was tense as he anticipated the sound of the other door opening, so when he heard the squeak of the hinge it came as a weird relief.

'Tyler.'

He breathed and turned to face Barry in the doorway. He was wearing a muscle T-shirt with a boxing gym logo on, something generic and fake American. Black joggers and bare feet.

'In you come,' he said, standing aside to let Tyler past.

Tyler kept his stride steady as he passed Barry in the doorway. He caught a whiff of vodka, sex and sweat. The door clicked shut behind them and Tyler went into the living room, the layout of the flat an inverted version of the one he shared with Bean and Mum. This place was a tip, booze bottles and pizza boxes on the floor, white powder on the kitchenette worktop next to a rolled-up twenty.

Kelly was on the sofa, wearing one of Barry's T-shirts and nothing else, her bare legs lifted under her. She was stroking the ears of one of their dogs, a brown staffie with a bad attitude. They had two dogs, Ant and Dec, Tyler couldn't tell them apart. The other staffie mooched over, snarled then nosed Tyler's crotch so strongly that he was pushed off balance. He nudged the dog with his thigh and it snapped at him.

'Fuck off,' Tyler said.

'He likes you,' Barry said.

A gameshow was on television, a version of the penny-pusher games you got at the amusements on Porty Beach. Answer a question, stick a coin in, win a prize. Or not.

Barry made no effort to get the dog away from Tyler. Kelly looked up from the sofa. 'Hey, squirt.'

'Empty your pockets,' Barry said.

'What?'

Barry stepped closer. 'You fucking heard me.'

Tyler put on a face like the instruction was stupid. 'Why?'

Barry took another step, his fingers tapping on the kitchen worktop, neck muscles straining. 'Do it.'

Tyler thought about the money he still had tucked into the elastic of his underwear as he emptied his pockets onto the worktop. Loose change, chewing gum, his phone. And Pearce's card.

Barry picked it up. 'What's this?'

'I was just coming to see you. I was checking on Bean first, then straight over.'

Barry had seen everything from the window, Tyler had assumed that, so he might as well play it straight.

'What did you tell her?'

'Nothing.'

Barry played with the card in his fingertips. 'Think harder.'

'Obviously I didn't say anything, why would I?'

'What did she want?'

'She said she knew about last night's jobs.'

'Bullshit.' Barry crumpled the card in his fist. 'How could she?'

Tyler swallowed hard. 'The second job.'

'What about it?'

Kelly was paying attention now, as pennies tumbled on the television screen and a contestant jumped up and down, grinning like an idiot.

'It was Deke Holt's house.'

One penny was left dangling over the lip of the machine, tantalising.

'Fuck off it was.'

Tyler nodded. 'I heard it at school too.'

'What exactly did you hear?'

'Connell told me that Ryan Holt's mum was stabbed in a burglary. St Margaret's Road. Her car was stolen.'

'And what did you tell Connell?'

'Nothing, what do you take me for?'

Kelly spoke up. 'Shit, this is bad.'

Barry put a finger out for her to shut up. 'Let me think.'

The dog, Ant or Dec, nudged at Tyler's legs again. The power in those muscles. These bastards could rip a kid to pieces in minutes. He was glad they stayed here, nowhere near Bean. They should be muzzled, but of course Barry would never do that.

Tyler tried not to stare at Barry putting it all together. They were fucked either way. He glanced at Pearce's card in Barry's fist. Tyler had already put the number into his phone under an alias in the lift on the way up, so the card didn't matter. He didn't know yet what he might need Pearce for, but his way out of this was getting narrower every minute, so he had to keep his options open.

'So be it,' Barry said eventually.

'What does that mean?' Kelly said.

'It means what it means, you stupid cow. We're in something now, let's just ride it as far as it goes.'

Kelly didn't speak, knew better than to ask the same question twice. Tyler had seen the black eyes, the bruised arms. He'd had the same, of course. They had that in common at least.

Tyler wondered if Barry had a clue what to do. If he simply hadn't used the knife, they wouldn't be in this shit, but Tyler wasn't about to say that.

Barry took a swig from a vodka bottle on the worktop, sniffed and rubbed his stubbled jaw. He didn't seem to give a shit. He uncrumpled the card in his hand and stared at it. 'I'll keep hold of this.'

Tyler picked up the rest of his stuff and put it back in his pockets.

Barry took another swig and Tyler wondered how drunk he was. He was steady on his feet but he could drink like a fish and seem sober, so that didn't mean much.

'And you're sure you didn't say anything to this bitch cop?'

Tyler shook his head.

'How did she get here so fast?'

Tyler shrugged. 'Someone must've talked.'

Barry thought about that. 'I'll put some feelers out. Find out what's happening.'

'What about the Holts?' Kelly said, shrinking as she spoke.

'I'll deal with those cunts.' Barry didn't sound convinced.

'Have you shifted the gear from last night yet?' Tyler said.

'What's it to you?'

'It'll make us more traceable.'

Barry pulled a roll of tenners from his pocket. 'Tough tits, it's gone.'

Tyler felt another nudge from the dog.

'I need to go see Bean,' he said. 'She'll be wondering where I am.'

Barry narrowed his eyes. 'Sure. But don't go anywhere else without telling me.'

Tyler put his hands out. 'Where would I go?'

14

Bean was parked in front of CBBC eating Pringles from the tube. Tyler walked over and ruffled her hair and she smiled without looking up. He liked that she just trusted him to be there. Sometimes being taken for granted was OK.

'What are you watching?'

'*The Next Step.*'

'What's that?'

She rolled her eyes as if the question was stupid. 'It's about a dance studio. They have boyfriends and girlfriends and competitions and bad guys.'

'Sounds daft.'

'You're daft.'

Two airbrush-beautiful teenage girls, a blonde and a brunette, were arguing about something in a coffee shop. He tried to remember if the stuff he watched at Bean's age was any better or worse. He'd been allowed to watch anything, do anything, at her age. Angela had no control and Barry and Kelly didn't give a shit.

He weighed the Pringles can and put the lid on it.

'Hey, I'm eating them,' Bean said.

'You've already had half a tube. Have an apple.'

'Can you cut it up for me?'

He made a crazy sign with his hand to his head. 'That's what teeth are for.'

'Pleeeease.'

He got a knife and cut the apple into quarters. He looked over to the corner, the bags of stuff were gone, right enough. He thought of Barry and Kelly next door. The fact they were having sex and didn't even care if he knew, that was fucked up. He wondered what DI Pearce would make of incest.

He stuck the apple pieces on a plate and handed it to Bean.

'Is Mum in?'

'In bed,' Bean said. 'Vodka.'

Tyler had read online that the first ten years were the most impressionable for the human brain. What chance did that give Bean? Her mind was taking shape, her sense of self forming, and all of this bullshit around them was going into it. But then he had the same and he turned out OK. He thought about Monica Holt and wondered about that.

'Did you go in?' Tyler said.

Bean nodded. 'I couldn't wake her.'

'How hard did you try?'

'Quite hard.'

Tyler went to the bedroom, careful not to hurry, knocked, waited then walked in.

Curtains closed, stale booze and fags, the smell of sweat and piss.

Angela was naked on top of the bed, skin ghostly and blue, dark patch between her legs. He put his hand in front of her mouth, felt her hot breath. That was something. He saw a wet patch on the sheet spreading out from under her. He rolled her onto her front, got an old towel and placed it over the stain, then rolled her back on top of the dry towel. Threw a blanket over her and stood watching for a while. Deep lines around her eyes and across her forehead, even in sleep. Blood close to the skin in her cheeks and nose, a drinker's complexion. Sores on her upper lip and spots around her mouth. Two chipped teeth at the front from when she fell over trying to get her key in the door. Despite all of that she looked peaceful, no worries for now.

He picked up the empty bottle but left the half-smoked joint in the ashtray by the bed, having checked it wasn't lit. He went back to the kitchenette, placed the bottle in the recycling box under the sink. He stood with a hand either side of the sink for a while, thinking.

He went to his bedroom and got his phone out, looked up the number for Edinburgh Royal Infirmary.

'Hello, ERI?'

'Hi, I'm phoning about my mum, Monica Holt,' he said. 'I was just wondering how she's doing?'

'Just a second, I'll put you through to her ward.'

Hold music, too cheery, Ariana Grande.

'Hello, intensive care?'

Northern Irish accent, curling vowels.

'Hi, I was wondering about my mum, Monica Holt?'

'Ryan?'

Shit. 'Yeah.'

'No change since you were in this morning, love, sorry.'

'OK, thanks.'

'Your dad's still here if you want to speak to him?'

Tyler's throat felt like it was on fire. 'No, it's OK, I'll see him at home.'

'OK, dear, take it easy.'

He hung up and looked around the room. His hands were shaking. He took breaths, closed his eyes, thought about waves lapping on a beach. Eventually he felt the heat behind his eyes dissipate, so he went back through to the living room.

Bean had finished her apple. 'What's for tea?'

'Fish fingers.'

He stood in the kitchenette, his fingers touching the worktop, and tried to remember how to cook.

✳

Bean had been asleep for half an hour when Tyler's phone rang. Nobody ever called. He approached the handset like it was a loose tiger and stared at the screen. A string of numbers he didn't recognise. He thought about the hospital call earlier, patched through a switchboard. But why would anyone think that call was suspicious? His hand moved towards the phone like it was magnetically attracted.

He took the call but didn't speak.

'Hello, hello, this better be Tyler Wallace.'

Flick.

'Hey.'

'Is that you?'

'Yeah.'

'Just as well,' Flick said. 'If you gave me a fake number you'd be a dead man.'

Tyler thought about Monica's phone, Deke's message.

'How would you trace me?'

'I have your name, dummy.'

'What if that's fake too?'

'Are you an international spy or something?'

'Maybe I thought it best to give you a false name, given where we met.'

'Shut up, I already found you on Instagram.'

'Oh.'

'I bet you weren't expecting to hear from me.'

Tyler thought about what to say. 'I hoped I would.'

'Correct answer.' There was a pause, she was either drinking or smoking something. 'Listen, what are you up to?'

'When?'

'Now.'

He looked around the room for an answer. He thought about Bean, but she was settled. 'Not much.'

'I need to get out of this place,' Flick said. 'Fancy going for a drive?'

'Where to?'

'I don't know, around. It's a drive, that's the point.'

He didn't speak for a moment.

'Hello?' Flick said. 'Is this thing on?'

'Sure.'

'Great. Text me your address and I'll pick you up.'

*

He checked in on Bean. She was cuddling Panda, covers off, snoring softly. He pulled the duvet up and kissed her. He went into Angela's room, no change, then he got his jacket and opened the front door. Put the key in the outer side of the lock and turned it so the Yale didn't click when he shut the door. He stared at Barry and Kelly's place, imagined the spyhole watching him. He tiptoed away and pushed the stairwell door. He couldn't stand waiting for the lift, expecting Barry to clatter out at any moment. Down fifteen flights, dizzy at the repetition, then he was outside in the courtyard.

Five minutes later the Beetle bombed round the curve in the road then braked and turned into the car park. He glanced at the windows above him, wondered if anyone was watching.

Flick smiled as the passenger window buzzed down. 'Hey.'

She was wearing black leggings and a loose T-shirt with *Loser* across it in a heavy-metal typeface. Her hair was down and she wore eye shadow and lippy.

He got in and she looked at the tower block. 'You live up there?'

'Top floor.'

'Some view, I bet.'

'Yeah, of the building site across the road.'

She pulled out and followed the road. Tyler was glad it was dark, you couldn't make out the fly-tips and shit everywhere. They drove past the school then onto the main road, headed into town. Tyler thought about last night, this same journey in the dark, heading west to the posh houses, Barry and Kelly touching each other in the front, all the shit that went down. He couldn't believe it was only twenty-four hours ago, it seemed like he'd known Flick for weeks. It felt comfortable here with her shifting through the gears then back down at the Cameron Toll lights. He didn't ask where they were going, just allowed himself to be taken. They drove through Southside past student bars and takeaways, down to the Pleasance and along Cowgate, through the tourists of Grassmarket.

As they headed into Lothian Road he took Monica Holt's phone from his pocket. Switched it on. Sat waiting, holding the phone too tight. As it came to life, notifications scrolled up the screen. He went into texts, looked for ones from Deke:

This phone has been stolen, please contact this number immediately. There is a reward.

He stared at it for a moment, then realised there was a more recent one above.

If you took this phone you are dead.

Sent at lunchtime today. He looked at it until the screen went dark, then switched the phone off and put it back in his pocket. He looked out at the Meadows now zipping past, another piece of misdirection for anyone tracking the phone.

He realised they were heading back to her ex's house when she turned at the end of Marchmont Road. Off to the right was St Margaret's Road but they drove straight on then turned the corner, left again.

'What are you doing?' he said.

'Just driving around.'

'No, you're not.'

She touched his leg. He looked at her hand, dark purple nails, long fingers.

'I just want to see.'

Returning to the scene of the crime. As if he could talk, walking along St Margaret's Road earlier today with his hood up.

She turned into Clinton Road and pulled in across the road from Will's house.

'We shouldn't be here,' Tyler said.

'Just for a moment.'

The house was silent and dark, no sign of life. He remembered the soft piano of that music. Flick was peering across the road.

'Do you rob people?' she said.

He closed his eyes then opened them again. 'What makes you ask that?'

She gave him a 'well, duh' look. 'I found you inside someone's house today.'

'You broke in too.'

'I wasn't robbing him.'

'I wasn't stealing anything.'

'But you could've.'

Silence, just the windows fogging up from their breath.

'I didn't.'

She stared at him. 'I don't mind if you are a burglar.' She smiled and touched his shoulder. 'Actually, it's quite sexy.'

He shrugged her off. 'You don't know what you're talking about.'

She bristled at his tone. 'Take it easy, I was only teasing.'

'We should go.'

She looked at him for a long time. A middle-aged woman with a dog walked past, and Tyler turned his head to look the other way so that she didn't get a clear view of his face. Flick noticed, then turned the engine on and pulled out.

They drove to Blackford then round King's Buildings, heading east again. Tyler thought she was dropping him back home already, and he tried to think what to say. He wanted to stay with her, thought maybe he'd offended her. But she turned right early and went up the hill to Craigmillar Castle, pulled into the tiny car park at the top of the hill.

She cut the engine and got out. 'Come on.'

He followed without speaking.

She climbed over the low gate and walked past the gatehouse, the closed ticket office inside. To their right were fields and the large woodland park, then beyond that Arthur's Seat was a dark presence against the bruised skyline. They were up high enough that he could already see the Forth and Inchkeith, the wink of the lighthouse every few seconds. The lights of the city painted a handful of clouds orange, but further out over the water the sky was black. Up ahead was the castle, technically a ruin but most of it was in decent shape. Some of the walls and roofs were missing but large sections of the stonework were intact.

'What are we doing?' Tyler said, catching her up.

'I like it here.'

'It's trespassing.'

Flick rolled her eyes. 'That didn't stop you at Will's house.'

'There are cameras,' Tyler said. He'd spotted one at the gatehouse already.

Flick shook her head. 'They don't work. I've been here a dozen times, never got caught. No one cares as long as you don't vandalise the place.'

The latticed iron gate of the castle was locked. Flick went round the sidewall and clambered up the crumbling stones. She was onto the top of the wall in a minute, and Tyler followed. She walked along it for fifty feet to another crumbling corner, then used the tumbledown part as steps into the castle grounds. She was quick and precise, had obviously done this before. He followed suit.

'Why this place?' he said.

She held her arms out at the view spreading north to the sea.

'I can't believe this doesn't have better security,' Tyler said.

'There's nothing to steal.' Flick headed into the central tower. She switched on the torch on her phone and climbed the stairs. He followed, the bob of her torch beam disappearing round the spiral staircase. She was running so he ran too, caught her at the top of the stairs.

She leaned on the wall, looked out at the view, so much more impressive from a hundred feet higher up. The whole of Edinburgh before them, hundreds of thousands of souls going about their lives, never realising they could have moments like this in the dark, with a girl, in a ruined castle.

They looked at the expanse of the city in front of them for a long time. The longer they stood in silence, the more comfortable Tyler felt. He could smell her perfume, the same as earlier today.

'I love it here,' Flick said eventually.

'I can see why.'

She sighed. 'When everything at school is too much, you know? There are all these people about, so much gossip and bullshit. He said, she said, all day long, it never ends. There's no time to stop and think.' She laughed at the words blurting out of her mouth. 'Sorry, that sounds really stupid.'

'No,' Tyler said. 'I get it.'

She threw a smile at him in the gloom. 'I knew you would.' She turned back to look at the view. 'That's why you were in Will's house this morning, wasn't it? Time to stop and think.'

Tyler thought about what to say. 'I can't really explain it. I've never talked about it before. It's like escaping.'

'Escaping what?'

'Life.'

'What do you need to escape from in your life?'

'All of it.'

She put her arm through his and leaned in a little.

'Tell me about your family.'

'What makes you say that?'

'Everyone's problems come from their families.'

'I have a little sister, Bethany, we all call her Bean. She's seven.'

'I don't have any brothers or sisters,' Flick said. 'Classic only child – overconfident, self-centred and narcissistic.'

'Bean's great, we're really close. I have an older half-brother and half-sister, Barry and Kelly.'

'What are they like?'

'Pricks.'

'I'm sure you still love them.'

He shook his head. 'You have no idea.'

'You haven't mentioned parents.'

Tyler glanced behind him at the central tower, lightning rod running up the side, a needle into the dark.

'Never had a dad. And Mum's got problems.'

'What sort of problems?'

Tyler shook his head. Silence spread between them. Out at sea he could see a ship, lit up like a ghost. A couple of cars came up the road to their right, headlights splitting the night, then over the brow of the hill and gone. It was so peaceful here, just the wind through the oak trees in the park.

'Well my parents are a fucking nightmare,' Flick said, raising her voice, trying to make a joke of it. But there was an edge to her tone. 'For a start they abandoned me at that shithole school. Dad was an officer in the Marines for years, so they moved around a lot. Now he's some kind of special private military consultant. He's out in Afghanistan at the moment. Mum's out there too, working as his PA. She could've stayed here and I wouldn't have had to board with all those stuck-up arseholes. She chose to be with Dad over me. Mind you, she's a high-functioning alcoholic. It's easy when you're well off, drinking all day is socially acceptable. And she takes a ton of pills to get to sleep, to wake up, to level out her mood, to take the edge off the day. It's pathetic. Dad doesn't even know. He has PTSD after a stint in Iraq, night terrors. He has his own shit to deal with.'

Tyler wondered how to describe his own home life and have it make sense. He couldn't even think of the words to use. Flick had her whole situation mapped out in her head, the hard-done-by abandoned daughter. But she had money, friends, got her meals cooked for her. She had routine, classes, extracurricular shit, her life regimented, structured.

He liked school because, when he didn't have to bunk off for his own sanity, it gave him the same thing, structure. He liked maths and science especially, the way the laws of nature and mathematics obeyed rules, there was logic to them, cause and effect, the neatness and symmetry of it.

'Sorry for mouthing off,' Flick said.

'Don't be,' Tyler said. 'I like hearing your voice.'

She laughed. 'It's just a voice.'

'It's not an accent I'm used to,' Tyler said. 'You sound like a weather presenter.'

She laughed again and pulled at his arm. 'Come on.'

She walked round the walled exterior of the keep, looking first northwest at the illuminated slope of the Royal Mile and the knuckle of Edinburgh Castle, then southwest, the Pentlands sprawled in the distance. Then she stopped at the southeast corner. Nearby trees blocked the view of Greendykes House. She looked in that direction.

'What's it like, living in Niddrie?'

'Not as bad as it used to be.'

'There used to be a lot of gangs, right?'

He nodded.

'Are you in a gang?'

'Fuck that,' Tyler said. 'Quick way to get yourself stabbed.'

He instantly regretted the word. He looked to his right, saw the spread of the hospital in the valley below them, glowing radioactive with hundreds of lights. Monica Holt was in there somewhere fighting to stay alive. Waiting to wake up and tell the world what she'd seen. A gaping knife wound that would take weeks or months to heal, if she ever came round. He thought about Ryan and Deke sitting seething at her bedside, desperate for revenge on the bastards who did it.

'Maybe I should come and stay with you at Inveresk,' he said after a while.

'You might not get stabbed,' Flick said. 'But, believe me, we have our own shit there too.'

He made a sceptical face, couldn't help himself.

She grinned. 'I know how it sounds. Poor little rich girl with all her emotional problems.' She waved her arms around, mocking herself, then put the back of her hand to her forehead like she might faint. 'Oh my!'

She rubbed at the stonework with a finger, head down. 'But that doesn't make the problems any less real.'

Tyler watched her for a moment, then put his hand on top of hers.

She leaned in and kissed him on the cheek, taking her time.

'I like you Tyler Wallace,' she whispered, her face close to his. 'I would hate it if you got stabbed.'

He held her gaze and realised he didn't even know her surname.

15

Tyler eased the key in the door, turned it and stepped into the flat. He went straight to Bean's room to check on her. She had the covers off again, the girl couldn't lie still for two minutes. She was breathing deeply and snuffled as he pulled the duvet back up. He leaned in and brushed his lips against her hair, stood looking at her for a second, then left.

He went to Angela's room next, hit by the smell as he opened the door. No worse than when he left, that was the main thing. She hadn't vomited or pissed any more by the looks of things. He rested his fingers on her wrist and felt a strong pulse. Her breath was pure vodka.

He pulled the door behind him then went to the living room, switched on the light and jumped. Barry was sitting on the kitchenette worktop smoking a fag. The TV remote was in his other hand but the television was off.

'Where the fuck have you been?' he said, gripping the remote.

'Just out for a walk.'

Barry shook his head and inhaled. 'Just out for a walk.'

'Yeah.'

'Where, exactly?'

Tyler looked out of the window. 'Up towards Craigmillar Castle.'

'Up towards the castle?'

'That's right.'

'Have you ever been to that fucking castle before in your life?'

Tyler shook his head, kept his distance. 'Don't think so.'

'No, I don't think so either. So why the fuck did you go there tonight?'

Tyler was motionless, as if he was wary of setting off a landmine underfoot. 'Just needed to think.'

Barry jumped down from the worktop with the cigarette hanging from his mouth, still clutching the remote. 'Why do you need time to think?'

Tyler didn't answer, there wasn't an answer.

Barry took a step closer. 'You don't need to think, bruv.' The last word was soaked in sarcasm. 'I do all the thinking in this family.'

Barry took another step.

Tyler stood his ground in the doorway. 'No worries.'

Barry sucked on the cigarette. 'What did I tell you?'

'Not to think.'

'You cheeky cunt. I mean earlier tonight. What did I tell you?'

Tyler stayed silent.

Barry raised his eyebrows. 'Well?'

'I don't know.'

'You don't fucking know.' Then again, much slower. 'You don't fucking know.' He rubbed at his eyes and looked tired. 'The shit I have to put up with, honestly. Your dumb slag of a sister, our fucked-up mum, even that wee bitch asleep through the way.'

Tyler stood taller at the mention of Bean, tried to fill the doorway. 'Sorry, Barry.'

'You're sorry, that's lovely.' He tapped the remote control against his thigh. 'What exactly are you sorry for?'

Tyler shook his head.

The fag was burning down in Barry's lips, not much more than filter now. 'What's the point of saying sorry if you don't know what you're sorry for?' Barry held his arms out wide, looked around the room for answers. 'Are you maybe sorry because I told you not to go out tonight, and yet you still fucking did?'

Tyler rubbed at the palm of his hand.

'Are you sorry because you're lying to me about where you were?'

'I'm not, honest.'

Barry stepped closer, pointed the remote control.

'You're a lying piece of shit,' he said under his breath. 'I heard you sneak out and I saw you get in a car downstairs, so you weren't out getting some air or clearing your fucking head.'

He lifted the remote and swung it at Tyler's head. Tyler flinched and ducked but it connected with his ear. Two more swipes, the plastic edge of the remote smacking into Tyler's temple and the corner of his eye. Tyler was hunched over, arms raised against the blows, but they came anyway, bang-bang on the back of his head, then again catching the edge of his eye as Tyler tried to look up, blood dripping from a cut there now as more blows came down, again on the ear then the base of his skull.

Barry dropped the remote and grabbed Tyler's throat, pushed him against the wall, choking him. Vodka and fag ash on his breath as he spat in Tyler's face. 'So why don't you tell me exactly what you were doing tonight.'

'I was out with a girl.' Tyler's voice was cracked.

Barry smiled. 'A girl? I always thought you were bent.'

Tyler struggled to breathe, put his fingers to Barry's on his throat but couldn't get purchase.

'Where did you meet her?'

'Online.'

'On a website?'

Tyler tried to nod.

'Where's she from?'

'Mussy.'

'Driving a car like that?'

'It's her mum's.'

'Must be fucking loaded.' Barry had eased off on his throat and Tyler gasped. 'Where did you go?'

Tyler gulped between words. 'We really did go to the castle.'

'Did you ride her?'

Tyler didn't respond so Barry squeezed his throat again.

'Nothing like that,' Tyler said.

Barry frowned. 'Maybe you are bent after all.'

Blood ran into Tyler's mouth from his cut eye. He sucked it in and swallowed. Taste of rust.

Barry relaxed a little but kept his hand on Tyler's neck. 'What's her name?'

'Fiona.'

'Fiona what?'

'That's all she's told me.'

'Probably wary of a prick like you. You seeing her again?'

'Not sure.'

'If you do, I want to meet her, right?'

Tyler didn't speak until Barry put more pressure on his neck. 'Of course.'

'Can't have just any cunt finding out about us, especially at the moment.'

Tyler nodded and Barry let go of his throat. Tyler collapsed and gasped in air, touched the corner of his eye, his hand coming away red.

Barry took the fag end out of his mouth and dropped it on the carpet, ground it in with his foot.

'Now don't be a cunt about that,' he said, pointing at Tyler's eye. 'It's just a scratch.'

He turned to leave the room but kept his eye on Tyler.

'It'll be worse for you if you ever lie to me again. Got it?'

Tyler didn't move, just watched his brother leave the room. He heard the front door close, then slumped to the floor and began crying.

16

He was woken by the smell of eggs frying. He touched the corner of his eye, which was half shut, felt the tender skin, the cut along the brow. He eased out of bed, aching, pulled on a T-shirt and went to investigate.

He stopped in the doorway of the living room. Angela was hunched over the stove singing 'Angels' by Robbie Williams under her breath. He hadn't seen her up at this time in weeks.

'Hey, Mum.'

She looked at him. For a moment it seemed as if she didn't recognise him, then she smiled. 'My beautiful boy, let me look at you.'

He took a couple of steps forward and she left the frying pan and met him, held on to his forearms like she was trying to stop him escaping. The pan hissed and spat behind her. Her eyes were glassy, either hungover or still drunk, or maybe already drunk again this morning. The smell of it on her breath.

'I'm so proud of you,' she said, pushing her hair out of her face. 'You know that?'

Tyler pulled his arms away. It was weird being touched by her after so long without contact. Like she wasn't entitled. But she was his mum, he had to keep reminding himself about that.

She looked disappointed that he'd pulled away but she tried to cover it, put on a smile. 'Fried egg on toast OK for you?'

'Sure.'

She turned back to the cooking. 'Wake your sister or she'll be late for school.'

Bean was sitting up in her bed playing with her slime, gloop stretched between her fingers.

'Time to get up,' Tyler said. 'Mum's cooking breakfast.'

'Shut up.'

He raised his eyebrows. 'No joke.'

'Why?'

Tyler shrugged. 'Just get your stuff on.'

'What happened to your eye?' Bean said.

'Nothing. Just bumped it last night.'

It was only when he was out the room and in the hall that he realised Angela hadn't mentioned the eye. Maybe she hadn't noticed.

He flinched at the sound of a key in the front door. He should get the locks changed but then Barry would be pissed off and take it as an insult. Anyway, changing the locks cost money and Barry could just kick the door in.

The door opened and it was Kelly. Tyler tried to think of the last time he'd seen her without Barry but he couldn't remember. She was bleary-eyed and wore a thick sweatshirt and jeggings.

She closed the door behind her, looked at him and put a hand to his cheek. 'What happened to you?'

'Bumped into a cupboard in the kitchen.'

She tried to run a fingernail along the cut but he flinched. She gave him a look. 'It's best just to do what he says.'

'You think?'

She sighed. 'He's got our best interests at heart.'

'How can you say that after the other night?'

'I don't know what you're talking about,' Kelly said. 'Nothing happened the other night.'

Tyler shook his head. 'I can't get it out of my mind.'

She lowered her voice. 'Well try harder or you're going to get us all killed.'

Talking to her was like talking to Barry's sock puppet, she just agreed with everything he said.

Kelly looked through to the living room. 'What are you making for breakfast?'

'It's not me, Mum's cooking.'

'Nice one.'

'Really.' He waved towards the kitchenette.

Angela was putting a bottle of wine back in the cupboard when Tyler got to the doorway. He was disappointed but not surprised. And wine wasn't that bad, considering.

Bean came in behind him and stared at her mum.

'What are you doing?' Kelly said.

Angela turned. 'I didn't realise it was such a big deal, cooking for my kids.'

'You don't normally,' Kelly said.

Angela got plates out of the cupboard, threw toast and eggs on them. The toast was burnt and the eggs were rubbery on the bottom and raw on top. Angela moved with the rhythmic sway of a constant drunk, like she'd spent a long time at sea dealing with the shift of balance on deck.

Bean made a face at the plate in front of her, and Tyler gave her a look to at least try. He leaned in. 'I'll get you something else to eat on the way to school.'

'I heard that,' Angela said. 'Fuck's sake, I'm trying my best.'

Tyler gave Bean another look, turning the two of them into conspirators. 'Sorry.'

Kelly watched all this with her eyes wide. 'I'll leave you guys to it.' She headed towards the door then pretended to remember something. 'Tyler, can you pop in and see Barry after school? He wants to talk about something.'

'Sure,' Tyler said.

Kelly left and Bean pushed a knife into the runny white on the top of her egg. 'What does Barry want?'

'How would I know?' Tyler said. 'Now eat up.'

Bean shook her head, trying to hide it from Angela.

'Fuck this,' Angela said. She opened the cupboard, took out the wine and went to her bedroom, slamming the door like a stroppy teenager.

Tyler put his knife and fork down.

'Forget that,' he said, looking at Bean's plate. 'Let's go.'

17

Bean gave him a hug then darted across the playground to join her pals. The other three girls had those bows in their hair in various luminous shades. Miss Kelvin caught Tyler's eye and gave him a wave, that look on her face. He was sick of sympathy but he supposed it was better than apathy or aggression. If only he could translate sympathy into a way out of this. He returned the wave as the bell went and watched Bean shuffle into the line. A boy was kicking off, throwing his schoolbag around, showing off to the girls. Another one was crying and holding on to his mum, who rolled her eyes. No such drama with Bean, so grown up already.

Once she was inside he headed out of the gate and towards the high school, but then walked past the entrance and plugged his earbuds into his ears, put on Four Tet, ambient dance with some weird strings over the top. He cut along the path that split the woods from the fields. This close to the school the woods were full of crap, burnt-out remains of fires and barbecues, piles of beer and cider cans, used condoms, melted bits of plastic and twisted metal. As he got further away the rubbish cleared and he pretended he was somewhere calm and secluded. The trippy beats in his ears helped.

He emerged from the trees on the road opposite the castle. He stood looking at its outline against the sky, remembered walking round the battlements last night.

He strode down the road then he cut back in again through the woods, over the fence by the ambulance helicopter pad, then he was into the ERI grounds. He followed the signs to the entrance, the doors flanked by people smoking fags in dressing gowns, one woman with a drip on wheels next to her, the tube feeding into the folds of her nightie.

Once inside he followed the signs and the coloured lines on the floor to Intensive Care. Thousands of people in this building, each with their own problems and worries, their own dramas and catastrophes, heart attacks and cancer, bowel or urinary infections, broken bones, replacement joints, varicose veins, brain tumours. Nearly fatal stab wounds.

He went up to the desk where a nurse not much older than him was making notes on a piece of paper. Her nametag read 'Justyna'. He'd figured that the nurse from his phone call last night, who knew Ryan by name and sight, would be off shift by now. This one looked a lot younger than the voice on the phone. She looked up and gave him a tired smile.

'Can I help you?' Strong East European accent, definitely not the same nurse.

'I've forgotten which room my mum's in, Monica Holt?'

'Shouldn't you be at school?'

'Study period.'

Justyna looked at the whiteboard behind her. It was a mess of symbols and acronyms, a secret language between doctors and nurses.

'Room six,' she said, pointing down the corridor. 'Third door on the right.'

'How is she?'

Justyna checked the board, then shuffled some papers on her desk to find something. 'No change, I'm afraid, she's still in the induced coma. But the consultant will be round to check on her at lunchtime, there might be news then.'

'Thanks.'

He tried to give her a smile but she was already back to her paperwork, tapping a pen against her teeth and thumbing through beige folders, slotting papers inside.

He stared at the board behind her, frowned at the hieroglyphs, then walked away, taking a big breath and blowing it out. He closed his eyes for a second and imagined standing on a snowy mountaintop, fresh Alpine air burning his lungs.

He was at her room. Four beds, two empty. One had an old woman in it, white hair like candyfloss, sunken features, badly bruised eyes and face. The other was Monica Holt. Her hair was down, not in the ponytail she'd had the other night. She was propped up a little and he wondered about that. She had a plastic tube running into her mouth, taped at her cheek, attached by a corrugated tube to breathing apparatus. She wore a loose hospital smock, her bare arms by her sides, a drip running into a raised vein in her hand.

She looked younger than he remembered, as if all the worry had fallen from her face. The nurse had said she was in an induced coma. He made a note to look it up when he left.

He inched towards her bed, looking around with every step and expecting someone to come in and grab him. The mechanical breathing apparatus wheezed and he flinched. Her chest rose and fell and he wondered about her muscles, sliced apart and put back together under the smock and bandages.

There was a plastic seat next to the bed. He looked at it but didn't sit down. He took another step towards her, stared at her face. He noticed the smoothness of her cheeks, the dry skin on her lips, the swirl of her hair follicles. Her eyebrows were neatly shaped, her nails shiny red.

'I'm sorry,' he said.

His hand hovered over hers, and he rubbed his thumb against his fingers, scratched his forehead, then returned his hand to just above hers. He stroked the back of her hand with two fingertips and thought about her lying on the floor in her own house. Thought about his own mum, imagined her lying in a pool of blood. He remembered flinching from Angela's touch this morning.

'I didn't know. Barry...' He took deep breaths as his eyes stung. 'I phoned the ambulance, I know that's not much. I don't know if you can hear me, I guess not. I'm so sorry.'

He stood watching her chest rise and fall for a few minutes, touching her hand with his fingers.

Eventually he turned and left. Along the corridor, a middle-aged man was leaning against the reception desk, chatting to the nurse and smiling. Tyler knew from the back of his head and stocky build that it was Deke Holt.

He turned and walked in the other direction. It was only ten feet to the corner, eight feet until he would be out of sight, five feet, one step in front of the other, all it would take was for the nurse to look past Deke and point him out, there's your son now, and he was a dead man, two feet, no shout from behind him, one foot and round the corner, breaking into a run, trainers thumping on the floor, heart throwing itself against his ribcage as he bombed down the corridor and threw himself against the security door, pushing the green button to open and bursting through and away, running and running as patients and staff stared at him until he found an exit and was outside, sucking in air, hands on his knees, feeling sick but holding it in, the fresh air electrifying his lungs.

His phone pinged in his pocket and he pulled it out. A text message from Flick.

Meet me at 20 Hope Terrace, asap. Fxxx

18

He scoped the street out of habit as he turned in from Kilgraston Road. Behind him was the high wall of Grange Cemetery keeping the dead in their place. Hundreds of souls he would never know. Hope Terrace was only a couple of streets over from Flick's ex-boyfriend's place, the houses not quite so huge, the owners maybe not millionaires but still not short of a few quid. These were Victorian four-bedroom joints, bay windows, small driveways, old gardens with oak and pine trees. The street was narrow, the houses keeping an eye on each other over the setts, a delivery van rattling over the surface as it passed him.

Number twenty wouldn't have been a target if he was on a job. ADT alarm box over the front door, newly bolstered windows. Low hedges meant you were exposed out front, no obvious entry points at the side of the house or any way to get up to the first floor. Just too risky.

He had his hoodie up as he entered the driveway, resisted the urge to look around. If someone was curtain-twitching they'd see his face more clearly. He checked the windows of number twenty for movement, for any sign that Flick had broken in, but there was nothing. Blossom from a cherry tree drifted across the stonework under his feet as he reached the front door. He breathed in and out then pressed the doorbell. Old-school ding-dong tone. If this was a set-up he would just say he was looking for a friend and had the wrong house.

He waited and listened then eventually heard footsteps. The outer door was closed, white-painted oak, no glass so he couldn't see inside. The door swished open and there was Flick, mussing her hair, in skinny jeans and a white strappy top that showed off a flat stomach with a silver belly-button ring.

'You took your time,' she said.

'Some of us have to get the bus.' He looked around. 'Where's your car?'

She looked both ways, comically, like a paranoid cartoon character. 'I parked it in the next street. I'm not supposed to be here.'

'Is this another ex-boyfriend's house?'

She smiled and ushered him inside, scanning the horizon again. 'How many ex-boyfriends do you think I need to get revenge on?'

'Could be hundreds for all I know.'

'Fuck you.' She held her hands out like a magician and looked around. 'Welcome to Chez Ashcroft.'

Tyler took in the hall. 'This is your home?'

'The one and only.'

A landscape in a frame on one wall, a formal family picture on another, Flick much younger, maybe eleven, braces on her teeth. Her dad was in uniform, her mum in a simple green dress, both handsome, ordinary people trying to raise a girl.

'Don't look at that,' she said, running over and lifting the picture off the wall. She turned it and put it on the floor, giving it a considered glance as she did.

'But you stay at Inveresk,' Tyler said.

Flick walked through to the kitchen at the back of the house and Tyler followed, watching the bounce of her hair.

'Correct.' Flick turned at the island worktop in the kitchen. The room was large, French windows out to a neat lawn, landscaped garden up both sides, a fishpond down the bottom by a shed. 'I'm not supposed to be here while my folks are in Afghanistan.'

Tyler shook his head. 'You're old enough to look after yourself, surely?'

Flick widened her eyes. 'Thank you, yes. I've told them a thousand times. But they think I won't be able to motivate myself to go to classes if I stay here.'

Tyler held his arms out. 'Well, they have a point.'

'You're not in school either,' Flick said. 'You don't have the moral high ground.'

'You called me.'

'You didn't have to come.'

He looked at the pots and pans hanging along one wall. The marble worktop, Smeg fridge. 'Why did you text me?'

She made a dumb face. 'Because I wanted to see you.'

He looked away, embarrassed by her honesty. 'Why?'

She sighed theatrically. 'Oh my God.'

She opened the fridge, which contained just basic stuff, cheese and butter, jars of pickles and mustard. She pulled open one of the drawers in the bottom.

'Fancy a drink? I have beer, cider or white wine.' She looked at him, then at a wine rack along the back wall. 'Or red. Or champagne. Fancy a mimosa?'

He shook his head, didn't want to ask what that was.

'Come on, live a little,' she said.

He spotted soft drinks in the fridge. 'Just a Coke, thanks.'

'Jeeze.' She handed it to him and cracked open a bottle of Chenin blanc, poured herself a large glass. She held the glass out. 'Cheers.'

He clinked self-consciously and swigged from his can.

She took a long gulp of wine. 'Do you want the tour?'

'Sure.'

She led him round the house, mocking herself and her family as she went. But she didn't really mean it. She was aware of how well-off they were, acted a little embarrassed about it. In the living room Tyler noticed Bluetooth speakers and a large, chunky set of audio equipment, Cambridge Audio. A small selection of CDs, old indie like Radiohead and Blur, other stuff he hadn't heard of. A sleek coffee table with hi-fi magazines on it, a small wooden sculpture of Buddha. The kind of stuff you saw in show homes on television. There was no sense of people living here, ordinary people with their ordinary shit.

There were a couple more family pictures in small frames on a bookshelf. Flick skipped across and blocked his view, turning them facedown before he could see.

'What does your dad do exactly?' Tyler said.

'Orders people about in the desert.'

'He actually fights?'

'He has done. So he says.'

'I didn't think we were still at war over there.'

'Logistics,' Flick said, moving on. 'Support. I don't really know. Mum Skypes every now and then but she never says anything. It's like they don't care about me at all.'

'I'm sure they do.'

Flick led him round a dining room with an oak table and chairs, flowery wallpaper, then an office with more dark wood, black leather chair, box files on shelves. Tyler wondered if there was anything worth stealing in the desk drawers, or hidden amongst the files.

'What about your mum?' Flick said, heading up the stairs. 'You said she had problems.'

She hesitated on the landing, took a drink of her wine. He watched her drink then followed. He stared at the landing window, noticed the reinforced locks that had been added to the original wooden frame. 'She's ill.'

'I'm sorry.'

'Don't be.'

There were four bedrooms but they only needed two, so one was a guest room and the other had been turned into a makeshift gym, free weights in one corner, a running machine in the other, bits of kit scattered around.

'They're both superfit,' Flick said. 'It's tiresome. It's just something to fill up the emptiness of their lives.'

'So?'

'It's lame.' She took another drink. Her glass was almost empty.

'And what are you filling up your emptiness with?' Tyler said, glancing at her glass. He regretted it immediately.

She registered surprise, then it was gone. She slid towards him and touched his cheek in a mock-sexy gesture. 'You fill the emptiness in me, darling.' Then she flounced out of the room. Everything with her was a performance, layered in irony, wrapped up in too much self-awareness.

It was sweet but fucked up, tiring to go along with, like he was supposed to dig around for the real her.

He tried to pick up the largest dumbbell but it didn't budge from the floor. He tapped it with his toe, imagined hurling it out of the window, then left to find her.

She was in her own bedroom, sitting on the double bed, her wine glass empty. She tossed the glass between her hands, daring it to drop and smash on the floor.

'You think I'm an idiot,' she said.

'Not at all.'

There wasn't much to see in here, presumably most of her stuff was at Inveresk. Along one wall was a giant map of the world, six feet wide, dozens of red pins stuck in it.

'Everywhere Mum and Dad have been,' she said. 'Mostly without me.'

He went over and touched a pin in the UAE, then one in the Philippines. Looked at the distance from Kabul to Edinburgh.

'I can't imagine going to all those places,' he said.

'Me neither, that's the sad thing.'

She had a dresser with a mirror, white wood. An old gymnastics certificate, a couple of photos of her with medals round her neck, bright-red leotard, smile on her face.

'Oh God,' Flick said. 'There are so many pictures of me around this house.'

'So?'

'I can't stand seeing myself.'

'I like it,' Tyler said. 'You're cute.'

She was watching him in the mirror, mussing her hair, blinking.

'Why don't you come over and see the real me,' she said, patting the duvet next to her. She was taking the piss but serious at the same time. Make a joke of it, then if you get rejected, pretend it was for laughs.

He stared at her for a long time until she looked away.

'Fuck's sake, I won't bite,' she said.

He took two steps towards her, hands trembling.

The doorbell rang.

Flick rolled her eyes. 'It's the postman, ignore it.'

It rang again, three times, then a thud on the door, hard.

'What the hell?' Flick went to the window. 'Oh shit.'

Her phone rang and she declined the call.

The doorbell again, then more thumps, a fist on the door over and over.

'It's Will,' Flick said.

'The ex?'

A voice came from outside, shouting up to her bedroom window. 'I know you're in there, Flick. I saw your car round the corner. And I know what you did to my house.'

Flick raised her eyebrows and smiled at Tyler. He didn't return it.

'How could he know?' Tyler said.

Flick shrugged.

'Did you tell him?'

'Of course not, he must've guessed.'

'How?'

Flick looked irritated.

Will was back to smacking the front door, sending reverberations through the walls. 'If you don't come down and talk to me, I'm going to do the same to your house.'

Tyler thought about the rugby type he'd seen in the family pictures at Will's house.

'He's bluffing,' Flick said.

A stone clattered against the glass of her window and she jumped. Tyler wondered if there was a way out through the kitchen patio doors without being seen.

'The next one's a rock,' Will said.

Flick sighed and went to the window. 'Just a minute.'

She turned to Tyler at the door. 'Wait here, I'll get rid of him.'

Tyler walked to the doorway as Flick ran down the stairs. He listened as she opened the door, heard them arguing. He shouted at her, called her a psycho bitch. She denied anything to do with the break-in at his house, but she couldn't hide the sarcasm in her voice, couldn't help herself letting him know she was responsible.

It sounded like she hadn't let him in, that all this was happening in the doorway. His voice became quieter, still pleading but calmer. Tyler heard her counter him, complain in return. He kept asking to come inside but she said no. Then there was a smack of wood on plaster that made the house shudder, a scuffle of feet on the floor.

'What the fuck?' Flick, trying to sound composed.

'You think you're such a smart bitch, don't you?'

'Get off me.'

'You think you're better than everyone. You think you're better than me.'

'You're hurting me.'

More scuffing of feet then a thud against a wall. This was inside the house now, for sure. Tyler moved to the top of the stairs and began walking down.

'Well, you're not in charge now,' Will said, voice level and calm. 'I can do anything I want to you.'

'Let go, you're scaring me.'

'Good,' Will said. 'About time someone made you realise you're not fucking untouchable. Stuck-up bitch. You can't walk about like a prick-tease and expect to get away with it.'

'Will.'

Tyler was on the landing, could see them now. Will had Flick pushed against the wall, his arm across her chest, pinning her arm. With his other hand he was grabbing at her crotch.

'Leave her alone.' Tyler stood with his fists clenched.

Will stopped and turned. Flick turned too, but Tyler couldn't work out the look on her face. Will eased off the pressure on her chest and dropped his other hand.

'Who the hell are you?' he said, catching his breath.

'Get out,' Flick said, her voice shaky.

Will kept his arm across her chest, enough to stop her breaking free. He had his eyes on Tyler as he spoke. 'A new guy already? You don't hang about.'

'It's nothing to do with you,' Flick said.

Tyler took a few steps down the stairs and Will raised his eyebrows.

'Get your hands off her,' Tyler said.

Will smiled. 'A tough guy. Surprising, given you're half my size.'

'Just leave.'

Will finally dropped his arm and Flick staggered away, swiping at his chest as she went.

'You're such an arsehole,' she said. 'Get out of my house.'

Will stood there, enjoying not doing as he was told. Tyler came down a few more steps until he was almost at the bottom.

Will pointed at Flick but didn't say anything, then pointed at Tyler. 'A word of advice, little man. This bitch is more trouble than she's worth.'

'Fuck you,' Flick said.

'Leave,' Tyler said.

'Are you going to make me?'

'If I have to.' Tyler was surprised at the conviction in his own voice. The menace. Hanging around with Barry was rubbing off. He tried to stay focused.

Will had his chin out, chest puffed, all the alpha-male bullshit. Tyler thought about how Barry would kill him in ten seconds. He pretended he had the same skills, the same determination.

Eventually Will deflated a little, stood down from high alert.

'You're not worth the hassle,' he said, looking around the hallway as if only just realising where he was. 'But if I see you again you're dead.'

Flick shook her head and Tyler remained motionless, face impassive. Sometimes, the best thing to say is nothing.

Will turned to leave, but pointed at Flick one last time. 'I'm sending you the bill for my house, for the window. You fucking psycho.'

Flick didn't answer as Will left, leaving the front door wide open.

Flick waited until his footsteps had faded then turned to Tyler. 'Thanks, seriously.'

Tyler sat down on the step and breathed, tried to loosen his fists, tried to stop his legs from trembling.

19

The playground was hoaching, a gang of younger boys kicking a ball around on the concrete, older girls reapplying make-up and laughing in a corner, a couple of stoners sharing a joint out of sight of the staffroom.

He'd made Flick drop him off round the corner from the front gate. It just seemed easier not to have her involved in this place, in his life. Yet he dropped everything whenever she called.

He found Connell and a couple of other boys hanging out at the edge of the staff car park, doing nothing. He'd missed lunch by now but he didn't feel hungry, the adrenaline from earlier still pumping through him. His veins felt tight and full.

'Where you been?' Connell said, kicking an empty Irn Bru can at him. Tyler had a couple of wee kicks then knocked it back to him. Connell flicked it to one of the other boys.

'Bean was playing up this morning,' Tyler said. 'Said she felt sick.'

'Was she?'

'Na, just at it.'

Tyler drifted in and out of the conversation as Connell and the other boys bounced chat between them, Hibs' chances this season, who they might sign, then something about Louisa who Connell fancied, a party at her pal's house coming up and how they could wangle an invite. Gentle piss-takes and ribbing, the mulch of friendship. He joined in on the surface but felt a rock in his stomach through the whole thing, a dread that wouldn't shift. He wondered about CCTV cameras at the hospital, about the death threat on Monica's phone. He thought about Barry hitting him for seeing Flick, pictured Flick pressed up against the wall by that twat Will.

The bell went and they trudged towards the entrance. As the streams of kids merged, he spotted Ryan Holt up ahead, talking to his stupid cousin Lee. They were equally as hard but Ryan had brains. Smart tough guys always need a dumb sidekick to make them feel better about themselves. Just like Barry and Kelly.

He headed in Ryan's direction.

Connell grabbed his arm. 'What the hell are you doing?'

Tyler shook him off and kept walking. He could sense Connell shrinking into the background behind him, the other guys too, they didn't want any part of this. Nobody wanted a piece of Ryan Holt, that was crazy.

Ryan was stubbing out a cigarette, unbothered about a teacher seeing him. He would soon be out of here and into the family business, making serious money. Meantime there were good contacts to be had at school, plenty of kids after drugs or other contraband.

'Ryan.' Tyler raised his voice over the chatter of the playground. A few girls in between them melted away. Ryan looked up, narrowing his eyes. Lee watched his cousin, gauging his body language. People didn't usually bother Ryan Holt.

Ryan stuck his chin out, a challenge for Tyler to explain himself.

'I heard about your mum,' Tyler said.

Ryan's shoulders went back. 'What?'

The playground felt very quiet, as if they were in a sci-fi film and everyone else had disappeared, transported to the mothership.

'I heard she's in a bad way in hospital.'

'What the fuck is it to you?'

'I just wanted to say I was sorry, that's all.'

'What exactly did you hear?'

Tyler pictured her lying there, the look on her face. Barry stepping round her, blood on the floor, Kelly's idiotic look at Barry.

He felt strong, the power of not giving a shit. The power of knowing you're in the wrong and whatever comes, you deserve it.

'I heard your house got robbed and your mum was stabbed.'

'Who told you that?'

Tyler looked around. To his surprise, there were dozens of kids milling about pretending not to watch. He searched the faces for Connell, spotted him with his head down, then turned back to Ryan.

'You know what this place is like,' he said.

'Tell me.'

'Word gets round.'

Ryan lengthened his neck. 'So every cunt is talking about my family, that right?'

'Not like that.'

'Slagging me off, slagging my mum off.'

'Not at all.'

Tyler was surprised he didn't feel scared. Lee was at Ryan's shoulder, too close, invading his space. Tyler wanted to push him away, make it just about himself and Ryan, strengthen the bond between them. He pictured Ryan sitting at his mum's bedside, holding her hand, head down, praying for her to get better. Or cursing the bastards who did this, promising violent revenge, torture, murder. Rumour was that his dad had killed enemies, and nobody doubted it. A couple of rival thugs over the years had died, one in a hit-and-run, the other stabbed outside a pub. Another up-and-coming wide boy just went missing a few years back. Some said he'd fucked off to Amsterdam to work the angles there, but a stronger rumour said he was at the bottom of Duddingston Loch.

Was the ability to kill genetic? If Deke did it, could Ryan? Maybe it was down to how you're brought up, a lack of respect for human life, bad role models and all that. Tyler thought about Barry in the Holt place with that knife, with a baseball bat another time, some poor bastard bad mouthing him, jumped and battered as Tyler watched, left for dead, now in a wheelchair and fed through a tube. He thought about Bean, seeing Barry and Kelly and Angela fucking up time and time again.

'What else did you hear?' Ryan said.

Lee was grinning behind him, showing off jumbled teeth.

'Nothing,' Tyler said.

Ryan grabbed the front of Tyler's shirt, pulled him close, spoke soft. 'Tell me.'

Tyler could see Connell at the back of the crowd over Ryan's shoulder, shaking his head, concern and fear.

Tyler held his hands out but didn't try to wriggle out of Ryan's grip. 'That's all. I just wanted to say I was sorry to hear about it.'

'Are you taking the piss?'

Lee leaned in. 'Sounds like it to me.'

'Fucking shut it,' Ryan said, turning.

Lee's grin disappeared and he slunk back.

Ryan turned back to Tyler. 'You think you're better than me, don't you?'

Tyler wondered where that came from. 'No.'

'You do,' Ryan said. 'Swanning about here like you're above it all. Well you're no better than us, you're right in the fucking shit with the rest of us. Got it?'

'Take it easy.'

'Take it easy,' Ryan mimicked. 'Take it fucking easy. I will not take it easy. My fucking house got robbed and my mum got knifed and when we find the cunts they're dead.'

'OK.'

'What?' Ryan said. 'I didn't hear you.'

'I said OK.'

Ryan threw a punch into Tyler's gut, winding him. He doubled over, gasping. Finally it was going to happen. All this talk, just do it already. He waited for more punches, a kick in the balls, a knee to the face. But nothing came. He stayed hunched over trying to get air into his lungs, but they wouldn't work, his throat closed and he made choking sounds.

Ryan leaned down and whispered in his ear. 'I'll be seeing you.'

He straightened up and walked away, Lee dancing after him.

Tyler finally caught a breath and wheezed, his lungs burning. He looked around. The crowd was a mess of uniforms and schoolbags, faces turned away. As he breathed in he felt strong, empowered.

20

A police car waited outside the school gate, DCI Pearce leaning against it and smiling. It was a squad car not the Ford from last time, so she was making a show of the police being interested in him. For a moment he imagined she wasn't here for him, maybe she was here to tell Ryan that his mum was dead or that she'd come out of her coma. But the look on her face as he approached made it clear she wanted to speak to Tyler. He tried to walk past but she pushed herself off the car to block his way.

'Just a minute,' she said.

'This is harassment.'

'I can harass you much better than this.'

'Leave me alone.'

She looked behind him but Tyler resisted the urge to turn. His schoolmates would be checking him out talking to a cop, who needed to see that?

'Get in.' Pearce indicated the front passenger seat.

Tyler noticed she was on her own, no uniformed officer for company.

'No thanks,' he said.

She touched the handcuffs dangling from her belt. 'If you don't get in, I'll have to use these.'

Tyler stared at her. 'Really?'

He felt the crowd of kids now streaming out of the school gates around them, eyeballing Pearce, commenting under their breaths, two boys in the year below him running hands along the squad car paint-work as a wind up.

'If I have to,' Pearce said.

'Outside the school gates? Classy.'

Tyler finally looked behind him. As he expected, Connell and the others were watching him, some of the girls from his year too.

He turned back and pointed left. 'I have to pick up Bean from primary.'

'Just five minutes.' Pearce clanked the handcuffs again. 'Once round the block for a chat.'

He sighed, walked to the passenger door and got in.

Pearce climbed in and started the engine.

The car smelt of blueberry Jelly Beans and was surprisingly clean, no Burger King wrappers or Krispy Kreme boxes.

'Seatbelt,' Pearce said, pulling her own one on.

They headed down Greendykes Road, away from both schools. Tyler thought about Bean waiting in the classroom with Miss Kelvin.

'Interesting times,' Pearce said.

'Get on with it.'

Pearce glanced over as she drove past a fly-tipping site, then the building work.

'We had a report of another break-in,' she said eventually.

'Good for you.'

'Sometime in the last twenty-four hours.'

'There must be dozens of burglaries in the city every day.'

'This was in Clinton Road. Sound familiar?'

Tyler stared out of the window. They passed the derelict house where Snook would be suckling her pups.

'No,' he said.

'The house belongs to a Mr and Mrs Fotheringham.'

Tyler didn't speak.

'It was phoned in by their son,' Pearce said.

'This is fascinating.'

'Clinton Road is just round the corner from St Margaret's Road in Church Hill.'

Tyler sighed. 'Not this again.'

He pictured Flick, blood on her hands, glass on the floor, that piano music playing.

'Strange one, though,' Pearce said. 'The boy said nothing valuable was taken.'

'Lucky for him.'

Pearce passed the Greendykes block where Tyler lived and kept going, round into the newer houses, speed bumps on the road, small gardens, social housing. She stopped at a junction and stared at him.

'Why would someone break into a house and not take anything?'

'Beats me.'

She pulled out from the junction and headed up to Niddrie Mains Road. 'Me too.'

Silence in the car as they drove, making their way back towards the schools.

Eventually Tyler spoke, his voice flat. 'So did you get anywhere with the St Margaret's Road thing?'

Pearce changed up a gear and looked at him. 'CCTV and forensics, you mean?'

Tyler shrugged.

Pearce indicated left, heading back into the neighbourhood. 'We're getting there.'

Which meant they weren't getting anywhere. If they had something, he, Barry and Kelly would be at Craigmillar Station right now asking for a solicitor.

They were back where they started. The crowds of kids had dispersed, just a few stragglers outside the gates, two boys joke fighting, some girls pretending not to watch them.

Pearce pulled the car into the kerb and killed the engine. Tyler went to get out but she put a hand on his arm. She nodded at his face, and it was only then that he remembered his bruised eye. His hand went to it.

'What happened to you?'

'Nothing.'

'A Barry-shaped nothing?'

Tyler stared at her and removed her hand from his arm. 'You don't know anything.'

'I know a lot more than you give me credit for.'

'That wouldn't be hard.'

Pearce sighed. 'You're fucked, you know that? We're going to get Barry and Kelly for this. If you don't give them to us, tell us what happened, then we'll fuck you too.'

Tyler sat in silence.

Pearce shook her head. 'Your sister will go into care without you. Is that what you want?'

Tyler had the car door open. 'You've already said this. Save it. I have to get Bean, she'll be wondering where I am.'

He was out the car now, his hand on the door, about to close it.

Pearce leaned over to see him better.

'You know what you need to do to protect her.'

'See you,' Tyler said, and closed the door.

He turned towards Craigmillar Primary and didn't look back. Eventually he heard the engine start up and the car pull away, leaving just silence.

21

The place was really starting to smell of shit and piss. Bean didn't seem to notice as she scurried over and gave Snook a hug. The dog fussed over her, tail flapping, snout nuzzling her neck, her tongue licking at Bean's face and making her giggle. Two of the puppies were watching their mum and nosing around the girl, mimicking her interest. The third just lay on the mattress next to a smear of her own poo. There were two male puppies and one female, so Bean had named them Mario, Luigi and Peach. It was Peach who didn't get up, just lifted her head and angled it to see where her mum was.

Bean noticed. 'What's wrong with Peach?'

Tyler knelt down and stroked her. Her brothers snuffled over, sniffing at his hand as it ran through her fur. He placed the palm of his hand against her chest, felt a racing heartbeat. He did the same to Mario to compare, but it felt the same. Peach's eyes were milky, like she couldn't focus. Tyler knew nothing about raising dogs, house-training, any of it. Snook ambled over and nudged Peach, licking her face, and the puppy responded with a faint flick of the tail and a high-pitched keen.

'Tyler?'

There was worry in Bean's voice.

'Maybe she's just tired,' he said.

But it was obviously more than that.

'Should we take her home, feed her up?'

Tyler shook his head as he stroked the pup. 'The best place for her is with her mum.'

Bean made a show of covering Snook's ears as if the dog could understand them. 'Mums are not always the best at looking after their children.'

Tyler gave Snook a stroke of her muzzle and moved Bean's hands away.

'Peach can't eat anything we give her,' he said. 'Puppies only drink their mother's milk until they're stronger.'

Bean stared at Peach, who had put her head back down on the mattress. Luigi stumbled and fell on top of her, and Tyler lifted him off.

'But what if she doesn't get stronger?' Bean said.

Tyler took a deep breath. 'Let's just wait and see, OK?'

Bean frowned, knew she was being fobbed off.

She fussed over Snook and the puppies as Tyler got up and looked around. He picked up an old magazine and ripped out a few pages, used them to scoop up as much of the puppies' shit as he could, all the stuff that was on the mattress or nearby. The shit was runny and left dark stains behind as he piled up shitty magazine pages in the old fireplace full of masonry rubble and dust.

Bean's comment about mums not looking after their kids was obviously about Angela, but he pictured Monica in that hospital bed, Ryan holding her hand.

The puppies had gone quiet. Tyler saw that they were all feeding, Peach less enthusiastic than her brothers, Snook's teat occasionally falling from her mouth, making her search about, groggy and unfocused. Bean had her bottom lip sticking out as she gently stroked Peach, nudging her back towards Snook's teat.

He wondered how much Bean remembered. For a little while after she was born, Angela seemed to get her shit together. She stayed off the hard drugs and restricted herself to functional heavy drinking, enough to be able to keep a baby clean and fed, just about. Maybe it was having to focus on Bean that gave her the idea that life was worth sticking at.

But gradually she began slipping back into old habits. Barry and Kelly were teenagers by then and concentrated their growing anger on belittling their mum, with a lot of success, driving her back to smack and leaving Tyler to pick up looking after Bean. Angela became so incapable and incoherent that she was sometimes a danger to Bean. Ovens left on, cigarette scorch marks on the carpet, which could easily have become infernos. Once she forgot Bean in her buggy completely, leaving her in the car park outside the tower block. Tyler heard his sister's screams as he walked home from school, God knows how long she'd been there, her nose and fingers freezing in the winter weather, her bum red with nappy rash once Tyler got her upstairs and changed. Angela was asleep on the floor in Tyler's room, and he was unable to wake her. Next day he couldn't get any sense out of her, she claimed to have no memory of it. He suspected she'd gone out to score and in the adrenaline rush and alcohol haze she'd simply forgotten she had a baby to look after.

He should've reported it. Maybe Bean would've been better off in a foster home or with adopted parents. But he knew he wouldn't get to go with her, they'd be separated, and he couldn't stand that. Besides, he was doing a decent job of looking after her, cleaning up around Mum and making sure he and Bean got washed and fed every now and then. And the truth was, Angela would die without them. She might die anyway, of course, but it would happen quicker if there wasn't that tiny spark keeping her going, somewhere buried deep down, the idea that she was supposed to be a parent, supposed to look after these kids, even if the reality was the opposite.

And as time went on, Tyler was less likely to report Angela's failures to social services because it would be even more likely that he and Bean would be split up. He learned to cope with Angela's erratic behaviour, learned to watch out for his sister and make sure he had all eventualities covered. And Angela retreated, sensing his growing confidence and competence. She slumped further into self-pity and smack, the spiral of those two things. Tyler wondered if he'd made a mistake, maybe covering for his mum and looking out for Bean made Angela abandon her responsibilities, because she knew Tyler would pick up the slack. But what the fuck was the alternative – endanger Bean? He wasn't willing to do that, not back then and not now.

He sighed.

'Come on,' he said to Bean, still stroking Peach. He made a mental note to look into why puppies might get sick. 'Time to go home.'

22

He spotted Flick's car as they came round the bend. It was impossible to miss, a brand-new, bright-red, soft-top Beetle parked outside Greendykes House. It was like a beacon of affluence shining in the gloom. The sight of the car made him feel excited and sick at the same time. As they came closer he saw it was empty and he gazed up at the top floor of the tower block, wondering.

He led Bean through the ground-floor lobby, praying Flick was there. No sign. They got in the lift and Bean pressed the button, then they went up with a judder and scrape. At the top he went to the flat, opened the door, prepared himself. Bean went straight to the living room and he followed, no one around. She switched on the TV, a thing on CBBC called *Marrying Mum and Dad* where kids got to take over their parents' weddings. More happy families.

Where was Flick? And Angela?

'Hello?' Tyler said.

No answer, just hyperactive television presenters burbling on screen.

He went from room to room. No sign of anyone, the flat was empty. Then his stomach dropped. He went out of the flat and over to Barry and Kelly's place, leaned his ear against their door. Conversation, laughter. No, no, no.

He tried the door and to his surprise it opened. He heard the voices more clearly, recognised them both. He could hear the dogs snuffling around in Barry's bedroom, locked away, but the voices were coming from the living room. He went in and there was Flick sitting next to Barry on the sofa. She was in her uniform, that red blazer, Jesus, like a distress flare. Barry passed a half-empty bottle of vodka to her and she took a swig.

Barry had his arm along the back of the sofa, was sitting close to her, smiling. Something in his face changed when he realised Tyler was in the doorway. He didn't look round at first, just raised his eyebrows. Eventually he turned.

'Hello, little brother,' he said softly. 'Look who I bumped into.'

Flick turned, shuddering as the vodka went down. 'Hey, there.'

She sniffed, and Tyler spotted coke leftovers on the low table in front of the pair of them.

Barry smiled as he followed Tyler's gaze. 'Just having a wee party, aren't we, Flick?'

The way he said her name, he was letting Tyler know that he knew it. Tyler had made something else up, what was it? Fiona. This was bad, this was all bad.

Flick waved the vodka bottle at Tyler. 'Want some?'

Tyler shook his head.

'He doesn't drink,' Barry said. 'Bit of a goody two-shoes.'

Tyler thought he might be sick. Barry was doing all this for his benefit.

Barry took the bottle from Flick. 'He doesn't know how to have a good time, not like us, Flick.'

Her name again. Fuck. Tyler tried to gauge Flick. He'd told her Barry was a prick, but she didn't realise he was dangerous. Nothing good could come of this, for any of them.

Flick's eyes were saucers because of the coke, her cheeks flushed from the vodka. He had to get her out of here.

'Flick's been telling me all about Inveresk,' Barry said. 'Sounds like quite a place.'

The sight of her in that uniform in this shithole was like seeing a unicorn that'd wandered into a swamp.

'I was wondering how you two lovebirds met?' Barry said.

Tyler stared at Flick, who showed something for the first time, a look that said she needed help.

'Online,' Tyler said. 'I told you.'

Flick nodded too much. 'That's right.'

She wasn't a good liar.

Barry passed her the vodka and she held it, didn't drink. He put his hand on her knee, just lightly. 'It's obvious what he sees in you.' He looked up at Tyler. 'But what the hell do you see in him, Flick?'

Tyler saw her swallow, a nervous movement. 'He's kind.'

'Is he?' Barry smiled. 'That's nice. He's a bit rough around the edges though, compared to Inveresk boys, eh?'

'I suppose.'

'You suppose.'

Barry looked at the bottle in Flick's hands.

'Have a drink,' he said.

Flick put the bottle to her lips, took a sip.

'Come on,' Barry said. 'A proper drink.'

Flick took another slug. Barry's hand was still on her knee.

'Maybe that's the appeal,' Barry said. 'That Tyler isn't like the other boys you know. A bit of rough, eh? You like that?'

He squeezed her knee and took the bottle from her.

Tyler took a step forward and spoke to Flick. 'We need to go.'

She shared a look with him, then glanced at Barry's hand on her knee.

Barry shook his head. 'You can't leave already, we're only just getting to know each other.'

'I do have to get back to school,' Flick said, beginning to ease herself off the sofa.

Barry tightened his grip on her knee so that she froze.

'I don't believe you,' he said.

'What?'

He held Flick's gaze for a long time then eventually broke into a smile. 'I think you guys want to have a quick shag, right?'

'Barry,' Tyler said.

'What?' He put on an innocent face.

'Come on,' Tyler said.

Flick looked from one to the other, sniffed and swallowed.

Barry stared at Tyler for a long time, still holding Flick's leg. Then he loosened his grip and sat back. 'Never let it be said that I stand in the way of true love.'

He laughed to himself and took a big hit of vodka.

'Now go and fuck each other's brains out.'

Flick got up and took Tyler's hand and they left the flat and stood in the corridor.

'What the fuck were you thinking?' Tyler said.

'What?'

He kept his voice to a whisper. 'He's dangerous.'

'I didn't have any choice,' Flick said.

Her voice was louder and Tyler put out his hands to quieten her.

'Right, he forced you to drink his vodka and snort his coke?'

Her eyes widened. 'Pretty much.'

'Fuck off.'

She straightened up. 'I came here to thank you about Will, I wasn't expecting you to jump down my throat.'

Tyler shook his head. 'You have no idea what you're dealing with here. Barry is crazy.'

'I told you I didn't have a choice. He came out when he heard me at your door. Invited me in, said you'd be home soon. I tried to say no but he insisted.'

'Try harder next time.'

'Why are you being like this?' Flick said.

'Because.' He didn't know how to explain. 'You don't get it. This isn't a fucking game. This is not some poverty safari for you to tour around, in your uniform and expensive car. This is real life. This is my fucking life.'

Flick stared at him. 'Is that what you think I'm doing?'

'Isn't it?'

She shook her head. 'Fuck you, Tyler.'

She turned and pressed the button for the lift, stepped in and the doors closed.

Tyler watched the floor counter above the doors then heard the brake mechanism kick in as she reached the ground floor.

Barry's door opened and he came out. Tyler froze.

'Oh dear,' he said, close to Tyler's face. 'Sounded like a bit of a lovers' tiff.'

Tyler just stood there. Barry grabbed his arm, meaty fingers wrapped around the bicep as he squeezed. He leaned in and whispered in Tyler's ear.

'Fiona, aye?'

Tyler swallowed.

'You've been lying to me from the fucking start,' Barry said. 'I can't trust you.'

Tyler felt the spit from the words on his ear.

Barry nodded towards the lift. 'And I sure as fuck can't trust her. Have you told her anything?'

Tyler frowned. 'Of course not.'

Barry punched Tyler's stomach, doubling him over. He kept hold of the arm, hauled him back up again.

'You'd better fucking not have.' He straightened, stuck his chin out. 'I don't want you ever seeing that bitch again, do you understand me?'

Tyler thought about Flick already driving back to the safety of Inveresk.

'Do you?' Barry said, squeezing his arm till it burned.

'I understand,' Tyler said.

23

They drove past Blackford Pond then turned up the hill past the allotments to Hermitage Drive. There was no end to the big expensive houses in this city. Tyler couldn't believe they were out on the prowl again, it was madness only two nights after what happened with the Holts. But Barry and Kelly seemed oblivious. When Tyler had protested back at the flat, Barry gave him the stare, and they were in the car heading out of Niddrie five minutes later. Bean was asleep at least, that was something. Angela crashed out, as usual.

Rain smeared the car window which had fogged up inside from Tyler's breath. He wiped at it with his sleeve and peered out. They turned at Braid Hills then across the main road to Greenbank, more modest places but still worth tapping if the chance came up. He had an idea and pulled Monica's phone from his pocket, switched it on. Waited for it to boot up then went into texts again. A message from Deke:

I will torture and kill you.

Tyler switched it off and looked out of the window. They were out at the Napier Uni campus now. He counted up, that was five different locations for the phone, if anyone was following it, spread over miles of south Edinburgh, none of them Niddrie.

They drove along Colinton into Morningside, round the back of the psychiatric hospital. This was unfocused, they were going too fast to properly scope the houses, and the rain didn't help. Barry was obviously rattled by this Holt thing but couldn't say anything.

The radio was punting the new Taylor Swift song at them, Kelly and Barry laughing and drinking beer in the front. Drinking in the car now? Christ. They were asking to get pulled over. Tyler pulled the snapshot of him and Bean out of his pocket, the one she took with the stolen camera. She was smiling widely, eyebrows raised in delight. Tyler had a furrowed brow. The graininess of the picture made it seem like it was taken years ago. He rubbed his thumb across Bean's face, then put it away.

Kelly turned to the back. 'I heard you had a run-in at school today.'

Tyler swallowed. 'What?'

Barry frowned. 'What's this?'

Tyler looked out of the window. 'It's nothing.'

Barry indicated as they turned into Craighouse Road. These were terraced houses, no easy way in, safety in numbers.

'I'll decide if it's nothing,' he said.

Kelly touched his arm on the gearstick. 'Baby brother here got in a fight with Ryan Holt.'

'How the hell do you know?' Tyler said.

'Denise messaged me, her little sister saw it. Thought I should know.'

They turned into Morningside Drive, some bigger targets here.

'It wasn't a fight,' Tyler said.

Barry pulled in to the kerb and put the car out of gear. He made a show of turning to Tyler, shifting his body round and holding the headrest behind him. He stared at Tyler. 'What was it then?'

'Nothing.'

Kelly smiled. 'Denise said you took a punch.'

Barry shook his head. 'Why am I only hearing about this now?'

'There's nothing to tell,' Tyler said.

Barry stuck his chin out. 'You take a beating from a kid who just happens to be the son of the woman we...'

That Taylor Swift song was burbling away, the engine ticking over in neutral. Barry put a hand to his forehead. 'What the fuck were you doing talking to Ryan Holt?'

Tyler had his head down. 'I wasn't talking to him.'

'Then why did he hit you?'

'He's angry about his mum, that's all.'

Barry scratched his head. 'What are you trying to say?'

Tyler held his hands out in supplication. 'I'm not trying to say anything.'

'Are you saying I shouldn't have done what I did?'

Kelly tried to touch Barry's arm but he shook her off. The look he gave her made her turn away.

'Is that what you're saying?'

Barry's eyes were wide and Tyler wondered how much coke he'd had before they came out.

'Of course not.'

'I did what I had to do,' Barry said, talking to himself. 'She was going to call the cops. We would've been fucked. I didn't see either of you two cunts saving our necks.'

Kelly piped up. 'You did what you had to.'

'Shut the fuck up,' Barry said. 'This isn't about you. It's about this cunt, thinks he knows best.'

Tyler spoke. 'Barry, come on.'

Barry grabbed the front of Tyler's shirt, pulled him closer so that Tyler's chest was pressed against the back of Kelly's seat. The move was so quick and strong Tyler's breath caught in his chest. Barry didn't say anything for a moment, just stared into Tyler's eyes, breathing on him, beer and adrenaline.

'Stay the fuck away from Ryan Holt, OK?' he said eventually.

Tyler took a deep breath. 'Of course. Sorry.'

Barry let go and Tyler slumped back in his seat.

Barry turned and switched the engine off. 'Now let's go and rob some cunt.' He got out, Kelly and Tyler sharing a glance as they followed. This was nuts, they didn't have a target yet, it was raining, there was CCTV in the street, plenty of streetlights. Barry was losing it.

They walked past a couple of white detached bungalows, 1920s, then there was a row of older terraced houses, most with lights on. The end house was dark, had a way round to the back door, no sign of an alarm box. But the house next door to it was lit up, a television playing in the living room. Barry walked straight up the path of the dark house and stopped outside. He didn't press the bell, just looked up then headed round the back.

Tyler shook his head at Kelly. 'What the fuck?'

Kelly shrugged. 'Just come on.'

Tyler trudged after her, his instincts on fire. This was too dangerous, all their procedures for avoiding conflict had been abandoned. It was as if Barry was looking for trouble, hunting it down.

Round the back there were hedges preventing them being seen from the road. Barry was already into the shed at the bottom of the garden, and came out with telescopic secateurs. He barrelled to the back door and wedged the blade into the space between door and frame, heaved on the handles and the back door popped so easily that it banged against an inside wall. As Barry went inside, Tyler saw a light go on upstairs.

'Barry,' he said under his breath. 'Someone's in.'

Barry stood in the dark kitchen and turned to look where Tyler was pointing.

'Hello?' A man's voice upstairs.

Tyler stared at Barry. 'This is not how we do it.'

Kelly had a pleading look on her face.

Barry looked at them both but didn't move. He weighed the secateurs in his hands like a weapon.

'Is someone there?' The upstairs hall light came on, then the downstairs hall. Footsteps down the stairs.

'Fuck this,' Tyler said.

He turned to leave but Barry reached out and grabbed his arm, held tight. He waited a few seconds, looked towards the hall, listened to the footsteps, hesitated.

'I'm armed,' the voice said. 'And I'm calling the police.'

Kelly stared at Barry holding Tyler. 'Please, Barry.'

Barry seemed to notice her for the first time since the car. He turned back to the hall, then looked at Tyler. He took one last look around the kitchen then seemed to decide something. He picked up a small digital radio and a bottle of whisky sitting on the worktop and left, dropping the secateurs on the grass as he strode to the bottom of the garden then clambered over the hedge, Kelly and Tyler scrambling after him. Tyler felt wetness on the front of his jacket as he shimmied over the rain-soaked bush and down into the street behind.

Barry was already twenty yards down the road, swigging from the whisky. He didn't look back to see if his brother and sister were following. He turned at the end of the road, then again, and was back at the parked car in two minutes, Tyler and Kelly scurrying behind. Tyler hunkered against the rain and listened for sirens but there was nothing. Of course, the police didn't have the resources to send a car and officers to every attempted break-in across the city.

Barry opened the car and got in, Kelly and Tyler behind. They shook the rain off, Tyler running a hand through his hair. Barry swigged the whisky and threw the digital radio into the footwell by Kelly's feet.

'What the hell was that?' Tyler said.

Kelly turned and glared at him.

Barry switched the engine on and the radio started up again, Rita Ora this time. He didn't speak, just pulled out and drove east, heading out of Morningside and along Cluny Gardens. Somewhere to their left was Flick's house. And a couple of streets over was Will's house. And beyond that a few more streets was St Margaret's Road, where Deke and Ryan would be planning revenge.

They were at the King's Buildings crossroads waiting at the lights when the late-night news bulletin came on. Top story, the police were still appealing for witnesses to an armed burglary two nights ago, the woman who was attacked remained in a coma. They were still hot news. Kelly stared at the car radio. Barry just kept looking straight ahead, one hand on the wheel, the other clutching the open bottle of whisky by the neck as the windscreen wipers swished in front of him like a heartbeat.

24

Tyler checked on Bean, who had slid halfway out of bed onto a pile of clothes. For some reason she was also wearing an old scarf of Tyler's like a bandana. He wondered what went through her mind sometimes. He picked her up and scooped her back onto the mattress, and she snuffled into the crook of his arm. He waited a moment to make sure she'd settled and spotted a pile of Polaroid pictures next to her pillow. He picked them up and flicked through. They were mostly of her school friends, some with her included in them too. One of Miss Kelvin, one of Panda. She had used up over half the film already.

He checked on Angela next. She was lying on top of her covers, mouth open. He couldn't hear her breathing so he went over to check and her eyes fluttered open. It took her a moment to focus.

'My beautiful boy,' she said.

'Hey, Mum.' He was already heading towards the door.

'Wait.' She pushed herself up on her elbows, sat up on the bed. She shook the sleep from her head, blinking heavily. 'What time is it?'

'It's late, go back to sleep.'

Angela patted the bed next to her. 'Come and sit with your old mum for a minute.'

He hesitated at the door.

'Please.'

He sat at the bottom of the bed near her bare feet. She sometimes did this, drunken or high moments of affection, bittersweet because they never lasted.

'You're such a good boy,' she said, sniffing. There was a bottle of schnapps and some smack gear on the table next to the bed, and she kept glancing at it. 'What am I saying, you're a young man now.'

'Mum, I need to get some sleep.'

'Wait.' She reached for his hand and took it. The sores, the dry patches, were rough against his skin. 'Just listen.'

He sighed. She cricked her neck. 'I don't know what I would've done without you, Tyler, really.'

'Don't.'

She squeezed his hand. 'I mean it. Bean too.'

Tyler just sat there.

'When Barry and Kelly's dad left,' Angela said, 'I thought I would die.'

This was her sob story. Angela had Barry and Kelly when she was still a teenager, knocked up by an on-and-off boyfriend called Jay. He was a real ballbuster, in and out of young offenders' then proper prison for a series of violent crimes. In between spells inside he used Angela as a punching bag, but she put up with it. She started drinking heavily to take the pain away, then graduated to smack, which Jay was pushing on the side anyway, so there was plenty around.

Then along came Tyler. Problem was, he wasn't Jay's kid, couldn't be because Jay had been in jail, the dates didn't match. Angela didn't even know who the dad was, could've been any one of half a dozen candidates, because she went through a phase of screwing for a fix when Jay wasn't around, anything to keep the darkness away. When Jay got out and saw Tyler he gave Angela a final ferocious beating, breaking four ribs, and left her to deal with all three kids. Which she continued to do terribly.

After no contact for five years, Jay got back in touch, wanted time with his two kids again. Something about a legacy. So he got Barry and Kelly whenever he wanted, no official agreement, just on the hoof. And they learned from him, about booze and drugs, about theft, violence and intimidation. Leaving Tyler at home with Angela as she got more and more lost in narcotics and couldn't find a way out. By the time Bean came along – another unknown dad in the mix – Barry and Kelly were young teenagers, already helping Jay out on any number of dirty jobs.

Then one day Jay fucked the wrong guy's wife, gave her a small going-over into the bargain, and the husband came looking with two brothers and a cousin. The next morning a primary-school football team found Jay's cold body on waste ground next to the Jack Kane Centre. But he'd spent enough time drilling into Barry and Kelly that they had to carry on what he'd taught them, so the bullshit legacy continued. They treated Angela with disgust, Tyler and Bean too, although they'd kept a tighter rein on Tyler, using him and abusing him into the bargain.

'But you saved me, Tyler,' Angela said now. 'You gave me a reason to keep going.'

This was delusional, she'd kept going with drink and drugs. Tyler had lost count of the number of times he came in from school to find her crashed out, needle on the floor, vomit, and one time black smoke billowing from the grill pan so that he had to switch everything off and open the windows. He was Bean's age when that happened. But he never told anyone, not his teachers or social services, because if they took him away from her, she would die. He knew that because she'd told him often enough.

'Mum, it's late.'

She shook her head and squeezed his hand again.

'I've fucked everything up in my life,' she said. 'I've tried my best to fuck you up too, and Bean, but you're both so strong, so good. I'm a terrible mother.'

'Get some sleep,' Tyler said.

'The world will be a better place when I'm dead,' Angela said.

He turned to her. 'Don't say that.'

She reached for his face and stroked his cheek. He flinched. 'You're sweet, but you know it's true.'

'You're not a bad mother.'

She was crying now, swallowed hard. 'I'm just so weak. I've always been weak. Ever since I met Jay at school. I never stood up to him, never stood up to Barry or Kelly either. I've never stood up for myself in my whole life.'

'Things can change, Mum. You can change.'

She shook her head again. 'It's too late.'

Her hand was still on his face. He lifted it away and held it in his own on the bed.

'Go to sleep, Mum, you'll feel better in the morning.'

She seemed to deflate, like all the energy left her. She glanced again at the gear and the bottle on the table and Tyler sighed. He patted her hand and got up, then lifted a blanket from the bottom of the bed and pulled it over her. She smiled, her brow wet with sweat and her fingers drumming on the edge of the blanket.

'Goodnight, Mum.'

'Goodnight, love.'

He went to his room and lay down on the bed. He stared at the ceiling for a long time, but couldn't sleep. Eventually he got his phone out. Dialled and waited. Three rings then an answer.

'I wasn't expecting to hear from you after earlier.'

'I'm so sorry,' Tyler said.

'Really,' Flick said.

'Really.' Tyler stared at the ceiling. 'I need to talk to you.'

'So talk.'

He breathed in and out. 'Can I come and see you?'

'Now?'

'Yeah.'

'It's half one in the morning.'

'I know.'

A long pause. 'OK.'

25

Inveresk was like Hogwarts or some magical kingdom, hidden behind high walls in the downmarket centre of Musselburgh. Tyler walked up the High Street catching glimpses of mustard-coloured walls between the large oak trees. He had Jon Hopkins playing in his earbuds, sweeping synths and glitchy drums fading in and out, everything echoing and bouncing. He got to the front gate, closed and guarded. CCTV all over the place. His instincts were kicking in as he pulled his hood tighter round his head. He turned down Millhill. This was better, a lot less busy than the main street. Buildings from the school campus backed onto the street here, but had small barred windows like a prison. The same bright-mustard walls, so they weren't trying to blend in.

Tyler had checked out the school's website on the night bus on the way, downloaded the campus map. He laughed out loud on the top deck when he saw that they had tennis courts, a golf academy, music, dance and drama studios. A theatre and a chapel. A tunnel that ran under the High Street, for God's sake, from the hockey pitches on one side to the science labs on the other.

Then he'd checked the fees. Holy shit, eleven thousand per term meant over thirty grand a year just to go to school. And this was a family who had a house in Edinburgh anyway, a million-pound home lying empty. Christ.

He turned into Millhill Lane, pebble-dash terraces and flats, working-class homes right next to all this wealth. He found the black gate with the red cross on it, sent her a text and waited, took his earbuds out. Tried to make it look as if he had a reason to be there, checking his phone as if something had just occurred to him, pretending to send a message. He couldn't see any cameras from here but that didn't mean there weren't any.

A few minutes later he heard a bolt being slid back. The gate creaked open and there she was, hair up in a mess, wearing joggers and a hoodie as if she was just like him.

She signalled for him to come in. She did that thing of looking around to check the coast was clear, which was so suspicious. He walked past her. She locked the gate then turned to him with her finger at her lips. She took his arm and he felt a tingle at the touch.

They walked around the edge of a neat grass square, under the cover of trees, then they were at the chapel. She pushed the door and they went inside. It was a strange building, old and Gothic at one end, a huge triangular sixties mosaic window at the other. This had featured in the recruitment video Tyler watched on the bus, a bunch of kids with marbles in their mouths singing hymns and looking angelic. A faint light came through the mosaic, the spill of streetlights over the wall carving up the gloom.

Flick sat in a pew at the front. 'Sorry, I can't risk having you in Almond House, someone might hear.'

That was where the sixth-year girls boarded, Tyler had seen that on the map too. Each boarding house had a housemistress. A different world.

He sat down next to her on the cold wooden pew.

'I'm so sorry about earlier,' Tyler said, looking away down the church.

'I'm not on a poverty safari.'

'I know.'

'I'm not just slumming it,' she said. 'I know your life isn't a game.'

Tyler shook his head. 'It's just Barry. He pushes my buttons.'

'He's horrible.'

'I don't want him anywhere near you,' Tyler said. 'I mean it.'

'I can handle myself.'

Tyler let out a laugh and Flick looked offended.

'You don't think I can?' she said.

'It's not about handling yourself,' Tyler said. 'Barry's in a different league.'

'I've seen some things.'

Something in the tone of her voice made Tyler look up.

'Like what?'

Flick shook her head. 'My dad is a trained killing machine, remember? Seven years in the Royal Marines, where he picked up a metal plate in his leg, night terrors, anger management issues and, according to my mum, syphilis and gonorrhoea.'

'Jesus.'

'To be honest, the STIs were the least of my parents' problems. I'd like to say that the anger was down to his PTSD, but dad was always angry at the world. I think that's why he went into the Marines in the first place. War can definitely turn people psycho, but sometimes people are just psycho to begin with.'

'What are we talking about?' Tyler said. 'Has he hit you?'

'Not me, Mum.' Flick's eyes were welling up. 'Not that she'd ever admit anything was wrong with her perfect marriage, of course. Mum comes from a world where keeping up appearances is still a thing. Where it matters what people think of you. That's why I'm in this place. She doesn't give a shit about me or my education, just wants her army-wife pals to know she can afford a crazy expensive school for her beloved daughter. It's so cringy. She's utterly neurotic, scrambling around the whole time trying to keep her perfect life together, when it obviously fell apart years ago.'

'Sounds tough.'

'Oh, she has her coping mechanisms. The good thing about travelling to lots of war-torn, third-world countries is the availability of top-class pharmaceuticals, no questions asked. Uppers and downers and everything in between, all washed down with the best wines you can buy in Afghanistan, which are quite decent, apparently.'

Tyler rubbed his neck before speaking. 'I notice you like a drop of wine yourself.'

He could feel her tense up. 'Meaning?'

He put his hands out in supplication. 'I don't mean anything.'

'Out with it.'

He thought for a long moment. 'It's just, what you said about your mum. I know what booze and smack has done to my mum, and that's why I stay the fuck away.'

'I'm nothing like my mother,' Flick said.

'I didn't say you were.'

'Good.'

The silence seemed bigger in the expanse of the church. Awkward. Tyler didn't know why he'd brought it up. Flick unnerved him more than any girl at his school, more than anyone he ever met.

'Is that why you called me up in the middle of the night?' Flick said. 'To scold me about my drinking?'

'I just needed to see you.'

'And it couldn't wait till morning.'

'You didn't have to say yes.'

She looked around. 'That's right, I didn't, but I like you and I thought you liked me.'

'It's pretty obvious I like you,' Tyler said.

Silence, then a wooden creak somewhere. Tyler looked up but it was just the chapel breathing.

'Do you believe in God?' he said, staring at the cross in the nave.

Flick lifted her shoulders. 'I believe in something. Not some old guy in a cloud, but karma, maybe. Like, be good to people, try to do the right thing, and good things will happen back to you.'

Tyler stared at the cross. 'You really believe that?'

'Why not?'

'Maybe you think that because you've had a lot of good things happen in your life.'

Flick angled her head and frowned. 'I've had my fair share of shit things, as discussed.'

Tyler waved a hand around the chapel. 'You're doing all right.'

Flick took her arm away from his. 'You know, I've spent my whole life defending the fact my parents have money. I've been lucky, I'm privileged, so what? Doesn't mean I don't get depressed and suicidal sometimes. I don't need this shit from you.'

Tyler looked her in the eye. 'Suicidal?'

She looked away. 'I've never ... you know. But I've thought about it. As a way out.'

'A way out,' Tyler said. He thought about that. That's what he needed, a way out of all this.

'I mean, I'm not about to top myself, but I get really down sometimes. Just about everyday shit, you know? Abandonment issues, pathetic daddy issues, my mum being a bitch, all the backstabbing shit that goes on around here. Honestly, rich girls are the worst. And the boys, my God, they're awful. So much entitlement.'

Tyler laughed at her tirade. 'Sounds like it's worth thirty grand a year.'

'How do you know how much the fees are?'

'I looked it up on the way here.'

'The fees are the saddest thing about this place,' Flick said.

Something in the air had loosened. They weren't fighting anymore, if they had been earlier.

Tyler looked her in the eye. 'So this karma thing. If I've done something bad, I can expect bad things to happen to me?'

Flick put a hand on his knee. 'I don't know, it's just an idea. You're a good person, Tyler.'

'You don't know that.'

She took his hand in her lap. 'Yes, I do.'

He examined their hands together. Her nails were shiny, perfect curves, and her fingers were long and thin, freckles sprayed across the knuckles.

He looked around the chapel, a huge organ at one end, plaques covering the wall behind the pews. It smelt of old wood and polish.

'You know, I think this is the first time I've been inside a church in my life,' he said.

'Really? You lucky sod. We come every Sunday morning for service. It's unbelievably boring.'

'I can't imagine having a church in my school.'

Flick shook her head. 'They love all that shit here. Bringing us up in the correct manner.' She put on a pompous voice. 'So that we can be fully rounded citizens and contributors to society.'

Tyler pressed his lips together. 'But you're hidden away behind the walls in your own bubble, with your music studio and hockey pitches. I know guys from Mussy and they think you're an alien race or something, a bunch of snobs who never mix with the locals.'

Flick removed her hand from his. 'Do you blame us? Every time I walk down the High Street in my uniform I get catcalls and whistles from builders and workmen, teenage boys calling me a posh whore or a bitch or a fucking cunt, women staring at me like I'm running down the street naked trying to steal their men. I have friends who've been assaulted just for going to Inveresk.'

'I'm sorry, I didn't mean anything.'

He felt the chill in the air, the cold wood under him.

She stared at him. 'Is that what you think? That I'm a snob, a posh bitch? Are we back to the poverty safari thing again?'

Tyler shook his head. 'Of course not, I'm sorry.' He waved his hand around. 'I'm just not used to any of this. I'm not used to girls like you.'

The look in her eyes softened a little, but there was still tension in the air.

Eventually Flick spoke. 'I come here by myself late at night. That's why I thought to bring you here when you called. Sometimes in Almond House, it's chaos. So much noise, everyone shouting and screaming all the time, thirty girls at once. It's hard to get a moment's peace.'

Tyler wanted to reach out and touch her hand, but he was scared to.

Flick stuck the tip of her tongue between her teeth, sucked in. 'You know, in the Middle Ages you could ask for sanctuary in churches. They were supposed to be places to escape persecution and hurt. You could hide out in a church and no one was allowed to come in and take you.'

'I like that.'

'This is my sanctuary.' Flick turned her eyes to the ceiling. 'Even if I don't believe in the big guy upstairs.'

Tyler reached out now and touched Flick's hand. She smiled. He looked at the mosaic window.

'Someone is in hospital,' he said.

'Who?'

He hesitated. 'A friend's mum. She was stabbed.'

'That's terrible, how did it happen?'

Tyler shook his head.

'Do they know who did it?' Flick said.

'No.'

'Is she going to be all right?'

'They don't know. She's in a coma.'

'I'm so sorry. Is your friend OK?'

Tyler looked up at the window, cutting up the light from the street outside into coloured pieces. He thought about the idea of sanctuary, a place to escape from the world.

'He's coping,' he said.

✳

Tyler left the rear entrance of Inveresk and walked back round Millhill towards Mussy High Street and the bus stop. He could smell Flick's perfume in his nose, could still feel the touch of her hand in his. He pondered what she'd said about her family. We're all fucked up in our own ways. The only thing we can do is be there for each other.

He reached the wide junction by the racecourse entrance and saw car headlights behind him. He stood waiting for the car to pass before he crossed, but it slowed down to a crawl. As it got closer he saw it was a silver Skoda and he felt sick.

The car stopped in front of him and the passenger window wound down. Barry leaned over from the driver's seat.

'Get the fuck in this car now,' he said.

Tyler looked around. No other cars on the road at this time of night. A faulty streetlamp was blinking on the corner, sending out a random signal for help.

He got in.

Barry spun the car with a squeal of tyres and drove left, the opposite direction from home. Tyler pulled his seatbelt on as they zipped past the racetrack and old golf course. Barry took a left at the Levenhall roundabout, down the back road out of town. They quickly ran out of houses on the left hand side, replaced by scruffy parkland and waste ground, Barry racing at sixty, the engine whining, Tyler not even daring to look round in the car.

Then Barry pumped the brakes, throwing Tyler forward in his seat, and turned left onto a dirt track full of potholes. They rumbled along the track for a few minutes, the rattle of the suspension in Tyler's ears, then followed the path north as it narrowed. They passed a *Danger No Entry* sign and Tyler realised where they were going, the ash lagoons.

The track ended with a large turning circle for trucks and Barry thumped to a stop. He jumped out of the car and walked round, threw open Tyler's door, popped his seatbelt and dragged him out by his jacket.

'Barry, wait.'

Barry pulled him up a scrubby embankment, the pair of them staggering up the slope, then they were at the top and Tyler could see views out over the Forth. They were so close to the sea he could smell it. Even closer was a giant lagoon, grey banks of ash along its edge, a black expanse of calm water. Industry used this place as a dumping ground, tried to pass it off as a nature reserve. Signs everywhere warning about the unsteady ground underneath and deep water.

Barry yanked Tyler down across the ash, kicking grey up into their faces as they went, then they were at the water. Barry waded in, dragging Tyler behind him, then he dunked Tyler's head under, one hand holding his jacket, the other pushing on Tyler's head. The cold was shocking. Tyler struggled and kicked his legs but the ash gave way underneath and his footing slipped until he was horizontal. The water was gritty and grey from the stirred-up ash, Tyler scrabbling with his fingers at Barry's hands.

He felt himself being lifted up out of the water and he gasped in air.

'What the fuck did I tell you?' Barry said, his voice calm.

'What?'

'About that posh bitch.'

'I'm sorry.'

His head went back under and he swallowed dirty water, spluttered and coughed, felt more water slip down his throat. He kicked his legs some more, got a little purchase, but then the ash slipped from under him again.

He was hauled up, sucked in air.

'Barry, please.'

'It's like I'm talking to myself,' Barry said. 'No cunt fucking listens.'

'I'm sorry. I won't see her again, I promise.'

His head went under, the water tasted of soot and scum, his fingers shook with the cold, his eyes stung. He grabbed Barry's wrist and pulled, but his brother's hands didn't budge. Tyler felt the energy drain from his body, felt his lungs about to burst out of his chest. Eventually he was pulled up again.

'It's for your own good,' Barry said. 'Do you understand?'

Tyler breathed in and out, gulping in air. 'Please, I won't, I'm so sorry.'

Barry stood over him. 'You're a sorry wee cunt, right enough. Do you want to go under again?'

Tyler put his hands up. 'I'll listen. I'll do what you say.'

'You'd better,' Barry said. 'Or I'll go after her next, got it?'

Tyler's chest heaved up and down as he tried to calm his jerky breaths. Somewhere in the black sky overhead he heard geese calling to each other.

'I've got it,' he said.

26

Miss Niven was taking them through the steps for differential calculus, substitute x for $x+h$, subtract the original equation, single out h by algebra and the rest. Tyler would normally soak this up, immerse himself in the abstract world, but he couldn't get into it. He was only a third of the way through the exercise when the bell went. He shuffled his stuff together and pushed it into his bag, then headed outside for morning break.

Connell was waiting at their usual corner with another kid, Ahmed from his reggie class. They were talking about a girl Ahmed fancied from the year below, how he was planning to get in there. Tyler checked his phone alerts, a few dull Instagram posts, some Hibs gossip. Then he checked the local news and froze. Clicked through to the story and scanned it, his heart thudding.

The Holts were offering a ten-grand reward for information on the stabbing. Ten fucking grand. That was an insane amount of money, but of course Deke had plenty. Tyler had seen his house. There were just four paragraphs to the story, most of it recapping the original break-in and stabbing. It referred to Deke as Derek, a 'devoted husband and father', and mentioned Ryan too. It also gave details of Monica's car, the Audi, identifiable by its personalised number plate.

'Hey, man, you all right?' Connell said. He looked at Tyler's phone screen over his shoulder, took in the story.

'Ten grand,' Connell said. 'Holy shit, I could use some of that. I don't suppose you've heard anything?'

Tyler stared at him. 'Of course not.'

Connell held his hands up. 'Just asking.'

Tyler thought about the shotgun under the bed, then about

Monica's car, which they'd fenced to Wee Sam. He must've realised whose car it was by now. And all the stuff from the Holt house Barry had already sold. How many people did that involve? A lot of them would've sussed it. Some of them might've kept quiet to avoid getting involved, but now there was ten grand in the mix.

He looked around. A gang of younger boys were hunched over their phones in a corner. A bunch of girls in tight leggings and with sculpted eyebrows were taking selfies while smoking. The nicotine drifted to his nostrils and he was reminded of his mum. What that was doing to Bean's lungs in the house. They learned about that stuff in primary school. Bean asked about it at home one day and got the back of Angela's hand in response. It was the one time Tyler had been aggressive with his mum, hauling her off Bean and throwing her onto the sofa in the living room. He could take all the shit she threw at him, but not at his sister.

He had to tell Barry about the reward. He moved away from Connell, who raised an eyebrow, and called his brother's mobile. It rang five times, then Barry on voicemail, Ant and Dec barking in the background. He hung up. He looked around again, waiting for Ryan Holt or his dad to appear from nowhere and stab him. He realised he'd been chewing the inside of his cheek, so he released his bite. The flesh was raw. He poked his tongue at it.

He shook his head and turned to leave.

'Hey.' Connell behind him. 'What about geography?'

Tyler just kept walking out of the school gates and down the road.

✳

The dogs were barking before he knocked on the door. Sometimes, when they weren't locked away in the bedroom, they'd start before Tyler had even got out of the lift, like an alarm, letting Barry know when anyone appeared on their floor. The doorbell didn't work, ever since Barry ripped the wiring out as part of his campaign to get rid of the Syrian family. Tyler rapped on the door and the dogs got louder.

He could hear one of them slavering against the door, scratching at the paintwork. Barry must not have fed them. He did that sometimes as a training method, to make them angry and mean, more savage in the build-up to a fight.

There was a place out near Tranent, off the A1 at Carberry, where someone had dug a pit in the woods and filled it with concrete. Barry would take the dogs to fight. There was so much dead space in East Lothian it was easy to get away with stuff like that. This place was between a golf course and a historic mansion, farms and fields all around, and nobody gave a shit. Either that or they were too scared to confront anyone. Barry and Kelly had taken Tyler out there a few times years ago with a previous pair of dogs, now dead. It was like an initiation to toughen him up. He'd endured the spectacle a couple of times, the amphetamines for the mutts beforehand, the tweaking of bollocks and injections to give their dogs the edge, the lacerated throats and savaged ribcages, bones and sinew showing, raw muscle like webbing exposed beneath fur. It was intended to shock but Tyler was already close to unshockable. But he hated it all the same and made himself sick once in front of everyone. It earned him a beating, but Barry had been so ashamed at the mocking he got from the other knuckleheads that he left Tyler at home after that.

Still no one had answered the door. Tyler went to open it, but the jaws of Ant or Dec were immediately at the crack in the door, slobbering and fighting to get at him.

'Down.'

He could make out Kelly yanking on the dog's collar, heaving it away from the door and into the kitchen, where she shut it in. She came back and opened the door. She was wearing black shorts and an oversized pink sweatshirt with *Awesome* scrawled across it. She looked tired and her hair was greasy, a sheen of coke sweat on her face.

'There's a reward,' Tyler said.

'What?'

'Ten grand for information on the stabbing.'

'Shit.'

'Is Barry around?'

Kelly shook her head.

'Where is he?'

Her head went down. 'I don't know.'

Tyler's heart quickened for a moment. 'You think something happened to him?'

Kelly shifted her weight. 'Like what?'

'Like the Holts found him.'

'Nothing like that.'

'But you said you don't know where he is.'

'He's with Cherise.'

This was Barry's ex, who took out a restraining order on him years before but forgot about it when she was drunk and it suited her. And Barry would run back. Cherise didn't seem to mind that Barry was shacked up with his own sister the rest of the time. And Kelly was too weak to complain about it either. What a fucking mess.

'Kelly, what are you doing?'

Her face hardened at his tone. 'What do you mean?'

'You know what I mean.'

She stuck her chin out. 'Shouldn't you be in school?'

Tyler could still hear that dog in the kitchen, and he wondered where the other one was. Maybe they would kill each other, and they'd all get some peace.

'I came to tell Barry about the money. We're fucked now, you realise that?'

'No one will grass.'

'Of course they will, it's ten grand.'

'So what?'

'Just tell Barry and see what he says. Hope he doesn't shoot the messenger.'

He turned to go into his own flat, leaving her standing in the doorway.

'Tyler, wait.'

Something in her voice made him stop and turn.

She looked scared. That was pretty common around Barry but Tyler couldn't remember the last time he'd seen her like this. She placed a trembling hand against her forehead, through her hair, back to her face.

'What is it?' Tyler said, stepping back towards her.

'Nothing, I just...'

Tyler stood watching her.

'I can't sleep,' Kelly said, her head lowered, eyes darting. 'I keep picturing that woman in the house.'

Tyler sighed. 'I know.'

Kelly scratched at the doorframe. 'Why did Barry have to stab her?'

'Why does Barry do anything? Because he's Barry.'

Kelly shifted her weight. 'He's not all bad.'

Tyler couldn't believe what he was hearing. 'Kelly, stop kidding yourself.'

'There's another side to him, Tyler, you wouldn't understand.'

That got Tyler mad. 'Are you insane? He's treated us both like shit our entire lives. He's a bully and a psycho and now he's going to get us killed.'

'There's stuff you don't know,' Kelly said.

'Like what?'

Kelly took a deep breath, raised her head. 'He protected me.'

'From what?'

Kelly swallowed. 'Back when we used to stay with Dad. Years ago. Dad would come in from the pub hammered, come to my room. Wake me up, you know.' She picked at an invisible splinter in the doorframe. 'He would do things. And hit me too. But one time he did it, Barry came in with a kitchen knife and held it to his bollocks, said if he ever touched me again he'd lose them. It was the first time I ever saw Dad scared.'

'Christ,' Tyler said. 'Why did you never tell me this before?'

Kelly shrugged. 'I'm telling you because I want you to understand that Barry has always looked after me. And he'll look after us now, I'm sure of it.'

So Kelly had gone from being abused by her dad to sleeping with her brother. Tyler remembered once when Bean was a baby, he'd come home from school and found Kelly lying on the floor in the living room playing with her. She'd made a nest out of dirty cushions for Bean to lie in, and a wobbly mobile out of the taped-together bits of a ripped-up cardboard box, which Bean was swiping and giggling at. Kelly had looked embarrassed to be caught caring, but she didn't stop. Half an hour later Barry came in stoned off his tits and ripped the mobile apart.

Why couldn't she see he was fucking toxic? It was so obvious to Tyler, to everyone surely. But she couldn't see his manipulation for what it was, she thought she was standing by the man who looked after her.

'He can't protect us anymore,' Tyler said. 'Not from this.'

'Of course he can, he's Barry.'

'He's losing the plot. You saw him last night. That burglary job was nuts, he was looking for a fight, he wanted to get caught.'

Kelly shook her head. 'We just need to keep our heads down. Keep out of trouble.'

'And you think Barry's capable of that?'

Kelly nodded but it wasn't convincing.

Tyler narrowed his eyes. 'Maybe there's another way.'

'How do you mean?'

Tyler tried to think it through before he spoke. 'That woman in the hospital, she could die. Then it's murder. We didn't stab her, neither of us. The police are sniffing around, and there's a reward now. Maybe we just tell the truth.'

Kelly's eyes widened. 'We can't do that.'

'Why not?'

'We just can't.'

'We don't owe him anything, Kelly. He would sell us out without even thinking if it was the other way round.'

'No way.'

'He would.'

The look on Kelly's face hardened. 'If you grass on him, Tyler, he'll kill you.'

That was true and Tyler knew it. And still Kelly couldn't see what kind of brother that made him, like the two parts of her brain were disconnected from each other.

Tyler shook his head and stepped away.

'Tyler,' Kelly said as he reached his own door. 'We have to stick together.'

He didn't turn back, just got his key out and opened the door to his flat.

The smell hit him, something more than the usual stale booze and fags. It was shit and piss, and a sweet undercurrent of something rotten. He walked into the living room and the smell got stronger so that he had to hold the crook of his arm over his nose. Then he saw Angela on the floor. She was naked and he could see track marks on her arms and legs, open sores that pockmarked her body like craters. She had the ligature still tight around her upper arm and the lower part of the arm was dark blue, like the edge of a summer night. Her face was a paler blue, scabbed lips white. He noticed a runny shit staining her buttocks and leaking onto the carpet.

He ran over and loosened the belt from her arm, the marks from the buckle springing up white underneath, her skin slow to return to normal. He held a hand over her mouth and knelt there for a few seconds. He couldn't feel any breath. He did the same under her nose, nothing. He dug two fingers into the sinew at her neck and tried to imagine a pulse. He closed his eyes to concentrate better. He thought he felt something but wasn't sure. He tried to calm his breath, his own heart racing against his chest, the adrenaline rising up in him.

'Come on,' he said to himself.

He pushed his fingers in harder against the neck muscle so that he could feel her voicebox. He imagined ripping it out, then felt a low murmur, a throb against his fingertips. A pulse, definitely a pulse. But then nothing for a second or two, then maybe another beat.

'Fuck's sake.'

He took his fingers from her throat, grabbed her shoulders, lifted her and shook. Her neck was loose, her head lolling like it might come off.

'Wake up,' he said, and slapped her across the face. Her head offered no resistance, just flipped across, lank hair falling into her eyes.

He looked around the room for an answer – just unwashed dishes in the sink, fag ash and heroin gear on the carpet. The stench was making his eyes water.

He dropped her on the floor, her head landing with a thunk.

He pulled out his phone and called 999, got put through to the ambulance service, but when he explained it was a suspected overdose and gave the address there was a pause, estimated arrival time was forty-five minutes. She would be dead in forty-five minutes and they both knew that.

He hung up and ran to the other flat, thumped his fist on the door. 'Kelly.'

He heard the dogs then Kelly opened the door.

'It's Mum, she's OD'd again,' he said.

'Seriously?'

'Come on.'

'Have you called an ambulance?'

'They said three quarters of an hour. She'll die before they get here. Is Barry's car downstairs?'

Kelly shook her head. 'He took it to hers.'

Tyler took Kelly's arm and dragged her to his flat, into the living room. She put a hand over her nose. 'The fuck?'

She took in the scene for a few moments. 'Call a taxi.'

'You know they won't pick up from here.'

'Any bright ideas?'

Tyler looked at his watch, half twelve, lunchtime. He thought about Barry holding him in the water last night, what he'd told him. But he didn't have any other option.

He dialled and she answered. 'Hey, what's up?'

'I need a favour.'

27

Tyler and Kelly were standing in the street with Angela propped between them when Flick's Beetle tore into the car park. Tyler had pulled joggers and a sweatshirt on to Angela's body so at least she was covered.

Flick's face was shocked as she stepped out of the car. 'Christ.'

'I'm so sorry,' Tyler said.

Flick waved that away and pushed the driver's seat forward.

Tyler offered Angela's arm to Flick. 'Take her.'

Flick supported her as Tyler went round the other side, flipped the passenger seat forward too and clambered into the back, reaching out. The women lifted Angela to the car and tried to manoeuvre her into the space, her shoulder clunking on the seatbelt support as Tyler took her weight and fell into the footwell of the back seat. He heaved Angela's body onto the seat and scrambled up, lifting her head, sitting down and putting her head back down in his lap.

The two seats thudded back into place as Kelly and Flick jumped in.

Flick looked in the rear-view mirror at Tyler. 'OK back there?'

Tyler made a face and puffed out his cheeks. 'Let's go.'

They bombed out of the car park and fired over the roundabouts, then turned left along Little France Drive. The road became buses only but Flick went along it anyway, the alternative route along The Wisp added ten minutes to the journey. Two cameras flashed at them.

A&E was at this side of the hospital site, so they were outside the sliding doors in no time, Flick helping the other two lift Angela out of the backseat and into a wheelchair Tyler found inside the doors. Flick went to park somewhere as Tyler wheeled his mum to the front desk, Kelly behind shaking her head. When he explained what had happened to the woman behind the desk they were led through to a curtained area, where heavy-set orderlies lifted Angela onto a bed and a young woman doctor with purple hair and tattoos on her hands calmly injected something into her neck, arranging for an IV drip at the same time.

Tyler watched it all and thought about Bean, how he would explain this. He'd been in this emergency room before with Angela, first when Bean was born, then three more times with overdoses, but Bean had been too young to remember any of those. She was old enough and smart enough now to ask questions, and to deserve answers. They got drug and alcohol education early at school around here, so she already knew the basics, but while she knew Angela drank too much, Tyler had managed to keep the smack from her.

Then he thought about Angela, how she might not even pull through, and he felt ashamed. Guilty that he hadn't helped more, that he hadn't been more supportive. That he hadn't found her sooner. But fuck it, he didn't stick the needle in, she did that to herself. When she had a young daughter to look after.

The doctor handed them a leaflet that Tyler already had in a drawer at home, then moved on to the next emergency. What a way to make a living, in a constant sea of other people's stress and pain. There was some chat between the doctor and nurse about finding a bed in a ward upstairs, but it was clear from their tone that a self-inflicted junkie overdose was not a priority. Tyler didn't blame them for that.

Flick appeared and hovered outside the open curtain of the treatment area. Tyler saw Kelly looking at her and got up to put himself between them. He watched Kelly look her up and down.

Kelly pointed at the red blazer Flick was wearing. 'What school is that?'

'Inveresk.'

Kelly thought that over for a few moments. 'How do you know my brother?'

Flick looked at Tyler then back at Kelly.

She smiled. 'We just bumped into each other one day.'

Tyler thought about her standing in Will's living room, blood dripping from her hand. What did they even have in common?

Kelly shook her head. 'I never heard him mention you.'

Flick reached out and touched Tyler's arm.

Kelly's eyes narrowed. 'Are you his girlfriend?'

Tyler's heart was in his throat.

Flick smiled confidently. 'Yes.'

Kelly turned her attention to Tyler. 'Does Barry know about this?'

'Yeah.'

Kelly frowned.

Flick went to Angela's bedside. Tyler followed her. Angela was so emaciated and worn, almost a ghost already, scabby marks on her arms, sores on her face, greasy hair.

'How is she?' Flick said, not seeming to notice the state of her.

'She'll live,' Kelly said. 'It's not the first time and it won't be the last.'

Flick turned to Tyler. 'I'm sorry.'

'What do you have to be sorry for?' Kelly said. 'You and your posh car saved her life. Might've been better if you hadn't bothered.'

Tyler stared at Kelly over Angela's body. 'Don't say that.'

'What did she ever do for any of us except fuck us up?'

'Speak for yourself.'

Kelly's face went hard. 'Well she was fuck all use to me as a mum, that's all I know.'

Tyler thought about what Kelly had said earlier. 'You can't blame other people for your life.'

'Of course I can,' Kelly shouted.

A passing orderly glanced into the cubicle.

'You make your own decisions. If you don't like how things are, change them.'

Kelly laughed. 'Life lessons from a seventeen-year-old. Great. You can't talk. We're both in the same shit.'

Tyler glanced at Flick. He shook his head, his fingers gripping the edge of Angela's bed. 'Shut up.'

Kelly seemed suddenly deflated.

'I have to get back to the flat,' she said. 'The dogs will be tearing up the place, and Barry might be back.'

Tyler shook his head. 'You don't have to go back there.'

Kelly stared at him for a long time. 'Yes, I do.'

She turned and left, silence in her wake.

Eventually Tyler turned back to his mum. She was like a skeleton, something from thousands of years ago that had just been dug up. He found it hard to look at her. He tried to remember something happy, an early memory that might trigger something in him. The brief moments of coherence amongst the booze and drugs and chaos, the first few times she'd tried to go straight, only to fall back into the old patterns at the smallest setback. He didn't want his upbringing to harden him against her, against the world, but fighting that was a constant struggle.

He turned to Flick. 'My family is so fucked up.'

'All families are fucked up.'

'Not like mine.'

'They're all fucked up in their own special ways.'

Tyler rubbed at his forehead.

Flick made a goofy face. 'But yours does seem particularly fucked up, I have to admit.'

Tyler laughed.

Flick grinned. 'I think that's the first time I've heard you laugh.'

Silence for a moment then she spoke again. 'What did your sister mean about the shit you're in?'

Tyler watched the drip flowing into the needle in Angela's hand. 'Nothing.'

The nurse from earlier swished in through the curtains. She was only a few years older than Flick and Tyler, tiny with short fair hair and eyes like saucers.

'We've found a ward bed for your mum,' she said to Tyler, taking in Flick at a glance. She fiddled with the locks on the bed wheels, clicked them off one side then the other. 'Do you want to come up with her?'

Flick looked at her watch. 'I need to get back to class.'

'Thanks for everything,' Tyler said.

He reached a hand out towards her, then was surprised to find himself in a full hug, the smell of her hair in his nose, the feel of her arms around him, the beat of their hearts almost touching through their chests.

28

He sat by her bed for an hour in silence. It wasn't visiting hours but the nurse let him stay anyway. There were four beds in this room on the ward, Angela in one, an old woman sleeping in another. The other two had younger women in them, addicts too by the look of them. One was watching episodes of *Breaking Bad* on an iPad, headphones on. The irony of watching a drama about a drug dealer. The other was on her phone, scrolling and flicking, her head bent over so that her nose almost touched the screen.

The machines in the room produced a background thrum, the sense of a building working to keep people alive. He liked the white noise, it helped to wash away the bad thoughts. But they kept seeping back in.

He had nowhere else to be. He couldn't go back to school, no way he could handle that. He didn't want to go home, couldn't face the flat. And besides, Barry might be there. Flick was at Inveresk. He thought about Bean. It would be afternoon break now, she'd be cartwheeling with the rest of the girls, or they would be bossily telling each other what to do, sorting out rules for a chasing game, wasting half their time arguing about what was and wasn't fair. The sense of fair play in kids that age overwhelmed everything else. He remembered being told off for talking in class in primary school once, even when it had been Connell, and the injustice of it burned his cheeks for hours afterwards. What kids that age needed to learn was that life wasn't fair, so you'd better just suck it up.

He felt his stomach grumble. He stared at Angela, who hadn't stirred the whole time he'd been here, then left the room to look for a vending machine. He went out of the ward and round a corner, and he noticed that the number of coloured lines on the floor increased, like boats joining a stream. Then he remembered Monica Holt, still upstairs somewhere. It was a brown line for Intensive Care, and he found himself following it as if he had no control over his feet. Before he knew it he was at the ward door, then inside, no nurse at the station so he just kept walking until he was at Monica's room, then without hesitating he was in and standing at the end of her bed.

She was propped up higher than before, her eyes closed. There was a book open on her lap, something thick with an embossed cover. That meant she wasn't in a coma anymore, either that or the book was someone else's. He looked around but there was no one else in here. He turned back to her. She looked a damned sight healthier than Angela.

He came round to the edge of the bed and stood there, his hands by his sides, his fingers almost touching the covers. Her breathing was shallow, her eyes flicking left and right beneath the lids. Her hair was just as shiny as he remembered it that night, someone must've washed it for her. Must be nice having someone look after you like that. He thought about his mum's hair.

She opened her eyes and stared straight at him. He took a shaky breath but didn't speak. To begin with he thought she didn't recognise him, then something seemed to change in her face, a realisation. He was ready for her to reach for the emergency button at the side of the bed. He glanced at it, only a few inches away from her fingers. He was ready to hear her scream out for someone to come.

But she just blinked heavily, keeping her gaze on him. He wanted to look away, to run away, to be anywhere but here, but he made himself stay.

'You were there,' she said. Her voice was croaky and dry, but it was definitely the same voice that shouted at Barry that night.

Tyler just stared. Eventually he gave the smallest nod. His eyes flitted to the button, and she noticed.

She shook her head, a tiny motion. 'I won't.'

'Why not?'

Monica swallowed and sighed. 'It wasn't you.'

'What do you mean?'

'You didn't stab me.'

Tyler stayed silent.

Monica swallowed again, it looked like hard work.

Tyler reached for a glass of water on the bedside cabinet and held it out for her.

She took it, leaned forward and put it to her lips, then her head fell back onto the pillow. She handed the glass back.

'Is he your friend?'

Tyler shook his head.

'What then? Brother?'

Tyler nodded.

Monica looked around the room then at the doorway. Tyler turned but there was no one there. He could hear his blood roaring in his ears.

'You're in trouble,' Monica said. 'You know that, don't you?'

Tyler was still holding the glass of water, tremors on the surface as his hand shook.

Monica looked at his hand. 'When Derek finds you, I mean.'

Tyler rubbed at his thigh, breathed in and out.

Monica stared at him. 'Did you know?'

Tyler looked puzzled. 'Know what?'

'That it was our house. Was it deliberate?'

Tyler shook his head again, that's all he ever seemed to do.

Monica let out a breath. 'Just bad luck.'

Tyler offered her the glass again but Monica waved it away. He put it on the cabinet.

Monica's hand came to rest nearer the emergency button. Tyler glanced at it.

'Why are you here?' Monica said.

Tyler shrugged. 'I wanted to see you were OK.'

A cough slipped out the side of her mouth. She looked him in the eye for a long time. 'Someone called an ambulance.'

Tyler didn't answer.

'From my phone,' she said.

Tyler remembered picking it up from the floor in her house, her eyes flickering open and closed as he shut the door behind him.

Monica was still looking at him intensely.

'Thank you,' she said. 'Now go.'

29

He came out of the main entrance of the hospital, went round the corner and stopped. The sun was out and he stood still, eyes closed, face raised to the warmth like a gecko. He imagined his skin catching fire, the smell of pork as his face cooked and melted away. He rubbed his hands against his scalp, cricked his neck and breathed in the oddly gassy smell that drifted on the wind across the hospital grounds. Some researchers somewhere, mixing up chemicals.

He'd left Monica and gone back to his mum, but there was no change there. He'd sat for a few minutes then realised he had to go get Bean from school. He could walk back over the derelict ground to Niddrie quickly enough, then up the hill and over to Craigmillar Primary, shouldn't take more than fifteen minutes.

'Hey.'

He knew who it was just from that one word.

He kept his eyes closed for a few seconds, reluctant to face this.

'I'm talking to you, retard.'

Tyler opened his eyes. There was Ryan Holt with his dad and another man the same age. Deke was in a smart business suit like he'd just come from court, his thick neck and shaven head pure bouncer. No tattoos visible, which was unusual these days. The other man was taller, a trimmed beard, a slight quiff, wearing a black bomber jacket and jeans with cuffs turned up. It might've been a hipster look if he wasn't so muscle-bound. Ryan was striding ahead of them towards Tyler, flicking a cigarette butt into the gutter.

'The fuck are you doing here?' Ryan said.

Tyler took a deep breath in and out. He pointed as calmly as he could at the entrance. 'Seeing my mum.'

Ryan was in his face now. He didn't have any other gears, just straight intimidation. 'What's the matter with her?'

Tyler looked past Ryan at the older men, watching him silently. 'Drugs.'

'Which drugs?'

Tyler swallowed. 'Heroin.'

'Fucking junkie,' Ryan said. He turned to the other two. 'This is the cunt I told you about, asking about Mum.'

Tyler held a hand out. 'I was just saying how sorry I was about what happened.'

Deke's eyes were narrow, maybe against the sunlight bouncing off the white wall behind Tyler. 'Why?'

'What?'

'Why bother speaking to Ryan about his mum?'

'Seemed like the right thing to do.'

Deke nodded. 'Uh-huh.' He didn't sound convinced.

Tyler was ready to run. He was pretty fast but he wouldn't outrun these three all the way to Niddrie.

Deke threw a thumb in the direction of the other guy. 'This is Sonny, my brother-in-law.'

'OK.'

'That's his sister inside there with the stab wound. My wife.'

'Sorry to hear that.'

Deke rubbed the stubble on his chin, then pulled at his earlobe. 'It's a bit of a coincidence, us meeting you here.'

'Not really,' Tyler said. 'If you knew my mum. I'm here a lot.'

Ryan sneered. 'Junkie bitch.'

Deke looked at him, and his snigger died. 'That's the boy's mum you're talking about. Watch your fucking tongue.'

Ryan's head went down. 'Sorry.'

'How would you like someone talking about your mum like that?'

Ryan didn't answer.

'Well?'

'I wouldn't.'

Tyler felt like he was rubbernecking a road accident. Then Deke's eyes were on him again.

'What did you say your mum's name was?'

Tyler hadn't said and they both knew it. 'Angela.'

'Angela what?'

'Wallace.'

Deke glanced at Sonny. He was obviously going to check at reception that they had an Angela Wallace in for a drug overdose, so no point in lying.

'You got any brothers or sisters,' Deke said.

'Older brother and sister,' Tyler said. He deliberately didn't mention Bean, they didn't need to know about her.

He wondered briefly if Barry's reputation stretched as far as the Holts. Maybe not, the Wallaces were small time, the krill at the bottom of the food chain, and the Holts were the sharks.

Deke was nodding to himself. 'Well, look after each other, family's important. What happened to my wife, it puts everything in perspective.'

'OK.'

Silence for a moment, Ryan looking from one to the other of them, trying to work out some leverage.

Eventually Deke looked away, up at the large sign above the main entrance. He turned to go inside, the others following like pack animals. 'Look out for yourself, Tyler. And look out for your family.'

30

Tyler cut around the back of the hospital and up the hill past the helicopter landing pad. Hannah Peel was playing in his ears, a trippy soundtrack to a sci-fi movie that hadn't been made. He skirted the edge of the trees that ran along Craigmillar Castle Road, the open field to his right, the Barratt building site beyond. So much open space around here still, gradually getting swallowed by houses and offices. To his left he could see the highest crennellations of the castle, remembered being up there in the dark with Flick, staring out over the sleeping city. He wondered what she was doing right now.

He stepped away from the road and followed the rough path through the trees to the edge of his school, then out onto the road and down to Craigmillar Primary. They'd got out twenty minutes ago so there were just a few mums left blethering outside the gate, their kids mucking around in a muddy puddle next to the bushes. But twenty minutes wasn't too bad, Miss Kelvin would have kept Bean in as usual. He tried to think how he would explain to Bean what had happened to Angela.

He got to the classroom, knocked on the open door and went in. Miss Kelvin was putting the little chairs up on the desks, clearing the place for the cleaners. Tyler glanced around then caught the teacher's eye, and the look on her face made his stomach sink.

She stopped with a chair in her hand, her fingers gripping the plastic. 'She's gone.'

'What do you mean, you just let her wander off?' Tyler looked around the room as if Bean might pop up from under a desk and surprise him.

'She said you were outside waiting,' Miss Kelvin said, her voice wavering. 'I presumed that if you weren't there she would come back in.'

'You didn't check?'

Miss Kelvin was on the verge of tears. 'The playground's busy at home time, you know that. I'm sorry, but it's not really my job. There are thirty children in this class.'

Tyler stared at her and wondered how old she was. Maybe about the same age as Barry. He tried to imagine her and Barry having a conversation, but he couldn't bridge the gap in his mind, they were from different universes.

Miss Kelvin put the chair down and stood there, arms by her side.

Tyler looked around again, tried to think. 'I'm sorry, it's my fault.'

'Would she just have walked home?' Miss Kelvin said.

Tyler nodded, Bean was a sensible kid, she wouldn't walk off with strangers. He thought about the Holts outside the hospital. Deke had said, 'look out for your family'. Half an hour later his little sister was missing.

'Yeah,' he said. 'She's probably on her way home.'

If only he'd come the other way from the hospital, he would surely have walked right into her.

'Maybe her mum came for her?' Miss Kelvin said.

Tyler let out a laugh, picturing Angela in the hospital bed. 'No.'

'Is there anyone at home when she gets there?' Miss Kelvin said. So many questions and Tyler didn't have any answers.

'I'd better go find her.'

He was already halfway out the door when Miss Kelvin called after him.

'Let me know she's safe.'

He ran out of the playground, picking up speed as he turned along Greendykes Road, the downward slope forcing him forward, his trainers slapping on the concrete, mums with little kids staring at him as he passed. One he recognised, Aisha with her mum, holding hands, their arms swinging in unison. He slowed as he reached them.

'Aisha.'

Her mum jumped at his voice, pulling her daughter closer.

He was breathing hard from the exertion. 'Have you seen Bean? Bethany?'

He was talking to both of them, looking from one to the other.

Aisha looked confused. 'Not since class.'

He stared at her mum, who was beginning to realise he'd lost her. 'Sorry, I haven't seen her. Can I help?'

Tyler swallowed and shook his head. 'If you see her, bring her home. It's Greendykes House.'

He ran on, round the building site until he was at the tower. She wasn't waiting outside. She didn't have keys but maybe someone let her in.

He went inside and jumped in the lift, tried to get his breathing back as it chugged up the floors, frustrated at suddenly being motionless. He burst out of the lift doors and into the flat, went through every room, even checked under the beds, no sign of her. He went next door, his heart racing, and thudded on the door. Just the dogs barking, no answer. He thumped again but that just got the dogs more agitated. Still no answer.

'Barry? Kelly?'

She couldn't be inside, surely, it didn't make any sense. He thought about trying to hammer the door down, but that was a non-starter. He tried to think. She wouldn't be at a friend's house, would she? No mum would take her and not mention it. Maybe Barry or Kelly had her somewhere else. But why? And it couldn't be the Holts. If they knew anything, they would've killed Tyler at the hospital. The dogs were scratching at the inside of the door, slobbering and barking, yelping as they fell over each other. He couldn't think. Then it came to him. The dogs.

He ran down the stairs and burst out of the front door, running again, feeling the dampness in his armpits, the breath in his lungs burning as he gulped in air, along the road again to the derelict house. He slapped the wall with his palm as he headed round the back. The cardboard sheet was still in the window frame, which made him frown. He ripped it out and peered in. Too dark, couldn't see anything, couldn't hear anything over his own heartbeat and breathing.

'Bean?'

He clambered in, careful of the broken glass in the frame, and landed inside with a thud and a puff of masonry dust. Opened his eyes wide to get used to the dark, then spotted Snook over in the corner by the dog basket. He heard a whimpering noise.

'Bean?'

He walked over, saw the dog and her pups more clearly, but no sign of Bean. He leaned down and scratched behind the dog's ear. 'Where the fuck is she?'

He straightened up and looked around. Went to the window and stared out over the waste ground at the back of the castle.

Then his phone rang.

He swallowed as he took it out of his pocket.

On the screen was the alias he'd plugged in for DI Pearce's number.

He answered. 'What?'

'Guess who I have with me?' Pearce said.

'You bitch,' Tyler said. 'I was worried sick.'

'She's fine,' Pearce said. 'Come and meet us for a coffee.'

✳

The Starbucks at Fort Kinnaird was new – dark wood and uncomfortable plastic chairs, overly cheery staff, huge glass frontage looking out at a traffic jam and Primark.

Pearce sat at a window table with Bean, who was halfway through a syrupy caramel milkshake. She grinned when she saw him, a cream moustache across her upper lip. 'Hi.'

Pearce gave him a knowing look as he sat down.

'What have I told you about going off with strangers,' Tyler said to Bean.

She frowned and sucked milkshake through the straw. 'But she's a policewoman. She showed me her badge.'

Pearce put her hands out in front of her. 'I'm here to serve.'

'How dare you,' Tyler said.

Pearce widened her eyes. 'What? It's lucky I was there. No

responsible adult to pick her up from school. She could've got into all sorts of trouble.'

Tyler shook his head. 'Leave us alone.'

Pearce leaned forward. 'This is just the start. I want Barry.'

Bean perked up. 'What about Barry?'

Tyler frowned and looked at her. 'Nothing. Go get a napkin from the counter, you've got cream all over your face.'

She took the straw from her cup and sucked it as she traipsed across the café.

'You're fucking unbelievable,' Tyler said.

'Give me what I want and you'll be safe.'

'You can't keep us safe.'

'The police are the best chance you have.'

'You don't believe that any more than I do.'

Pearce leaned back. 'Maybe I'll take you in for questioning right now. Get social services to look after Bean.'

Tyler narrowed his eyes. 'You wouldn't dare.'

'Wouldn't I?'

'You say you're trying to help us, but it doesn't feel like that.'

Pearce shrugged. 'I can only do so much if you don't cooperate.'

Bean came back, making exaggerated swipes at her face with a napkin.

Tyler stood up. 'Come on, Bean, we're going.'

'Can I bring my milkshake?'

Pearce lifted the cup and handed it to her. 'Of course, dear. You look after your big brother, you hear?'

Tyler stared at her for a moment then took Bean's hand and left.

＊

The cardboard sheet was still away from the window frame, Tyler hadn't replaced it in the rush to head to Starbucks. He lifted Bean through the opening and placed her carefully on the floor inside, heard Snook whine.

He looked around, breathing in the fresh air, then pulled himself through the opening and dropped into the darkness. It took his eyes a few moments to acclimatise. Bean ran over and sat down next to Snook on the mattress, picked up one of the pups and stroked it in her lap.

'Bean?'

He went over. She looked up with tears in her eyes. In her lap was the sick puppy, motionless and curled into a ball.

'She's dead,' Bean said. 'Peach is dead.'

Snook let out a keening noise and licked at the pup in Bean's lap, who didn't respond.

The other two puppies shuffled nervously around their mum, sensing something was off.

'Why did she die?' Bean said.

Tyler crouched next to her and stroked the puppy's head. It already felt cold, or at least not as warm as a living thing. He brushed tears away from Bean's cheek.

'There's nothing we could do,' he said. 'Sometimes little ones just aren't strong enough.'

'We didn't look after her properly,' Bean said, her voice hard.

'No,' Tyler said. 'It's not our fault.'

'Then it's Snook's fault,' Bean said, staring at the dog. 'She wasn't a good mum.'

Tyler put a hand on Bean's shoulder. 'Look at me.' He waited until she held his gaze. 'It's not anyone's fault. Snook is a good mum. Look at the other two puppies, they're fine, aren't they? Sometimes these things happen. It's just life.'

Bean stared down at the dead puppy in her lap, played with its ear between her thumb and finger.

'Then life's not fair,' she said.

31

Snook sniffed around the corners of the living room then into the kitchenette, licked at some toast crumbs on the floor there. She padded about, checking out the new territory, the two pups lolloping behind and beside her, getting in each other's way. They seemed not to notice that the third one was missing. Was it that easy to move on?

Bean had insisted they bury Peach, so Tyler had gone into the allotment at the back of the tower block, busted into a shed for a shovel, and dug a hole away from the rows of runner beans and onions. He laid Peach in the hole, said a few words about doggy heaven, and Bean placed a Polaroid picture of Snook on top of the body. Tyler began covering her over. Bean stood impassive, staring into the hole as the dirt landed on top of Peach's fur.

Bean had also insisted they bring Snook and the puppies to the flat to keep a closer eye on them. When they'd come out the lift door into the hallway, Ant and Dec went crazy barking and yelping in the other flat, scratching at the door, making Snook cower into the opposite corner. Tyler expected Barry to come barrelling out, maybe let his dogs have a go at them, but the door remained closed.

Tyler lifted Snook in his arms and brought her inside, Mario and Luigi flopping in behind. They were too young and stupid to know the danger behind the other door, tails wagging at their new adventure.

Bean threw some cushions from the sofa onto the floor, making a nest for Snook to settle in, which she did after circling the room a few more times. Tyler got out food and water out for her and she ate greedily, gulping down mouthfuls and raising her eyes between bites. She lay down and the puppies began to suckle, more room now there was just the two of them. Survival of the fittest was brutal.

Tyler put the television on and Bean flumped into the sofa.

'Is Mum in bed?' she said.

Tyler pushed at his eyebrows. 'No, she's in hospital.'

Bean turned away from the screen, flickering light on her cheek. 'Is she sick?'

'Yeah, she's very sick.'

Bean considered this for a long time. 'Is it drugs?'

'What do you know about drugs?'

'We learned all about it in school. How they're really bad and can make you ill.'

'That's true.'

'I don't understand,' Bean said. 'Why do something that makes you sick?'

How to get into this? He wondered if he could just stay quiet, if she would be distracted enough, but she turned to him looking for an answer.

'Well?'

'It's complicated,' Tyler said. 'If you feel sad, sometimes drugs make you feel better but only for a short time, then they make you feel worse.'

Bean pursed her lips. 'That's stupid.'

Tyler looked at the TV screen. It was a clay animation about a bunch of kids who had all swapped bodies somehow. If only it was that easy to switch lives.

'It is pretty stupid,' he said.

'And Mum's stupid too.'

'Hey,' Tyler said.

She turned at the tone in his voice.

'Don't say that about your mum,' Tyler said. 'It's not her fault. Some people just aren't as strong as others, they can't help it.'

Bean stared at him, then glanced at Snook and the pups. 'Like Peach?'

'Like Peach.'

'Are we strong?' Bean said.

'Yeah, we're strong.'

Silence again, Bean thinking. 'Will Mum die?'

Tyler paused before answering. 'No, she won't die.'

'You promise?'

Tyler sighed and pulled at his earlobe.

'Just watch your show,' he said. 'I'll make us something to eat.'

✴

It was a sharp, cloudless night, stars like glitter glue spread across the blackness. Tyler felt Bean's warmth against his chest and lap. They had the blanket wrapped round them both as Tyler told the story again, this time giving Bean Girl even more powers than usual, battling and easily defeating all the evil monsters of Niddrieville. He skirted over the bit mentioning Angela giving birth to her. They could see the hospital from here glowing in the distance, throbbing with life, and he thought about Monica in there too, trying to get better, using every ounce of strength to heal herself. He wondered if Angela had come round yet, if she was going through withdrawal. He wondered if they gave her anything to help her get through it, whatever she was feeling.

Down below the lights from the building site reached into the sky like little fingers to heaven trying to commune with God. As if there was a big guy up there who could solve everything, just wave his hand and all the pain and hurt in the world would disappear.

Tyler added a canine sidekick to the story, Bean Girl supported in her adventures by Little Peach, her trusty puppy, getting her out of scrapes when she couldn't do it herself, saving the day more than once, and being rewarded with colossal hugs and doggy treats.

The metal door from the hatchway crashed open, a shocking clang in the darkness, and Tyler felt Bean jump in his arms.

'Fuck's sake,' Barry said, clattering out of the doorway and scuffing towards them.

Tyler pulled Bean close, a signal between them under the blanket. He rubbed her hands then interlaced his fingers with hers.

'You fucking cunts doing up here again?' Barry said, lurching towards them.

Tyler tried to breathe normally so that Bean wouldn't get scared. He didn't speak.

Barry was at them now, standing over them.

'I asked you a fucking question.'

Tyler could smell whisky on Barry's breath and sweat, something chemical to it, coked up again. He gave Bean's hand another squeeze. 'Just telling her a bedtime story, that's all.'

'Up here?'

Bean shuffled in Tyler's lap. 'I like it up here.'

Barry seemed confused that Bean had spoken and stared at her. Tyler could feel her muscles tense up. Barry shook his head, like he was trying to think straight.

'What the fuck is going on with the dogs downstairs?' he said. 'You running a fucking kennel?'

It took Tyler a moment to realise. Snook and the pups.

'We found them,' he said.

'Street dogs, are you mental? Mangy little shites, full of disease.'

Tyler felt Bean clear her throat.

'They're my pets,' she said.

Barry stared at her again like he couldn't believe she was real. 'Get rid of them. If you don't, I'll feed them to Ant and Dec, they won't last two fucking minutes with a couple of proper dogs.'

'Dogs shouldn't be for fighting,' Bean said.

Barry ignored her and turned to Tyler. 'I think they've almost got to us.'

'The Holts?'

'Who do you think?'

'How?'

'I was just at the casino with Gerry from Mussy. Says Wee Sam's gone missing from the garage.'

'So?'

'So either the Holts have found the car and traced it to him, or he's grassed us up and is hiding. Either way, we're fucked.'

'What does Kelly think?'

'I can't find her. You seen her?'

Tyler shook his head and felt Bean straightening in his lap.

'Mum's in hospital,' she said to Barry.

He seemed confused for a moment. 'I've bigger things to worry about than that junkie whore.'

'You're not nice,' Bean said.

Barry leaned forward and swiped the back of his hand across Bean's face, knocking her off Tyler's knees and onto the rough ground. Tyler sprung up and went to her, touched her arm as she lay there silent. Then the tears came, welling up in her eyes, a wail escaping from her mouth that drifted into the night. Barry's sovereign ring had cut her cheek and her eye was starting to swell above it, dark red as the blood gathered under the surface.

'Shut the fuck up,' Barry said. 'I hardly touched you.'

Tyler looked up. 'You've cut her face. Her eye's bruised.'

'She needs to toughen up.'

Tyler stood up. 'Don't ever touch her again.'

Barry swayed where he stood, raising his eyebrows. 'Or what, fucktard?'

'I'll kill you.'

Barry spread his arms wide. 'I'd like to see you try.'

Tyler lunged at him and shoved him in the chest. Barry's movements were sluggish and he took the hit square on, staggering back a few steps so that he was only a couple of feet from the roof's edge. Tyler pushed again but he had no run-up so there was no force behind it. Barry had regained his balance and sidestepped enough to make the blow glancing. He grabbed at Tyler's wrist on the way past and held on tight, twisting it so that shards of pain shot up Tyler's arm. He flinched and buckled under, Barry twisting his arm further so that Tyler had to turn and bend his knees in subservience, Barry rabbit punching Tyler in the kidneys then the back of the head, pulling at Tyler's hair, yanking his head backward like he was the loser in a cheap wrestling bout.

'You pissy little bitch,' Barry said, pulling Tyler's arm further behind his back until Tyler thought his shoulder was going to pop out of the socket, the pain burning through him. Somehow amongst the pain he realised his other arm was still free, and he flung his elbow round, catching Barry in the ear with a crunch so that Barry let go. Tyler staggered round and swung a punch at Barry's chin. It connected but Barry didn't flinch, his neck muscles straining as he threw a punch himself. Tyler ducked but not enough and it thudded into the temple above his eye, black sparks flashing across his vision. He crouched and threw himself forward into Barry's stomach, knocking the wind out of him with his head as the pair of them lurched backward. Barry lost his footing and collapsed, Tyler falling on top of him, the pair of them at the edge of the roof now, fifteen floors of nothing below them on the way to the pavement.

Barry heaved Tyler's weight off him, thrashing like a madman as Tyler tried to hold on to his wrists. Barry got his leg free and dug his heel into the back of Tyler's knee, making Tyler yell out and loosen his grip, then a fist came into his face from Barry's left, rattling his jaw and making him dizzy. Barry heaved again and rolled, and he was on top of Tyler, then he staggered onto his feet, dragging Tyler by his shirt over the edge of the roof, holding him there with his head hanging back, a rush of wind from below playing with Tyler's hair. Barry spat in Tyler's face, making him wince, and released one hand from gripping Tyler's shirt to slap him across the face. Tyler had no energy, beaten, and he wondered who would care for Bean when he was dead. He tried to look over to where she was but he couldn't see her.

'You fucking little cunt,' Barry said. 'After everything I've done for you. Both of you. I raised you when that junkie bitch wouldn't and this is how you repay me.'

Tyler couldn't think of anything to say and couldn't get his mouth to work anyway.

'Don't.' This was Bean, now gripping Barry's arm, trying to pull him away from Tyler. Barry swatted her away so that she fell backwards and hit the floor again with a yelp.

Barry stared at Tyler and seemed to be considering his options through the coke haze.

'I should just let go,' he said. 'Drop you over the edge.'

Tyler could hear Bean sobbing and wanted to comfort her.

'Barry, we're family,' he said. 'Family sticks together.'

Barry was still for a long moment. Tyler tried to work out what was going through his head. The family thing was bullshit of course but Barry had some faith in it, despite his attitude to Angela. Some bollocks about community, harking back to good old days that never existed.

Eventually Barry shook his head. 'I don't have time for this.'

He let go of Tyler's shirt and Tyler's head lurched back over the ledge. He scrambled with his legs until he was away from the edge, gulping in air.

Barry straightened his back and stood with his legs spread, getting his breath back. He ran a hand over his scalp and looked from Tyler to Bean, both of them cowering on the floor.

'If you hear from Kelly, let me know,' he said, walking away. 'And get rid of those dogs or I'll kill them.'

32

Bean stuffed Panda into the holdall Tyler had thrown onto the floor in the middle of her bedroom. She put in other stuff, the jar of slime that a friend at school made her, some cheap plastic necklaces, an unsuitable make-up set that Tyler had stolen from a teenager's bedroom in Comiston. She carefully placed the Polaroid, her stack of pictures and the remaining film in the bag. Tyler went through Bean's drawers pulling out jammies, school clothes, underwear, leggings and tops.

'Where are we going?' she said. It was the third time she'd asked.

'A friend's house, I told you.'

'Which friend?'

'You don't know her.'

'You have a girlfriend?'

'A girl who's a friend.'

'Isn't that a girlfriend?'

'No.'

He went to his own room and threw in some clothes, then the bath-room to get their toothbrushes and toothpaste, shower gel. He went back to his room and dug under the mattress, pulled out the small wad of money that was there, stuffed it inside a sock in the bottom of the bag.

His phone buzzed. She was downstairs. He looked out of the window but she'd parked round the corner like he asked. He couldn't see her or the car, which meant Barry hopefully couldn't either.

He went back to the living room where Bean was stroking one of the puppies.

'Shoes on,' he said.

She traipsed to the hall and came back, fumbling with them.

'Do the laces,' she said.

He sighed. 'You need to learn. I won't be around to tie your laces forever.'

He regretted saying that, given what'd just happened. His body was still shaking from adrenaline and shock. He tried to keep his voice level.

'Now, you've got a very important job,' he said. 'You have to keep the puppies quiet, OK? When we leave.'

She nodded gravely. 'I will.'

'Good.'

He looked around, went to Bean's room, emptied out a plastic box of beaten-up old toys and brought it back. Its sides were steep enough to prevent the puppies clambering out.

'Put them in here,' he said, handing her the box.

She did it diligently, Snook sniffing around her as she moved.

Tyler checked the food cupboards in the kitchenette, but there was nothing worth bringing. He went into a drawer and pulled out the sharpest knife, pushed it through the belt loop on his jeans. He got the holdall, zipped it up and threw it over his shoulder. When he came into the hall Bean was already there with her jacket on, holding the puppies in the box, Snook at her side.

He smiled. 'Ready?'

She nodded.

'We have to be super quiet, remember? Barry can't know we're leaving.'

'I know.'

'That means the dogs too. If Ant and Dec hear them, they'll kick off.'

Bean looked at the puppies, worried.

'We're going down the stairs. We can't wait for the lift. Ready?'

'You already asked that.'

'OK.'

He turned the latch on the door and opened it slowly. Put his key into the lock on the outside of the door so he could turn the mechanism and stop the door clunking shut. He pushed Bean out of the door and picked up Snook in his arms. She was lighter than he expected. Bean crossed the hallway towards the stairs, the puppies snuffling at their new surroundings. With Snook in his arms and the holdall on his back it was hard to get the key turned in the lock and pull the door shut. He kept at it and finally it closed silently. He slid the key into his pocket.

One of the pups let out a tiny whine, nose over the edge of the box, looking for his mum. Bean twigged immediately and tipped the box so he could see Snook in Tyler's arms. He panted and breathed, tail brushing the plastic of the box. Tyler looked at Barry's front door and turned to follow Bean, Snook fidgeting in his arms as he went, then he had the stairwell door open and they were both out in the echoing concrete of the stairs. The door was on a cushioned hinge, and Tyler tried to pull it shut as gently as possible but it was slow. It wasn't quite closed when one puppy yelped, a noise that reverberated around the stairwell like a gunshot.

A pause of a second then Tyler heard Barry's dogs barking and thudding down their hall.

He pulled the door closed and turned.

'Go,' he said, pushing Bean towards the stairs.

He overtook her as they went down the floors and had to keep stopping for her to catch up. He looked upward, expecting to hear the fire door swing open and Barry's voice come roaring down to them, or the dogs clattering with their paws on the concrete. But it didn't happen. As they approached the last few floors, he imagined Barry heading down in the lift with Ant and Dec, waiting for them when they reached the bottom. His heart thudded as he opened the door into the entrance, but it was empty.

Outside the door was Flick, smoking a cigarette and leaning against the wall like she was waiting on a date. She saw him, stubbed out the cigarette and smiled. When she caught sight of Bean holding the box of puppies her smile got bigger. She opened the tower block door for the pair of them with an exaggerated bow.

'Your chariot awaits,' she said.

✳

Bean looked tiny in Flick's double bed. Her eyes were sleepy but she was smiling as she hugged a cuddly elephant that Flick had given her. The white sheets on the bed and the classy bedside table and lamp made it feel like a hotel. Snook and the pups were nestled in a corner of the room, newspaper down on the wooden floorboards underneath them. Tyler said they should stay in the kitchen but Bean insisted, she wouldn't let them out of her sight, and Flick didn't care either way.

It was after midnight, way past Bean's bedtime. She had taken all of this in her stride. They were in a strange new home and she only had a few of her belongings with her, but she had taken to Flick immediately, her shiny hair, her big smile, her confident demeanour. Bean had insisted on taking her picture with the Polaroid, the picture now lying on the top of the pile next to her bed. Tyler glanced at it and realised that Flick seemed unearthly to Bean, a visitor from another planet. She had the same effect on him.

Bean was drifting off, failing to keep her eyes open.

'What if I have nightmares?' Her words slipped into each other.

'You won't, not here. Only good dreams come in this house.'

'But what if I do? Where will you be?'

Tyler pointed at the door. 'In the other bedroom, like I showed you.'

'Will Flick be there too? Is she staying here?'

'I don't know,' Tyler said. 'Now go to sleep.'

'Am I going to school tomorrow?'

'Of course,' Tyler said. 'Why wouldn't you?'

Bean's tongue poked from her lips. 'When Grace moved to a new house, she went to a different school, remember?'

Tyler touched her cheek. 'We're not moving house and you're not changing school.'

'Good.' Bean turned her head a little. 'Where's the toilet again?'

'At the end of the hall. You just went.'

'Oh yeah.' She opened her one available arm. 'Cuddles and kisses.'

He hugged and kissed her then she drew Nellie the elephant tighter to her chest and rolled over.

Tyler glanced at the world map on the wall, thought about distance, then went through to Flick's parents' room. Flick was sitting on the bed with a large glass of white wine, flicking through a guidebook to New York.

'Have you been?' Tyler said, looking at the book.

She nodded. 'It's not all that.'

'I'd love to go sometime.'

'I'll take you.'

'You've done enough for us already.'

Flick pointed in the direction of Bean's room. 'Is she OK?'

'She will be.'

'She's a lovely kid.'

'Yeah.'

'She's lucky to have you for a big brother.'

'I don't know about that.'

'Of course she is.' Flick patted the bed next to him and he sat down by her side.

They were silent for a while, Tyler aware that she was examining him, looking for something.

'I owe you an explanation,' he said finally.

She sipped her wine. 'You don't owe me anything.'

'I really do. You hardly know me.'

'I know enough.'

Tyler waved a hand around the room, at the expensive hardwood dresser, the memory-foam mattress, the writing desk by the window.

'Letting us stay here,' Tyler said. 'It means so much.'

Flick shrugged. 'It's lying empty. It's no bother.'

Tyler hung his head, thinking about Monica and Angela in their hospital beds.

'It wasn't safe for us back there.' He paused for a long time. 'With Barry. I've sheltered her from him as much as I can, but things have got worse recently. Much worse.'

'Has he hurt her?' Flick said.

'Tonight for the first time. I swore to myself if he ever laid a hand on her I would get her out of there. I can't protect her.'

Flick laid a hand on his and he looked up.

'But you are protecting her,' she said.

'Maybe I'm just bringing trouble to your door.'

Flick rubbed the back of his hand then pointed at his bruised eye. 'Was that him?'

'Yeah.'

'Has he done that before?'

A sarcastic laugh escaped Tyler's mouth. 'Just a bit.'

Flick sipped her wine then sucked her teeth. 'You should tell the police.'

'I can't.'

'Why not?'

'He would kill me. And Bean.'

'He wouldn't get the chance.'

'You don't know him.'

Flick sighed. 'You can't stay here forever.'

Tyler cricked his neck, suddenly exhausted. 'I just need some time to come up with a plan.'

Flick looked at a picture on the wall, her mum and dad looking uncomfortable. 'How's your mum doing?'

'Same, as far as I know. I left at three o'clock and they haven't been in touch. She might've come round by now. Do they call if patients wake up?'

'I don't know.'

Flick took a final gulp of her wine and set the glass down on the bedside table. Something occurred to Tyler, something Bean had asked. 'Do you have to get back to Inveresk?'

She thought that over for a moment. 'I don't think so. The girls will cover for me in the house.'

'It seems very easy for you to come and go from that place.'

Flick raised her eyebrows. 'They make the mistake of treating us like adults. As long as I'm back there early in the morning it'll be fine.'

Tyler couldn't help a smile coming across his face.

'Don't get any funny ideas, though,' she laughed. 'I'm not that kind of girl.'

'I never thought you were.'

Another wave of exhaustion swept over him and he felt his eyelids get heavy. 'I need to sleep.'

'Just get under the covers.'

He looked at her for a moment then kicked his shoes off. He pulled the sheets back and got in fully clothed. She did the same at her side, and slid across to hold him. The warmth of her body and the scent of her filled his senses, and he began falling asleep.

'Will I put the light off?' she said.

He was almost gone.

'Leave it on,' he said. 'In case Bean comes through. She's afraid of the dark.'

✳

He was woken by the sound of breaking glass.

He sat up in bed and looked around. Flick was out for the count next to him, her breath rattling in her nose. He flipped the covers off and strode through to the other bedroom. Bean was lying sprawled out, arms wide like she was looking for a hug, her face loose and relaxed. He lifted her duvet from the floor and threw it over her.

Maybe he'd imagined it.

Then he heard a thump downstairs. He knew that sound, as if someone had climbed in through a broken window. He looked around Bean's room for something heavy, something he could get a good swing with. Couldn't see anything. He thought he heard the crunch of broken glass underfoot. The number of times he'd heard that noise before, all the houses he'd helped rob with Barry and Kelly. He wondered if it was them, if they'd followed him somehow. Or maybe the Holts, finally catching up.

He opened the top drawer of a dresser and found a craft kit with scissors. He lifted them out, held the handles in his fist and left the room. Stood at the top of the stairs, listening. Wondered if he could go downstairs quietly enough to make it to the kitchen and get a proper knife. He'd stupidly left the knife he'd brought down there.

He started down the stairs and heard more noise from the living room. Someone swearing under their breath. He was halfway down the stairs now, his hand sweating on the handles of the scissors, his legs shaking as he tried to take deep breaths. There was no more noise for a few moments, only his heartbeat in his ears, the faint creak of the stairs under his feet. He'd read once that treading on the edge of a step rather than the middle would reduce the noise, but he'd never known it to work in all the jobs he'd been on. But he still tried it, hugging the wall as he crept down till he was at the bottom, readying himself, feeling his weight against the earth, his balance and poise.

He heard a dull thud, someone bumping into a piece of furniture in the dark maybe. He took a few steps towards the kitchen, away from the living room, keeping an eye over his shoulder as he went, and got as far as the kitchen doorway.

'What the hell are you doing here?'

He felt pressure lift as he recognised the voice. Not Barry or Deke but that posh kid Will.

He turned. 'I'm staying here.'

Will was incredulous. 'You're fucking Flick?'

Tyler lowered the scissors a little, felt his body relax. 'I just needed a place to crash for a bit.'

Will took a step towards him. 'And you and Flick are such good friends now.'

'She's helping me out.' Tyler frowned as Will took another two steps. 'Anyway, what are you doing here?'

Will looked smug. 'Just getting my own back.'

Tyler looked at him, then around at the darkness, the faint light from the upstairs landing striping between the banisters. 'You could've broken a window anytime. Why come in at night, particularly when Flick is here?'

Will stepped closer. 'You have a dirty mind. I'm not some sex pest.'

Tyler gripped the scissors tighter and raised them an inch or two. 'I saw you sexually assault her last time.'

Will checked him out, up and down. 'How old are you? She's a cradle snatcher.'

'My age is irrelevant.'

Will shook his head. Another step. 'You don't know anything about women.'

'Next you'll be telling me when they say "no" they mean "yes".'

Will raised his shoulders like a mob gangster. 'That's actually true.'

He looked at the scissors as he took another step. He was only a couple of feet away, moving smoothly and calmly. 'What do you plan doing with those? That's attempted murder.'

Tyler tried to keep his hand steady. 'Self-defence, reasonable force. You've entered the premises illegally.'

'Listen to the lawyer.' Will thought for a moment. 'You've been in front of a judge before, haven't you?'

He took another step.

'Stop right there,' Tyler said.

Will lunged at Tyler, slapping away the hand with the scissors so that they clattered across the kitchen floor. He pushed his shoulder into Tyler's chest, knocking the breath out of him as the two of them tumbled into the kitchen, Tyler's back slamming against the island worktop, Will over him, a forearm across his throat, his other fist connecting with Tyler's stomach. Tyler gasped and tried to breathe as Will kicked at his knee, more pain as Tyler looked around for something to give him leverage. Will was taller and had a couple of stone on him, a rugby player probably, used to rucking with the big boys, throwing his weight around. Tyler could see a block full of expensive knives but it was over on the other worktop, might as well be a million miles away. He began to feel lightheaded, blisters of light in his vision. Will leaned in to gloat and Tyler took his chance, aiming his forehead at Will's nose, which burst open in a spray of blood. But Will didn't loosen his grip, just pushed harder with his forearm into Tyler's throat, spitting blood into his face. His other fist connected again with Tyler's stomach, then with the side of his head, his skull thunking onto the marble worktop as another punch caught his eyebrow and he felt himself beginning to drift away from consciousness.

Then suddenly the pressure eased and Will stood back, releasing Tyler's throat and holding his hands up. As he backed away, Tyler saw Flick standing behind him with a gun pressed against his temple.

'Flick,' Will said, voice shaky. 'What are you doing?'

She was calm. 'Get away from him.'

'Take it easy.'

Flick removed the gun barrel from Will's head and came to stand beside Tyler, keeping the gun pointed at Will.

'I'll take it easy when you get the hell out of my house.'

Will had his hands in front of him like he could fend off a bullet if she fired.

Flick glanced at Tyler. 'You OK?'

He'd straightened up and was gasping, his hand at his eye. 'Fine.'

She looked at Will.

'I didn't mean anything,' he said. 'It was just a little fun.'

Flick held the gun steady. 'Get out.'

Will backtracked out of the kitchen, eyes on the pistol in Flick's hand. 'Do you know what you're doing with that thing?'

'Would you like to find out?'

'OK, I'm going.'

She walked to the hallway with Tyler following and watched as Will left through the front door. As soon as he was out she fastened the deadbolt and security chain, leaned against the door with her forehead and let out a breath.

Tyler stared at her. 'Thanks. Again.'

'No worries.'

'*Do* you know what you're doing with that thing?'

She lifted her head off the wood, looked at the gun. 'I do.'

'Where did you get it?'

She slid something across on the handle, Tyler presumed it was the safety. 'My dad got it in Iraq. Black market. He doesn't know I know about it. Mum told me, just in case.'

Tyler shook his head.

Flick smiled, looked at the door, then at him. 'Let's go back to bed.'

33

Bean was lining up to go into class. Tyler knelt down and straightened her collar, told her in a soft voice what he'd said earlier that morning about not telling any of her friends where they were staying. As he stood up, he got a call from an Edinburgh number he didn't recognise. He tried to think who it could be. He let it ring as Bean went inside, nattering to Aisha and smiling. He stared at his phone as it kept ringing, aware that he was getting looks from the mums in the playground. Eventually he pressed answer.

'Hello, is this Tyler Wallace?'

A woman's voice, not one he recognised. The sound of activity behind her, people being busy.

'Yes.'

'I'm calling from the Edinburgh Royal Infirmary about your mum, Angela.'

He tried to swallow. 'What about her?'

'She's being discharged.'

He looked at the women leaving the playground, the trees beyond swaying in a breeze, clouds crawling across the sky. He breathed.

'So soon?'

'She's recovering well.'

'Well' wasn't a word Tyler would use for her under the circumstances.

'But she's an addict,' he said. 'Isn't there a programme, some help for her?'

'She'll have to take that up with her GP,' the woman said. She had a kind voice but businesslike. She probably had this conversation ten times a day. 'That's not what we do here.'

'She won't go and see her doctor.'

He heard a sigh down the phone. 'Tyler, is it?'

'Yes.'

'I'm sorry, son, believe me. Have you spoken to social services?'

'They know all about us.'

'Well, it's more their kind of thing than ours, I'm afraid.'

'Can't you keep her in a little longer, give her more time to detox?'

'The doctor gave her the all-clear first thing. We're very tight at the moment and we need the bed. In fact someone else is already in it.'

'Then where's Mum?'

'At reception waiting for you.'

'Christ,' Tyler said. The playground was almost empty now, a couple of late stragglers traipsing into the entrance. 'Why didn't she call me herself?'

There was a pause. 'She has no money or phone. I offered to let her use this one.' Another pause, and Tyler wondered what it was like to be a nurse all day. 'I think she was ashamed to speak to you, to be honest.'

Tyler looked up at the clouds, scudding a little faster than before, heading east, chasing each other to the sea.

'I'll come and get her,' he said.

✳

She was sitting on the ground outside reception as if she was begging for change. She wore the same hoodie and sweatshirt that Tyler had thrown on her the other day, and was smoking a cigarette, sucking on it with thin cheeks.

'My boy,' she said. Her voice was croaky, hands shaking. Her skin was grey, deep bags under her eyes.

'Come on,' Tyler said. He held out a hand and she took it and got up slowly, grunting as she did.

'Can we get a taxi? I'm not sure I can walk.'

Tyler raised his eyebrows. 'Have you got any money?'

She looked at him like he was mad. Tyler still had some money that he'd skimmed from the Holts, but that was for Bean, he was damned if he was wasting it on this.

'Me neither,' he said. 'Let's walk.'

'Maybe Barry could pick us up.'

Tyler stared at her. They both knew Barry wouldn't help and that it was dangerous to even ask, unless you wanted an earful of abuse or worse.

It took them forty-five minutes to get home along Little France Drive, a walk Tyler could've done on his own in ten. Angela kept stopping and wheezing, looking around at the waste ground and the trees up the hill in the distance, Tyler standing waiting for her. He remembered the drive the other way, Flick behind the wheel and Angela in the back, drool from her mouth, her skin blue. He wondered if Flick got a ticket for pummelling down the bus lane.

He pictured her first thing this morning, slipping out of bed to the toilet, the sound of her brushing her teeth. She sneaked back in and saw he was awake, kissed him quickly on the lips then headed back to Inveresk before she was caught. Bean was disappointed Flick wasn't there when she woke up, asking when she'd get to meet her again.

When they got to Greendykes House Tyler held the door open, ushered his mum into the lift, then up and inside the flat. She put the telly on and crashed out on the sofa. This was the same room where he found her yesterday and it was depressing to be back here with her. The place stank of booze, shit and piss. He wondered how long before Angela got antsy and went out to score. Or if she would stave it off with booze. He tried to think if there was any alcohol in the flat, but what was the point? She would find stuff if she wanted to. She never had money but she always had money for smack and drink, that's how it worked.

He made her a cup of tea and placed it on the arm of the sofa by her head.

'Thanks, love,' she said, without looking at him. She was watching an episode of *Wanted Down Under*, wholesome British families out property hunting in Australia, contemplating emigrating to a better life.

He saw the shit stain on the carpet from where he'd found Angela lying yesterday. He went to the sink and soaked a sponge, then came back and got on his knees, started scrubbing at it.

Eventually Angela noticed. She looked confused then put it together. 'Leave that, I'll get it.' Her voice was so pathetic.

Tyler kept scrubbing. 'It's fine.'

'No, it's not.' But she didn't move to stop him, just lowered her head in shame and turned back to the television.

He finished up and was heading out the door when she spoke.

'Tyler?'

He stopped in the doorway and turned back.

She looked at him with deep sadness in her eyes, her body swamped in those clothes. 'I'm sorry.'

He didn't know if she was apologising for what she'd done, or what she was going to do. It didn't matter either way.

He chewed the inside of his cheek and left the flat.

*

He went in the school gates and saw a police car waiting outside the main entrance. He was twenty yards away when the front passenger door opened and Pearce got out, arching her back and stretching her shoulders.

He shook his head as he reached her. 'Please leave me alone.'

Pearce looked at him with sympathy. 'It's your sister.'

His stomach dropped. 'Bean? What's happened?'

Pearce shook her head. 'Kelly. I'm sorry, Tyler, she's dead.'

The blood rushed to his face and his legs felt like jelly. He was relieved about Bean more than anything else, and ashamed of that. Pearce had told him that way deliberately, to fuck with him. He blinked and tried to breathe normally.

'Are you sure?' he said.

'Barry has already identified her.'

'How did it happen?'

Pearce pointed at the police car. 'That's what we're trying to find out. You need to come down to the station and have a chat.'

Tyler looked past her at the school. From here, maybe a dozen classrooms were looking out on him talking to a cop. So that was over three hundred kids and teachers, all eyeballing this conversation.

He opened the car door and got in.

34

Craigmillar Police Station was an anonymous low-slung concrete sprawl, one storey high, clean brick and bright-blue trim around the doors and windows. It hunkered between a community centre for adults with learning difficulties and a sliver of ground where a handful of the travelling community permanently camped out. The only clues to the station's status were the high metal fences on either side and the two squad cars parked out front.

Tyler was led into a room at the side of reception. It was bland, metal desks in the middle, uncomfortable chairs, a projector and AV equipment for presentations. It smelled of bleach and there was a scatter of biscuit crumbs on the carpet. This was a meeting room not an official interview room, and Tyler wondered about that.

'Where's Barry?'

Pearce signalled for him to sit down. 'He's being interviewed.'

'He's surely not a suspect.'

'You don't think?'

'He wouldn't kill his own sister.'

Pearce raised her eyebrows. 'Are you implying he would kill someone who wasn't his sister?'

'That's not what I said.'

Tyler thought about Bean, the back of Barry's hand cutting her cheek open. He wondered if Miss Kelvin had mentioned it in class this morning, if Bean had told her anything. Something else occurred to him.

'Have you told Mum yet?'

Pearce shook her head. 'We tried the flat this morning at the same time as we got Barry. There was no answer.'

Tyler nodded. 'I was bringing her back from hospital.'

That got Pearce's attention. 'Is she not well?'

'OD'd again.'

'So where is she now?'

'On the sofa, drinking tea. Or maybe she's already out trying to score.'

Pearce bit at the corner of her lip. 'We'll send a uniformed officer out to speak to her.'

Tyler looked around the room. Outside the window two officers in stab-proof vests were climbing into a car with polystyrene cups of coffee in hand. They were laughing at a joke, unhurried, at ease with their authority.

'You said Barry was being interviewed,' Tyler said.

'That's right, with his lawyer.'

'Barry doesn't have a lawyer.'

'It appears there are some things you don't know about your big brother.'

'Half-brother.' Tyler frowned. 'Anyway, why are you not interviewing me?'

'Do you want us to?'

Tyler shook his head. He scratched at a piece of graffiti on the corner of the desk that said 'Debbie is a slag'. The letters had been gone over so many times they had etched the words into the metal tabletop. Outside, two seagulls were scrapping over a discarded burger.

Pearce leaned forward, opened her hands out. 'Look, I think we got off on the wrong foot.'

'Yeah?'

'I really want to help you, Tyler. And Angela. And especially Bethany.'

'OK.'

'Kelly is dead, doesn't that mean something to you?'

Tyler didn't speak.

'Apart from the fact your half-sister has been murdered, it also suggests that you and your family are in danger.'

'How so?'

Pearce sighed. 'You know how, I know you do.'

Tyler waved his hands, indicating for her to keep talking.

She looked at him. 'You and I both know who did this.'

'Do we?'

Pearce actually looked around, as if making sure no one was eavesdropping. Tyler wondered about bugging devices, was that legal? Inadmissible evidence anyway, he knew that much.

'This is revenge,' Pearce said. 'From the Holts. They've somehow found out that you and your siblings robbed their house and stabbed Monica, and this has escalated.'

'If you think it was the Holts, you should be talking to them.'

'We will be, don't worry.'

'But in the meantime, you're hassling me and my brother in the middle of our grief.'

Pearce got up and wandered round to the window, looked out for a moment. It was calculated, like she was thinking of something on the hoof, but it was obvious she had this all planned out.

'I'm giving you one last chance,' she said. 'That's what you're doing here. I'm giving you the chance to come out of this alive and in one piece.'

Tyler shook his head. 'No, you're not. You're trying to get me to grass on Barry.'

'It's not grassing if it saves Bethany's life.'

Tyler pushed his seat back from the table and the scrape of it made Pearce jump. 'You don't give a shit about Bean, so stop pretending you do.'

Pearce studied him for a few moments.

'I know what it's like,' she said eventually.

Tyler just stared. 'No, you don't.'

She swallowed, took a breath, seemed uncomfortable for the first time since he'd met her. She looked out of the window again and Tyler had the impression this was different from last time, this wasn't premeditated.

'I knew your mum at school, did you know that?'

Tyler scratched at the table. 'Everyone knows everyone around here.'

'We weren't mates or anything, but we were in a couple of the same classes. She dropped out when she got pregnant with Barry. Aged fifteen, I think.'

'That's a nice story.'

'By that same age, I had been regularly raped and sexually assaulted for three years by my stepdad. Every week since I was twelve, since I had my first period. I tried to tell my mum but I couldn't get the words out, and I knew she wouldn't believe me anyway, she would take his side. Eventually I ran away. Only then did the police get involved. They found me begging, living on the street, sleeping by the warm air vents at the Commie Pool. When they tried to take me home I freaked out, told them everything. They didn't believe me. My stepdad denied it, Mum said it was all nonsense, that I was just a difficult teenager making things up.'

She turned and held his gaze. 'So I know what it's like to have nowhere to turn to, Tyler. I really do.'

Pearce's eyes were wet and Tyler looked down at the floor.

'What did you do?' he said.

She walked back over to the table and pulled up her sleeves. Faded scars criss-crossed the inside of her wrists, healed over the years but still there as a reminder.

'I was lucky,' she said. 'Mum found me and I went to hospital. If my stepdad had found me I'm sure he would've left me to die. I refused to go home when the hospital released me, said I would do it again. They threatened to section me. So I ran away again. Lived rough until I turned sixteen, stayed on the floor of a friend's house on and off, when her parents let me. Then I got smart. Spoke to a social worker, applied for a council flat, got into the system.'

She pulled her sleeves back down but stayed looming over him at the table.

'I know it could easily have worked out differently. I could've died. I was only a whisper away from that. So I know about the situation you're in.'

Tyler shook his head. 'There's no situation.'

Pearce became angry, barely containing it. 'I can't help you if you don't talk, Tyler. I'm trying to save your fucking life, and your little sister's. Do you want to know what they did to Kelly? There were signs of torture, multiple stab wounds, strangulation, severe beatings about the face and body, then she was set on fire, most likely while still alive.'

Tyler tried to swallow but his mouth was dry. 'So go and arrest the guys who did it.'

'We will,' Pearce said. 'But you know how it works. They're smart, they'll have alibis. They'll have been careful about forensics, they know about that stuff. There's a reason we haven't caught them before. I need you to give me Barry first, that's my way into this.'

Tyler stood up. 'I don't know what you're talking about. And even if I did, you can't protect us.'

'We're the only ones who can,' Pearce said. 'Do you think Barry will protect you from Deke Holt? Do you think Barry wouldn't sell you in a second if it saved his skin? He's probably in the interview room right now with his solicitor working out how he can drop you in it, now that Kelly's out of the picture.'

Tyler shuffled from foot to foot.

'Who knows?' Pearce said. 'Maybe he killed Kelly because she was a witness. Maybe you're next.'

'That's crazy,' Tyler said. 'You said she was tortured.'

'You think Barry couldn't do that?'

He thought about those fucking dogs, and about Barry assaulting him and Bean. And his million other acts of violence against the world.

Pearce narrowed her eyes. 'He was sleeping with her, wasn't he?'

Tyler sat down.

Pearce sighed. 'Fucking his own sister. Christ, it's like the Wild West around here.'

Tyler rubbed at his forehead, felt a tightness across his brow.

'If you don't speak,' Pearce said, 'I have to let you go.'

'Great.'

She pointed out of the window. The seagulls had settled their argument over the burger, the bigger one had it. The bigger one always wins in the end.

'You think it's safer for you out there than in here?'

Tyler looked around the room, at the nothingness of it. 'I'll take my chances.'

Pearce paced up and down, like a detective in an old movie pretending to think something over. Or maybe she really was thinking things over.

'Where did you and Bethany stay last night?'

Tyler straightened in his seat. 'What?'

'It was early when we came round to your flat. You and Bethany didn't stay there last night, did you?'

Tyler looked at the table.

'My guess is that you didn't think it was safe.' Pearce moved closer to him, stood next to the table. 'Given what happened to Kelly, that was probably sensible.'

Tyler shook his head, to himself more than anything. 'We stayed at a friend's house.'

'You found someone willing to take that chance?'

'What chance?'

Pearce leant her knuckles on the table. 'Tyler, for a smart kid, you can be pretty stupid sometimes. If you're in danger, anyone sheltering you is in danger too. So this friend of yours better make sure the Holts don't hear about him giving you somewhere to hide out.'

'It's not like that.'

'No?'

Tyler rubbed at his palm with his other hand. 'It's just different. It's a different world.'

Pearce shook her head. 'Like you said earlier, everyone around here knows each other's business. That's the problem with this place, no one can keep a secret. That's why you and Barry are in the shit.'

'We're not in the shit.'

Pearce held her hands up. 'If that's how you want to play it, fine. I tried to help you, remember that. I tried to give you a way out.'

'By grassing up Barry.'

'By helping me get a psychotic maniac off the street and end this ridiculous vendetta.'

'You won't get Barry off the street, that's the problem,' Tyler said. His hand came up and touched his bruised eye. 'You'll fuck it up, then I'll be dead.'

Pearce gave him a serious look. 'I promise that won't happen.'

Tyler chewed at his thumbnail before he spoke. 'You can't promise that.'

Pearce sighed and straightened up, went back to the window for some more acting like a detective. 'Well, maybe we won't need you anyway.' She turned back. 'Did you know Monica Holt is conscious? Apparently her memory of that night is coming back. I'm heading to the hospital next to speak to her. I'm sure she'll have some interesting things to say.'

'I'm glad she's OK.'

Pearce raised her eyebrows. 'I'll bet you are. But when she tells me what happened, that's it. You and Barry will both go down.'

'It wasn't us, I keep telling you.'

Pearce looked insulted. 'Spare me, it's far too late for that shit. When you get put away, that'll leave Bethany being looked after by Angela, is that what you want?'

'Angela is her mum.'

'Angela's in no fit state to look after anyone, including herself. Without you around Bethany will be taken into care, you know that.'

Pearce stared at him for a long time. Tyler wondered what Barry was up to in the interview room. He couldn't be cutting a deal, surely. No, he would be sitting in silence. They didn't have anything, he just had to ride it out. But what about Monica?

Tyler thought about Kelly. She was a victim of Barry as much as anyone else. He tried to conjure up happy memories of the two of them as kids, but the truth was that Kelly had been under Barry's spell from way back. There were glimmers of a caring sister now and then, but mostly subsumed by the role she played with Barry, the pressure he put her under. Tyler remembered a few moments with her, but always when Barry wasn't around. Kicking a ragged old football around across the road before it was a building site, sharing a bag of stolen Haribo on the way home from school. One time, Kelly had tried to help him with his spelling homework, but despite being several years older her spelling was terrible and her handwriting even worse, and Tyler had to explain to his teacher why he'd done so badly.

But most of the time, when Barry was around, Tyler was treated as the runt of the litter, ignored or abused by the pair of them. Until Bean came along and replaced him in that role. He couldn't let her go through the stuff he went through, so he'd spent the last few years taking care of her. He wasn't about to stop now, just when she needed him most.

Pearce eventually turned away.

'Just go,' she said.

Tyler stood up. He reached the door, his fingers on the handle.

Pearce turned back to look at him. 'Good luck, Tyler, I mean it.'

35

Tyler answered his phone after a deep breath.

'Where the fuck are you?' Barry said.

Tyler looked around at the big Victorian houses of Cluny Avenue. He'd come here straight from the police station, jumped on a bus then just wandered around the streets, soaking up the affluence. He needed to pretend for a few minutes that he wasn't in the middle of all this. He imagined a parallel universe where one of these houses was his home, maybe he was attending Inveresk, maybe he was even friends with that prick Will, playing rugby on a Saturday morning, attending chapel on a Sunday, singing hymns and hanging around afterwards to claim sanctuary from all the murderous bastards out to get him and his family.

'Nowhere,' he said.

'Well, you've got to be somewhere, cunt.'

'Just out walking.'

Barry was sniffing down the phone, permanently coked. 'They killed Kelly.'

'I know.'

'How do you know?'

'The police told me.' Tyler thought about what Pearce said. Kelly had been beaten and stabbed, tortured and choked. He felt his own breath catch in his throat, tears coming to his eyes. His hand shook, rattling the phone against his ear. He felt his legs become unsteady, the trees towering over him, wavering on the edge of his vision. She had never been much of a sister to him, but Christ almighty.

'Cunts had me in for two hours, as if I did something wrong,' Barry said. 'As if I was to blame.'

Tyler let that slide. If he said anything Barry would rip his head off.

'I want you back home,' Barry said. 'Now.'

'Why?'

'We've got a job to do.'

Tyler's heart was a rock in his chest and he felt bile rising in his throat. 'What is it?'

'Just fucking get here.'

Click.

Tyler felt dizzy as he looked around, his legs weak. He put a hand out against the wall next to him, then doubled over and puked against a lamp-post. His eyes watered and his nose ran as he spat and tried to breathe. Eventually he straightened up, saw an old woman passing with her small dog, giving him a look of revulsion. He didn't belong around here.

✳

Barry had the Skoda engine running in the car park outside Greendykes House. Tyler craned his neck and wondered about Angela up in the flat. Behind him the diggers on the building site were throwing mounds of earth around, making the ground quiver under his feet. The crash and roar of it filled his ears.

Barry jumped out of the car. Tyler had never seen him as bad as this, coke sweat drenching his forehead and arms, his eyes tiny black holes, arms and legs jittery.

'Get in,' he said.

Tyler got into the car. There was a baseball bat and a can of petrol in the footwell in front of him. Ant and Dec were slobbering and pawing at each other in the back seat, the feral stink of them filling the car. Barry got in and screeched off, burning rubber, the acrid stench of it mingling with the dog smell.

'Fucking cunts,' Barry said under his breath. 'Deke Holt thinks he's God. Fuck him, fuck his ugly wife, I should've finished her off when I had the chance. Fucking snobby pricks think they're too good for Niddrie, fuck's wrong with them, no sense of community, abandon the place as soon as they have a few quid. Dirty fucking Holt bastards.'

It was a psychotic mantra. He was winding himself up more and more as he muttered and shouted, barely looking at Tyler. He drove like a maniac through a red light on Niddrie Mains Road and round the roundabout at Cameron Toll. Tyler prayed for an accident, imagined a delivery truck smashing into the side of them, pushing them off the road into the trees, anything to take the terrible momentum out of this. He pictured himself reaching over and pulling at the steering wheel, but he didn't move.

Too soon they were past Kings Buildings and into Blackford. They'd robbed houses around here for years without thinking, without consequences. Not anymore.

'We're going to their house?' Tyler said eventually.

Barry grinned. 'What do you fucking think?'

'They'll kill us.'

'Not if we kill them first.' Barry lifted his T-shirt to show a gun tucked into the waistband of his jeans.

'Christ,' Tyler said.

Barry frowned and pointed at the bat on the floor. 'Just back me the fuck up.' He tilted his head to the dogs in the back, their breath steaming up the windows. 'Maybe I'll let these guys have a go.'

'Where did you get a gun?'

'What do you care? Fucking goody two-shoes.'

'This is insane.'

Barry was still driving recklessly, cutting in front of oncoming traffic, swerving up Kilgraston then into Strathearn Road. He pulled the gun from his waistband and pointed it at Tyler, the barrel pushed into his cheek. Barry's other hand was on the wheel, his gaze switching between the road and Tyler.

'Just back me up,' he said.

Tyler edged back in his seat, away from the barrel. 'Take it easy.'

They were there, St Margaret's Road. Barry pulled up in the street outside number four. There was no car in the driveway, no obvious sign of life. Tyler tried to breathe, tried to stop his hands from shaking.

Barry handed the bat to Tyler then skipped out of the car and let the dogs out the back. They clambered over each other and tumbled out, ready. Tyler followed with the bat hanging down by his side. He watched as Barry rang the doorbell.

'This is your plan?'

Barry sniffed and smiled. 'They won't expect it.'

Tyler was either going to get killed or be an accessory to murder. He thought about running, but pictured Ant and Dec chasing him down the driveway, ripping him apart in the middle of the street in front of passers-by.

Please no one be in. Please.

Barry rang the doorbell again.

Tyler imagined the neighbours' curtains twitching, thought about CCTV in the street. This was too exposed. He prayed that a neighbour didn't come out and get involved. He just wanted this to end one way or the other.

'Fuckers aren't in,' Barry said. He was almost dancing on the spot like he was barefoot on hot sand. He scratched the side of his head with the gun and Tyler imagined it going off, spreading his brains and skull across the lawn and the gravel drive.

Barry stuck the gun back in his jeans and grabbed the bat from Tyler. He turned and smashed in the bay windows of the front room, the crash of it excruciating, making the dogs jump and act even more jittery. No alarm went off because they had no alarm. If they'd just had an alarm in the first place their house wouldn't have been a target and none of this would've happened. Tyler remembered being here that first night, the shotgun under the bed, the money clip, Monica Holt lying in the hallway staring at him. Kelly stepping past her body, Barry already out the door. He felt a twinge about Kelly and wondered how long it would be until they were all dead.

Barry went to the car and lifted out the petrol can. He came back, unscrewed it and poured petrol in the smashed windows, over the rugs inside, splashing it onto the nearest furniture. The dogs recoiled at the stench of the fuel. Tyler wondered if anyone was upstairs sleeping, maybe Monica was already discharged from hospital, resting up with painkillers and sleeping pills. Barry led a trail of petrol away from the window frames and into the driveway then got a lighter out.

Tyler looked at the house then back to Barry who was smiling like he'd just won the lottery. He lit the petrol trail and it whooshed into flame, tearing along the gravel and up into the window frames, the curtains catching the fever and spreading it inside the house.

Barry watched for a moment then turned towards the car and clicked his fingers for the dogs to follow. He turned to Tyler and pointed at the flames in the living room.

'Don't fuck with the Wallaces, eh?'

36

Bean clattered up the rough stone steps in her school shoes and disappeared around the corner of the spiral staircase.

'Come on,' she shouted.

Tyler and Flick gave each other a look and followed, disappearing into the gloom themselves, the narrow slits for archers throwing slivers of light into the tower. Halfway up the steps Tyler felt Flick take his hand, and a trill ran up his arm straight to his heart.

They hadn't paid entry to Craigmillar Castle, it was easy to sneak past the old woman at the front gate, just walk through the field further down the hill, reach the cover of the trees, then you could pop up at the side wall and clamber over.

Tyler had persuaded Barry to let him out of the car at the high school, telling him it would look less suspicious if he attended a couple of classes this afternoon. He hadn't gone to class, obviously, just walked through the woods at the back of the school until it was time to pick up Bean from primary. Just as he was standing waiting in the playground Flick had called, keen to meet up, and he couldn't think of a reason not to.

So here they were like a bizarre family, mum, dad and little daughter, exploring the medieval ruins at the top of Craigmillar Hill. Tyler remembered being here at night with Flick – how long ago was that? He was losing track of the days, drowning in time, unable to get a clear view of a future.

Halfway up the tower they came out into a great hall, high ceilings and a ten-foot wide fireplace. Bean stood in the fireplace, stretched her neck and shouted at the narrow chimney slit way above. She came out and darted off to the side, found another staircase and steps. Tyler and Flick smiled and went after her. They found her in a smaller room down some steep steps, a sign on the wall saying it had once been a prison. From here the prisoners could've heard the sounds of partying from the main hall, would've smelt the roast boar. Tyler thought about prisons as Flick pretended to lock Bean inside and throw the key out of the window.

Then Bean was off again, up and up until they were at the top of the tower, where Flick had kissed him that night.

Flick was holding his hand again by this time. Bean noticed, smiled and took Flick's other hand. But she had to let go when they scrambled up the last battlements and round to the front of the ramparts overlooking the city.

Tyler looked west, searching for smoke in the air, but he couldn't see anything. He hoped that meant the house hadn't gone up, the flames had somehow stopped spreading, or someone had got there in time and doused the fire.

'This is amazing,' Bean said, running up and down the narrow path cut into the rampart. Like Tyler, she'd lived in the shadow of the castle but had never been here. It was amazing what could be right in front of you the whole time that you never even noticed.

There was an information sign about how rival armies used to try to take the castle, and how the people inside would fire arrows at them, pour boiling oil down on advancing soldiers. Flick read it out to Bean, who grimaced and laughed, acted out getting burned alive, gargling and giggling. Tyler thought of Kelly and grabbed the handrail to steady himself against a gust of wind. He would have to tell Bean that Kelly was dead. She hadn't been a big part of Bean's life, Tyler had shielded her, but she was still her half-sister, it still mattered. But he didn't want to break this fragile moment between him, Bean and Flick. He tried to imagine the three of them heading off somewhere together, a remote cottage in the Highlands or a small apartment by the sea in Greece. But he couldn't picture it. Couldn't see them any place where Barry wasn't lurking in the shadows, where the Holts weren't looking to take him out.

'You OK?' Flick said.

Bean had run off to the adjacent wall of the tower, singing a song under her breath as she trailed a hand along the stonework.

'Sure.'

'You look worried. Is it your mum?'

He thought about Kelly and Barry, how to explain it all. He thought about the Holts, and what Pearce had said at the station, that whoever was helping him and Bean was putting themselves in the firing line too. When Flick had called him, he hadn't had the strength to say no. Now he was regretting that, wondering if somehow the Holts were watching them, closing in on Flick and Bean.

The wind whipped round from the west and Flick pulled a strand of hair from her mouth. She was still in that bright-red uniform, unafraid to show people where she was from. He admired that confidence, wanted some of it for himself.

'I was at the police station earlier,' he said.

'Why?'

He looked out to sea. Inchkeith hiding out there, shrouded in fog.

'Kelly is dead.'

'Oh my God, Tyler. I'm so sorry.'

She hugged him. He tensed up at her touch, then tried to relax. Eventually he pulled away. She was looking in his eyes, so he had to turn away to the view of Arthur's Seat and the Crags.

'What happened?' she said, watching him.

'She was murdered.' He couldn't bring himself to tell her the details.

'Is this to do with Barry? Why your house wasn't safe?'

She looked over to where Bean was pretending to have a sword fight with an invading knight.

'Maybe.'

'You can't go back there,' Flick said. 'You and Bean can stay in Hope Terrace as long as you like.'

'But your parents.'

'They won't be back for months. We can work something out before then.'

Tyler shook his head. 'We can't impose on you like that.'

She touched his arm. 'Of course you can.'

'This is crazy, we've only just met.'

She held his other arm too now, as if she was going to shake him. 'Tyler, you're the best thing that's happened to me in years.'

He frowned and turned away.

'I'm serious,' she said.

'All I've done is bring you trouble.'

'That's not true, you saved me from Will.'

'Then *you* saved *me* from him.'

'There you go, we're perfect for each other.'

Tyler looked at Bean, who looked over and waved. He waved back. Behind her was the hospital, the clutter of white rooftops in the hollow of the land. Rainclouds were sweeping in from that direction, they'd get wet here soon.

'My mum is at our flat.'

'They let her out of hospital already?'

'They needed the bed.'

'Then bring her to the house.'

'I can't do that.'

'Of course you can. There's plenty of room.'

'She's...' He didn't know how to end that sentence.

'She's your mum,' Flick said. 'And Bean's mum. That's all that matters.'

Tyler stared at her. She was so much more together than him.

'Let's go and get her now,' Flick said.

Tyler frowned. 'You take Bean back to the house, I'll bring her.'

'Why?'

He didn't want Flick anywhere near Greendykes House, the Holts might be waiting there. Or Barry. And even if they weren't there, Angela would take some persuading, if she was in any fit state to be persuaded.

'Just do it, please,' he said.

Bean ran towards them and Tyler stepped back from Flick to accept a hug from his sister. He looked up and Flick was smiling at him, just as he felt the first drops of rain on his face.

37

He walked home looking for signs, waiting for a car to screech up beside him and the Holts to bundle out. The noise from the building site was monstrous today, the ground shaking under him as diggers fussed over huge piles of dirt, guys in hard hats and ear protectors shouting at each other. One day this would all be beautiful new family homes, too expensive to live in, then in another fifty years they'd be old and get knocked down and something else would be thrown up in their place, and over and over until we were all dead and the last houses crumbled into nothing and the animals and plants could reclaim it all for themselves.

It was raining steadily now, the stench of wet earth rising from the piles of rubble and dirt beyond the razor wire to his left. The cloud was low and pressed down on him, sucking light from the sky. He had his hood up, felt the gentle patter of raindrops against the material, imagined the drops driving through his scalp into his skull.

A car swished past from behind and he tensed up, half expecting it to swerve onto the pavement and take his legs from under him, push him into a whole new future of pain.

At the tower block, nothing seemed suspicious. Maybe the Holts hadn't worked out where they lived after all. Maybe they hadn't traced the stolen car, or the rest of the fenced stuff. Maybe Kelly hadn't said anything as they beat her. He felt sick at the thought of that.

Tyler went up the stairs so that the mechanism of the lift wouldn't sound in the hallway on their floor. He wondered if Barry was in there with the dogs right now, or out somewhere plotting more insanity.

He opened the stairwell door at the fifteenth floor and crept across the landing to the flat. No dog noise from Barry's flat. He slotted in his key and opened the door, slipped inside and closed it behind him. Pushed his hood down and took a second to acclimatise. This place felt like someone else's home already. He'd only spent one night at Flick's house with Bean, but he'd already become used to the luxury, the space to stretch out, a bedroom with enough floor space for a dresser, a whole room used as a study. That's what money bought you, space. Space made all the difference, gave you the chance to escape into your own world for a moment, gave you inner peace. That's the reason he'd started breaking into people's houses on his own in the first place, the opportunity for space, time and emptiness. Things he never got in normal life.

He expected Angela to be crashed out, either in bed or in front of the TV, maybe even OD'd again. But he opened the living-room door and she was standing in the kitchenette with a spread of ingredients in front of her, eggs, mushrooms, milk and ham.

She looked up.

'You can't make an omelette without breaking eggs,' she said, cracking a shell and emptying the contents into a bowl.

It was corny and she knew it, but she was clear-eyed and functioning, no sign of booze or drugs in her face. By the look of it she'd even washed her hair.

'Do you want one?' she said.

'I'm OK.'

'There's plenty.'

He walked to the kitchenette, placed a hand on the worktop. 'Mum, we need to go.'

She frowned as she whisked the eggs. 'Go where?'

'A friend's house.'

'What are you talking about? This is our home.'

Tyler took a breath. This would've been easier if she was stoned out of her head and unable to comprehend. Tyler felt guilty for that thought.

'It's not safe here.'

'What do you mean?'

Tyler sucked at his teeth. 'Barry has done something.'

She moved the pan over the gas ring, poured the egg mix in and swished it around to the edges. 'What?'

'Mum, there's something I have to tell you, please.'

Something in the tone of his voice registered and she turned to face him, rubbing her hands on the front of her jeans. 'What is it?'

Tyler held her gaze. 'Kelly's dead, Mum.'

He could see her swallow and breathe. 'What?'

'She was murdered,' Tyler said. 'The police found her this morning.'

Angela looked at the omelette then back at him.

Tyler moved towards her and took the pan away from the heat, turned the gas off.

Angela's hands were shaking. 'I don't believe you.' She lifted a hand to her eyes, rubbed at them, then the bridge of her nose.

She looked at him. 'Was it Barry?'

Tyler shook his head. Of course she knew what her son was like, that he was capable of this. If Tyler hadn't known the circumstances, he would've put Barry at the top of the suspect list too.

'I don't think so,' he said.

'Then what?'

'Barry did something crazy, Mum. He made some bad people very angry. I think they killed Kelly.'

'I don't understand,' she said, reaching out and touching the bowl.

If anything was going to send her back to heroin it was this. He wished he didn't have to tell her, and he hated Barry for putting him in this position, for making him break the news. He hated Barry for every single thing he'd done over the years, the drip-drip of bullying and intimidation, the beatings and threats, coercing him into breaking into houses, the insinuation that Bean would be next, the perpetuation of all his bullshit.

'Why don't you sit down,' Tyler said, leading her to the sofa. The television was on, sound down low, some low-rent antiques thing, contestants in matching fleeces and some posh guy smarming over them. Everything was about aspiration on daytime TV, turning a few quid at auction, doing up a shithole house, moving your family to the other side of the world. But what if you had nothing to start with? Or less than nothing, what then?

'Kelly,' Angela said.

Tyler wondered if she was trying to remember Kelly as a baby, a toddler. When had it all got away from her? Imagine having kids who you barely remembered about half the time. Now dead, too late, no chance to make it right.

'We need to go,' Tyler said as softly as he could manage.

She stared at him, but it was as if she couldn't see him, her mind drifting.

His phone rang. Flick.

He got up and turned away, answered.

'Hey.'

'Hello, Tyler.' A man's voice, one he recognised from outside the hospital. Deke Holt.

Tyler thought he might be sick. 'Who is this?'

'You know who it is.'

'Where's Flick?'

'She's safe. Same goes for your wee sister. Lovely girls, the pair of them.'

Tyler looked at Angela, in a trance, staring at nothing.

'Don't hurt them.'

Deke threw out a croak of a laugh. 'Like you didn't hurt my wife?'

'That wasn't me.'

'I don't care.'

'How did you find us?'

'The car. Wee Sam gave you up. We found your sister at the flat. Her bad luck. Sonny picked up your trail at the girl's primary school earlier.'

Tyler swallowed. 'So what now?'

Static on the line for a second, maybe the crackle of a lit cigarette. 'Bring your brother to me. Once I have you and him, I'll let the girls go.'

'How can I trust you?'

'You can't.' Another suck on the cigarette. 'And obviously, if you go to the police, I'll kill them.'

'You're bluffing.'

'Was I bluffing with Kelly?'

Tyler swallowed and looked around the room for answers. Just egg congealing in a pan, his mum on the sofa in a trance, the television burbling away.

'Where are you?' he said.

38

He scoped the house out of habit as he strode up the driveway then took out the key Flick had given him and opened the front door. The house was silent. He walked down the hall and looked in the kitchen. Snook and the pups were sleeping on the floor next to a bowl of water. It felt weird being here without Flick and Bean.

He had to find it. Think, Tyler. She came downstairs with it, which meant it's kept upstairs. Most likely in the parents' bedroom.

He took the stairs two at a time and went to the bedroom. The covers were still a mess from last night, it seemed like a lifetime since he'd crashed out here, like it happened to a different person entirely. A guy who's half-sister hadn't been murdered, who hadn't been questioned by police, whose mum was still in hospital, who hadn't tried to set fire to a house, who's friend and sister weren't being held hostage by the biggest hardman in the city. But he was all of those people now, and he had changed.

He checked under the bed first, seemed reasonable of Flick's dad to want it nearby in case of a break-in. But there was nothing except dust bunnies and a couple of suitcases. He tried the bedside tables too, nothing.

He started going through the drawers as carefully as he could, didn't want to leave a mess. It felt invasive, trawling through Flick's mum's underwear drawer, touching the bras and knickers. He slid his hand into the corners of the drawer but came out with nothing. Then Flick's dad's drawers, same result.

Into the wardrobe, riffling through dresses and jackets, trousers and shirts. Boxes of shoes at the bottom. He flipped each one open and scanned the contents. Nothing. He looked around, the only storage space he hadn't checked was a large chest sitting at the bay window. He went over, slid the catch and opened it. Spare blankets and sheets. He hoofed them out of the way, ran his hands around each layer, down to the bottom, then his knuckle hit something.

He lifted it out. A leather cloth folded around something heavy.

He unwrapped it and stared at the gun. It had *U.S. 9mm M9-P. Beretta-12486* embossed along the barrel. He felt the heft of it in his hand, the curve of the grip, the sleek coldness of the metal. He examined it. There were several switches and clips on the handle and barrel. He checked inside the leather cloth, no ammunition.

He got his phone out and Googled 'how to load and fire an M9 Beretta'. Hundreds of YouTube hits. He watched the shortest one, under a minute. Copied it, opening the slide and setting the slide catch. Popped the magazine out of the well with the catch at the base of the grip, checked the bullets, the well and the barrel, popped it back in. The safety was by the thumb, up was ready to fire, down was safe. Easy.

He carefully placed all the blankets back in the chest and closed it.

He picked up the gun and tried to get used to the weight and shape of it. Pointed at himself in the mirror and tried to imagine firing it, the glass shattering his reflection.

He got his phone out and called.

It rang for a long time, but eventually he picked up.

Tyler stared at himself in the mirror.

'Barry, I know how we can get the Holts.'

39

Tyler stared out from the roof. Not towards the hospital and castle, but in the other direction, further out of town to the southeast. Over the park to the new houses being built on The Wisp, Fort Kinnaird beyond that, the brown belt wastelands and fields, factories and offices being thrown up quick and cheap. He wondered how far you'd have to go before you reached a place where there were no signs of human occupation, where the planet was being left alone. But that's not how cities worked, they spread and spread until everything was infected, compromised.

He kept pulling the gun from the waistband of his trousers, fiddling with it, getting used to it. It was uncomfortable and awkward, and he thought about all those dumb movies where tough guys had four weapons hidden on their bodies. So ludicrous. When he had it in his waistband with his hoodie pulled down and over his belt it seemed so obvious, like it was glowing, sending out a signal to the world.

'The fuck you doing up here?'

He jumped at the sound of Barry's voice. He hadn't heard the metal door opening. He had his back to Barry, and touched the gun barrel through the material of his jeans.

He turned. 'Just needed some air.'

'Air,' Barry said, as if air was the enemy. 'Fuck's sake.'

Tyler thought about Bean and Flick, if they were tied up, drugged, beaten. He'd been in the Holt's place and he tried to think which room he would keep captives in if it was him. He wondered if it would be possible to sneak in somehow, surprise Deke and the rest in their own home. Crazy. He had no idea who was even there, let alone whereabouts they were in the house. And he couldn't risk Flick and Bean. He had to get them out of this, that was the only thing that mattered.

'You took your time,' Tyler said.

Being bolshie was a gamble, but he had to show he was up for it.

Barry grinned. 'I was getting this.'

He pulled a sawn-off shotgun from his coat pocket. Tyler raised his eyebrows. Seemed it was easy to hide a gun after all.

'Where from?'

'Never you mind,' Barry said, wielding it like he was in a gangster film. 'The Holts are fucked, that's the main thing.'

Tyler nodded.

'So where are they?' Barry said.

Barry was wide-eyed and sniffing, coked to the eyeballs, his legs shaking, his neck muscles straining. Tyler gazed over Barry's shoulder at the west of the city, the hundreds of thousands of people just getting on with life.

'Come on,' he said, walking past Barry as confidently as his legs would let him. 'I'll show you.'

✳

'Tell me again, from the start.'

Barry was trying to get Tyler to slip up, either that or his coke-addled brain couldn't keep a single piece of information in it for longer than ten seconds. The car tore along Duddingston Road West past the police station where Tyler had started the day, past the golf course and playing fields then Duddingston Loch on their left. Just one of the countless pockets in the city where the urban suddenly gave way to wildlife, trees and parks and enough quiet space to get away with shit while no one watched.

'They phoned me. They want to meet up, make a truce.'

They were back amongst houses just as quick, sitting at the cross-roads with the A1, Barry tapping the steering wheel, his foot revving on the accelerator. Tyler was surprised he hadn't just piled through the lights regardless, that's how unhinged he seemed. Ant and Dec were restless in the back, mirroring Barry's edginess. Tyler hadn't thought about the dogs coming, they made things more complicated.

'How did they have your number?'

Tyler stared at the red light, willing it to stay that way forever.

'From Kelly's phone, I presume.'

'Fucking truce.' Barry said the word like he was disgusted at the concept. 'They killed Kelly. Fuck a truce.'

As if Barry had ever cared about Kelly. She was just an excuse to be angry, the latest in a long list of things to be outraged and violent about, the world out to get him, everyone in his way, life as constant combat. It must be so wearing, Tyler thought, being full of rage all the time.

Barry had the shotgun in his lap as he drove, resting his hand there between gear changes. They reached sixty up the A1 in a twenty-limit area, then screeched to another halt at the lights at Jock's Lodge. There was a gastropub on the corner that until recently had been an old man's place, a good bar to get a beating. It closed when someone was finally stabbed in the toilets. Only five minutes to the destination and Tyler felt the hot metal of the Beretta stuffed inside his jeans, his crotch sweating up, his stomach like it was full of concrete. One of the dogs barked in the back and Tyler jumped. The other dog snuffled around the first one, pawing at him aggressively.

Red, amber, green and they were off, turning left at Meadowbank towards Holyrood Park then another left up the single-track road that climbed round the back of Arthur's Seat. The road was narrow and curved, they were going too fast, Tyler thrown this way then that in his seat, feeling the stab of the barrel into his crotch. The dogs tumbled around in the rear footwell and one yelped and snapped as its tail was squashed by the other's bulk.

'Why here?' Barry said.

Tyler shook his head. 'No one around, I guess. No witnesses.'

'Suits me. They think they're fucking smart, top-dog wankers, I'll tear them new arseholes.'

They were almost there. Arthur's Seat loomed black against the purple evening sky, darkness overwhelming the streetlight glare from down below as they climbed. Tyler caught a scent of something like coconut from the yellow bushes that lined the road.

'What's your plan?' Tyler said, nodding at the shotgun.

'All guns blazing,' Barry said. 'Then let the dogs tear them apart.'

Christ almighty, some plan.

Barry cut his lights and blackness poured into the car from outside. He pulled into one of the lay-bys before the car park at Dunsapie Loch, killed the engine.

'What are you doing?' Tyler said.

'Element of surprise. Fuck's sake, don't you know anything?'

Barry got out with the shotgun then opened the back door for the dogs. They were about fifty feet from the meeting place, round the bend in the road, tree cover in between. Maybe he wasn't so stupid or coked after all.

Tyler got out and followed as Barry ran in a crouch along the bank of the loch with the dogs at his heel. Swans were out there on the nesting platform built in the middle of the inky water, slashes of white in the shadows. The smell of coconut was stronger now, gorse bushes all around them. Tyler ran too, lifting the pistol out of his jeans in readiness.

Then they were by the car park, in the thick grass at the back, bramble bushes tangled alongside. The car park was empty.

'What time is it?' Barry said.

Tyler looked at his watch. 'We're early.'

Barry looked around them, checking all sides for movement, but there was nothing. There wouldn't be, of course. He turned back to the car park as the dogs snuffled in the bushes.

Tyler lifted the gun and pointed it at the back of Barry's head. He was two feet away. The gun shook in his hand, his arm with a will of its own. He had to do it. This solved everything. He heard the whump of a swan flapping its wings behind him but he didn't turn. The dogs were ten feet away to his left. If he had to, he would do them too.

Barry shifted his weight, eyes forward, looking along the road for a car, a sign of the Holts arriving.

Tyler pulled the trigger.

At least he tried to. It didn't budge. He remembered the video, the safety. He moved his thumb up the grip to the switch and slid it down.

It clicked.

Barry turned and looked straight down the barrel at him.

Tyler's hand was shaking even more now. He began to squeeze the trigger again but Barry reached out and slapped the gun so that the barrel pointed away from his head. The crack of a gunshot barrelled around the hills, shredding the quiet. Crows lifted from the trees and the dogs yelped and snarled at each other.

'You fucking cunt,' Barry said.

He twisted Tyler's arm so that his grip on the gun loosened. He grabbed the gun by the barrel and swung the handle into Tyler's face, crunching the bone in his cheek, blood spraying from his nose. The dogs perked up as Barry pistol-whipped Tyler about the skull, each blow sending shuddering pain through his head. He fell back into the grass as Barry kicked at his ribs and back.

'You ungrateful cunt, fuck you, think you can pull a gun on me, you pathetic little arsewipe.'

This was in time with the punches and kicks, staccato insults and pain until Tyler had his head covered, his body curled into a ball. More kicks to the back of his head, his kidneys and spine, his body flooding with pain.

Eventually Barry stopped. Ant and Dec snuffled around Tyler's body, tugging on his clothes with their teeth, but only playfully. If Barry gave the word, they'd kill him.

Tyler could hear Barry breathing heavily. Barry spat at him, then kept panting and swearing.

'After everything I've fucking done, doss wee cunt. You're a traitor to your family.'

Tyler brought his arms away from his face and looked up.

Barry had the pistol tucked away, the shotgun pointing in Tyler's face. He reached down and clutched Tyler's hair in his fist, pulled him to his feet.

'This was all a set-up?'

Tyler didn't speak. Barry smashed the butt of the shotgun into his nose, more blood dripping onto the grass.

'Where are the fucking Holts?'

Tyler spat blood and wiped at his face. 'They're at home. It didn't burn.'

Barry grabbed Tyler and pulled him towards the car.

'Come on,' he said. 'You're going to help me kill them.'

40

Barry made Tyler drive so he could keep the Beretta pointed at him, the shotgun at his feet, the dogs getting more and more agitated in the back. After they came down from Arthur's Seat and passed the Commie Pool it was basically one long, straight road until they were there. Tyler toyed with the idea of jerking the steering wheel to the right, throwing the Skoda into an oncoming car, but that could kill the other driver. Maybe go the other way, onto the pavement. They were passing Grange Cemetery, a long high wall that would take the impact. But he didn't have the bottle. And anyway, if he didn't deliver Barry to the Holts, Flick and Bean could die. And, of course, if Barry survived the crash, he would shoot Tyler on the spot. He might shoot him anyway once this was over. Tyler thought back to Dunsapie Loch, pointing that pistol at the back of Barry's head, his hand quivering.

They were there too quick. It seemed as if all the traffic lights turned green just as they arrived at the junctions, like they were fated to get through.

They turned into St Margaret's Road and Barry made Tyler pull over in the street a couple of doors before the Holt place.

'Out.'

Barry was quick out his side then round the car, pulling Tyler up and out. The dogs snarled, sensing Barry's rage. He dragged Tyler up the driveway, their steps crunching as they went, signalling their arrival if anyone was listening. This was Barry's plan, to just barge in and start shooting. Barry had switched guns, had the pistol in his jeans, the shotgun pointed at Tyler. They reached the front door.

Barry jammed the shotgun into Tyler's neck.

'Wait thirty seconds then ring the doorbell.' His voice was quiet. 'Got it?'

Tyler swallowed, the barrel against his Adam's apple.

'I want to hear you counting,' Barry said.

'One, two, three...'

Barry clicked his fingers and darted round the side of the house with the dogs at his side, taking the same way they'd gone that first night here, not knowing whose house it was, what they were getting into.

Tyler continued counting under his breath like a game of hide-and-seek. Coming, ready or not. He took a step to the side and tried to see in through the edge of the curtains. He saw Flick and Bean sitting on a sofa together watching television. Monica was sitting alongside them, her gaze in the same direction. She was out of hospital, that meant she was getting better. That was good. The three of them looked like an ordinary family. He appreciated that Monica was sitting with them, trying to keep things normal for Bean's sake. Bean was still in her school uniform and had a little smile on her face. She laughed at something on screen and looked at Flick to share the joke. Flick smiled at her but it was a thin gesture. He tried to read Monica's face, whether she was sympathetic with these two, or burning up because of what Barry had done. She'd seemed passive in hospital, but she was just out of a coma, that could change you. Maybe she'd had time to think things over, maybe she wanted Barry and him dead, just like Kelly.

Tyler guessed that had been thirty seconds. He wondered what would happen if he didn't ring the doorbell. He thought about what Barry had planned. He thought about the two guns and killer dogs.

He rang the doorbell.

Waited.

Expected an explosion, something dramatic.

Silence.

He hoped the girls stayed on the sofa, kept their heads down.

He heard a click behind him.

'Don't move.'

A figure emerged at his side. The brother-in-law Sonny. He had a handgun pointed at Tyler's head, finger on the trigger.

The front door opened and there were Deke and Ryan, both holding sawn-off shotguns. One thing was for sure, even if Tyler survived this he could never go back to school, could never sit in the same building as Ryan Holt again.

'Barry is at the back door,' Tyler said.

'We know,' Deke said. 'Come in.'

There was an explosion that made the house shake and everyone flinched. Sonny grabbed Tyler's jacket and hauled him inside, using him as a shield. The gunshot had come from the back of the house, then the sound of wood splintering, Barry kicking the back door in. There were more shots. Tyler could see right down the hall to the kitchen. Two big guys with pistols were there firing at the swinging back door.

As Tyler was hustled into the hall, he saw Ant and Dec lunging through the doorway straight for the thugs, one going for a gun hand and ripping at it, the second launching himself at the throat of the other guy. Both guys were muscle-bound and hard but they weren't expecting this. A psycho with a shotgun was fine, but trained fighting dogs were a different matter. Both of them were on the floor already, the dogs snarling and tearing at their hands and faces, one taking a chunk out of a guy's neck, the other moving down the body to sink its teeth into the meat of his man's midriff. He screamed and writhed, trying to get away. Both of them had dropped their guns, which lay on the floor waiting to be grabbed.

Sonny still had a hold of Tyler, shoving him further into the hallway.

Ryan stood with his mouth open watching the dogs slaver and snarl, while Deke took aim and shot, grazing one of the dogs' rumps, making it yelp for a moment, then return to thrashing at the guy under him.

Barry emerged through the kitchen door and fired, the blast from the shotgun zipping past Tyler's head. Deke and Ryan ducked into the doorway of the living room, Ryan disappearing inside and Deke staying in the doorframe and returning fire. Sonny was crouched behind Tyler, who was the only one exposed to Barry's fire now. Two more shots roared out from the kitchen.

Deke returned fire from the living-room doorway and so did Sonny, the pistol next to Tyler's right ear, the crack of it deafening.

Barry fired again, this time with Flick's Beretta, short, punchy sounds that shook Tyler and felt so close to him that he wondered for a moment if he'd been hit.

Sonny had loosened his grip at the sound of Barry's shots so Tyler saw his chance and wrenched himself free, running down the hallway past Deke and sliding into the kitchen, tumbling onto the tiles. He reached for one of the guns on the floor and grabbed it, scuttling backwards into the corner of the room.

He saw Barry emerge from the other corner of the kitchen to fire again down the hall. A shot came from behind Tyler, Deke or Sonny, and shattered the kitchen window behind Barry's head.

Barry spotted Tyler in the kitchen with him, holding the gun, and he grinned.

'Don't fuck with the Wallaces,' he shouted. He had a gun in each hand now, a swagger in his movements, both dogs still tearing into the guys on the floor.

Tyler took a quick look back down the hall at Deke hiding in the doorway and Sonny now crouching behind the bottom of the stairs. From this angle, Tyler could hit both of them. He thought about Ryan in the living room with Bean and Flick, Monica too. He turned back to Barry, who let two shots off down the hall, making the others duck back.

Tyler lifted the gun and pointed it at Barry's face.

Barry's smile faded and he shook his head, more in disappointment than fear. He swung both his guns round to point at Tyler but Tyler pulled the trigger, once, twice, three times, plugging bullets into Barry's face and chest, throwing him backward against the dishwasher and the sink with a clatter, then he fell forward onto the floor, the guns skittering away from his body.

Tyler stood and strode towards Ant and Dec, pointed the gun at the first dog's head and pulled the trigger, a spray of blood and brains over the guy underneath him, then he took two more steps and did the same with the other dog, catching it between the eyes, it's face splitting open, bone splintering and blood splashing against the kitchen cupboards.

The vacuum in the air after the shriek of gunfire was painful. Tyler's ears sang, his heart roared with blood. The two guys on the floor were moaning, curled up, the mass of the dead dogs lying on top of them. The tang of blood and gun smoke hung in the air. Tyler stood there amongst the bodies and breathed. He looked at the dogs, their heads half missing, blood splattered across the sheen of their coats, their muscled legs. He turned to look at Barry. Blood pooled under his hair, spreading down and out around his face. His eyes were open, staring at nothing. A bubble of blood escaped his mouth, burst and dribbled down his cheek.

'Don't move.'

Deke was behind him. Tyler turned and saw him approaching with his shotgun, careful steps into the kitchen. Behind him Sonny had crouched down to check on the nearest of the guys savaged by the dogs. He pushed the dog's body off him and helped him to sit up against the cupboard door, a hand on his neck failing to stop the blood oozing out of the wound.

Deke was just a few feet away now.

Tyler looked at him, then down at his own hand holding the gun. It felt like it didn't belong to him, like it was a separate entity. He opened his palm to get a better look at the gun he'd used to kill his brother and the dogs.

He looked up at Deke again, then dropped the gun with a clatter on the kitchen tiles and raised his hands.

Deke kept the shotgun on him and went to Barry's body. Nudged it with a toe, then again, harder. Barry moved like a lump of meat, then flopped back. Deke grabbed Barry's scalp and lifted his head, looked into his eyes. He crouched there for a moment in silence, then dropped the head in a splatter of blood.

He stood up and waved the gun at Tyler.

'Through there.'

He walked Tyler out of the kitchen and into the living room.

When Deke came in, Ryan straightened his back. He was stand-ing in the middle of the room, shotgun pointed at Flick on the sofa. Monica had her arms around Bean, who was crying. When Bean saw Tyler she tried to get up and run to him, but Monica held her where she was, whispering in her ear and stroking her arm, calming her. Bean took gulping breaths, her face puffy.

Tyler shared a look with Flick. She was relieved but angry too. And scared. He didn't blame her.

Moans came from the kitchen where Sonny had stayed to check on the other mauled guy.

'What happened?' Ryan said.

Deke waved his gun at Tyler, smiling. 'This cunt shot his brother. Dropped him like a sack of tatties. Three shots, clinical. Then he exe-cuted the dogs.'

Ryan frowned. He looked edgy, his shotgun swaying between Bean and Flick on the sofa.

Tyler pointed at him and spoke to Deke. 'Can he lower that gun?'

Deke looked at Tyler then turned to Ryan. 'Put it down, you're as likely to shoot your mum as anyone.'

Ryan lowered the shotgun but kept his eye on Tyler with a look of resentment.

It was only now that Tyler noticed the bay windows. They'd been replaced already since Barry smashed them earlier. There was a smell of petrol in here but no sign of damage to the carpet, curtains or fur-niture. Who can get fire damage and panned windows fixed so quick? Someone with a shit ton of money and connections. Someone not to be fucked with.

Tyler looked at Bean and Flick. He tried to think what to say but nothing came to him.

Sonny appeared in the doorway. 'The boys need help.'

Deke frowned. 'Get Malone over here.'

Sonny got his phone out and went back to the kitchen.

'I did what you asked,' Tyler said. 'I brought you Barry.'

'You let him shoot the back door in while you stood as a decoy at the front.'

'He had a gun on me.'

'Not when you were alone at the front door.'

'I told you as soon as I could.'

Deke scratched his chin, thinking.

Monica was still holding Bean, comforting her. Flick sat motionless on the sofa, looking at Tyler.

'You said you'd let the girls go,' Tyler said.

Deke smiled. 'I also said you couldn't trust me.'

'I could've brought the police. I didn't.'

'I would've killed the girls.'

Tyler glanced at Bean. 'I dealt with Barry for you.'

Deke nodded to himself, still thinking.

Monica spoke up, her tone calm. 'What are you going to do, Derek?'

'They've seen too much,' Deke said.

Monica patted Bean on the arm and got up. She approached Deke slowly, holding her back at the stab wound.

'There's been enough violence here,' she said.

Deke pointed at Tyler. 'They violated our home. They almost killed you.'

With Monica off the sofa Bean ran over to Tyler, the sudden burst of movement making Ryan raise his gun at her. She clutched at Tyler's waist, pressed herself into his chest.

Tyler raised a hand at Ryan's gun. 'For fuck's sake, please.'

Ryan hesitated but eventually lowered it.

Monica pointed at Tyler and spoke to Deke, low and soft. 'He didn't stab me, you know that. The other one did and now he's dead. He killed him.'

Deke thought that over.

Monica rested a hand on his shoulder. 'He called the ambulance, Derek. He saved my life.'

Tyler closed his eyes and squeezed Bean.

Monica spoke again. 'It's over. Please.'

Deke thought about that for a long time. He looked at Monica then Flick, then at Tyler and Bean. He looked around the room. Tyler followed his gaze and noticed splintered wood in the doorframe from Barry's shotgun blasts, stains on the carpet from his own bloodied shoes. He thought about the mess through there. So much to clean up, so much to forget about.

Deke looked at Monica who still had her hand on her back.

'OK,' he said eventually.

He turned to Tyler. 'You were never here.'

Tyler nodded.

'We've never met,' Deke said. He looked at Flick. 'Any of us.'

Tyler felt Bean clutching at him, and he rubbed her back in reassurance. 'Got it.'

Deke touched his forehead. 'If I ever come across your name or face again, you're dead.'

'Of course.' Tyler swallowed. 'What about Barry?'

Deke looked into the hall. 'I'll deal with that.' He gestured towards the doorway with the gun. 'Go. All of you.'

Flick jumped from the sofa and walked towards the door. Tyler followed, holding Bean's hand as she kept her head down. He paused at Monica and Deke.

'Thank you,' he said.

41

He was wrestling with a two-headed dog, its faces snouted versions of Barry and Kelly. Their fangs snapped at his face, tearing skin from his neck and cheek, claws ripping his body. Another dog with Bean's face had his arms pinned while the first one savaged him. Bean smiled at him as all the flesh, sinew and muscle was torn from him, leaving only a blood-soaked skeleton. Bean-dog leaned down and licked the blood from his skull then sucked at his eyeballs until they popped out.

His phone was ringing. He bolted awake and looked round. He was in Flick's parents' bed, with Flick at the other side and Bean snug between, hugging Flick's elephant. Lying across the bottom of the bed were Snook, Mario and Luigi.

Light slipped through the gap in the curtains, it was morning already. He grabbed his phone and looked at the screen. A quarter to nine, Bean was late for school, not that he had any intention of taking her today. Then he remembered it was Saturday. The weekend. When real families did stuff together, went out on their bikes, trips to the park or beach, shops or the cinema.

He recognised the number calling him. He worried that the ringing would wake the girls so he got out of bed and answered it as he left the room.

'Tyler?' Pearce. Voices in the background.

'Yeah.'

'Where are you?'

'What's it to you?'

'We've been to your flat this morning, your mum doesn't know where you or Bethany are.'

'She's safe with me.'

'Where?'

'A friend's house.'

A pause down the line. He couldn't work out if she was sighing or talking to someone else with the mouthpiece covered.

'The same friend as before?'

'Maybe.'

This time definitely a sigh.

'I need you to come back to the station.'

Tyler pinched the bridge of his nose. 'Why?'

'I think you know why.'

'Try me.'

'Barry is dead.'

A long pause. 'How did it happen?'

'We don't know yet. He was found in his burnt-out car along with his dogs.'

'Right.'

'You don't sound very upset.'

'Should I be?'

'Or surprised.'

Tyler looked at the doorway of the bedroom, where Flick and Bean were still sleeping. He heard a gentle thump then one of the pups came tottering out of the room and up to him, tail wagging. He bent down to stroke it and it snuffled at his fingers.

'Barry was into a lot of bad stuff,' he said. 'You know that as well as I do.'

The puppy licked the palm of Tyler's hand and it tickled.

'Just get down here,' Pearce said. 'Do I need to send a car?'

Tyler looked around at the Ashcrofts' house. 'I'll get a bus.'

✳

Same meeting room as before, so still not an official interview. The door opened and Pearce came in carrying two mugs of coffee. She hadn't asked if he wanted anything, had just presumed. She put one in front of him then sat down across the table, blowing on her own. Like two pals having a chat, apart from all the dead bodies they had to discuss.

'So,' she said.

Tyler raised his eyebrows. He looked out of the window, remembered the squabbling seagulls from last time, wondered if they hung out in the car park all the time, creatures of habit like the rest of us. Or if they'd managed to break the cycle of their lives. If that was even possible.

'So,' he said.

He sipped the coffee. It was too milky. He put the mug down.

Pearce studied him over the steam of her mug. 'What can you tell me?'

'About what?'

'The death of your brother.'

'Are you sure it's him?'

Pearce nodded. 'Your mum identified the body this morning.'

Tyler swallowed. 'How was she?'

Pearce paused and stared. 'How do you think she was? It wasn't easy, given the nature of his remains. Want to know the details? The top half of his body was completely burnt, pretty much a melted puddle of flesh. But bodies burn in weird ways, and there was less damage to his lower half. She mentioned a birthmark on his foot and there it was, a bit charred but recognisable.'

Tyler hadn't even known that Barry had a birthmark on his foot. It made him feel queasy. Of course Angela had known, Barry was her son just like Kelly was her daughter. She wasn't the best mother in the world but she was the only mum they ever had. Her two eldest children were now dead. Tyler tried to get his head around that.

Pearce took a sip of coffee. 'So what do you know?'

'Where was the car?'

'You tell me.'

'You think I did this?'

'You know more than you're telling me.'

Tyler wrapped his hands around his mug.

Pearce examined him. 'The car was in Craigmillar Castle Park, hidden in the woods.'

'How do you get a car in there?'

He looked around the room at the dull walls and furniture. Pearce kept her eyes on him the whole time.

'It appears the car smashed through a single bollard across the footpath next to the Old Dalkeith Road recycling centre. It's at the end of a dead-end road, the centre was closed. The bollard was loose in the concrete anyway, according to complaints to the council.'

Once you were inside the park grounds in a car you could hide it anywhere, it was a labyrinth with a hundred different cubby holes and quiet spots. At night no one would be there to see the flames, and the smoke wouldn't register in the dark skies. It could burn for hours, destroy as much evidence as possible. Deke had been smart.

'And the dogs were in the car too?' Tyler said.

'They were in the back, badly burnt.'

'So what do you think happened?'

Pearce was lifting her coffee mug to her lips when she hesitated, then lowered the mug back onto the table without taking a sip. 'Forensics will find out. And phone records. Police work, you know.'

Tyler tried to think. Presuming the Holts hadn't reported anything about the attempted arson, that left the sound of gunfire at the house. Maybe the family's reputation would mean that neighbours kept their noses out of business that didn't concern them. If any of them reported anything, the Holts would soon go round and have a word. So that left CCTV and phone records. He couldn't think if there was CCTV of him anywhere near the Holt house, but it was everywhere these days, it seemed likely. But how would the cops know exactly when and where to look? He thought about the phone. He'd called Barry yesterday evening, that was the last time. And the Holts had called Tyler, but using Flick's phone, so there was no connection to Barry there.

Pearce leaned forward. 'Where were you last night?'

'I told you, me and Bean stayed at a friend's house.'

Pearce shook her head. 'You're going to have to do better than that. I need a name and address, this is your alibi.'

'I don't need an alibi, I haven't done anything.'

Pearce fixed him with a stare and lowered her voice, looking at the closed door behind him before she spoke. 'Look, don't you get it yet? We don't give a shit about Barry. Why should we care when a nasty little prick like him dies? And we don't want you either, you're just trying your best as far as I can see. But you need an alibi so we can do this properly. I need a name and address, someone who will confirm your story.'

Tyler looked out of the window and saw a seagull lifting into the sky, just one. He wondered if it was one of the same ones from the other day, without its adversary. Maybe it didn't know what to do without that daily struggle against its nemesis, maybe it had lost its purpose.

'The Holts have an alibi,' Pearce said.

Tyler turned back to Pearce. 'What?'

'The whole lot of them, Deke, Monica and Ryan were at home all night watching television. It's not airtight, but unless we come up with evidence it'll do them for now.'

Tyler thought about Monica, Flick and Bean on the sofa, Barry and the dogs soaking in their own blood through in the kitchen.

'Her name is Felicity.'

'Surname?'

'Ashcroft.'

'And you and Bethany stayed at her house last night?'

'Yes.'

'All night?'

'Yes.'

'Felicity will confirm this?'

Tyler nodded. 'There's no need to talk to Bean, is there? She was asleep all evening anyway.'

Pearce stayed silent. Eventually she spoke. 'No. We won't have to speak to your sister. Little kids can get confused anyway, can't they?'

Tyler rubbed at his forehead.

Pearce had a pen and pad out. 'What's the address?'

'20 Hope Terrace.'

'In Morningside? No offence, but how do you know a Morningside girl?'

Tyler pictured her standing in the living room surrounded by broken glass, her hand dripping with blood, and smiled.

'We just bumped into each other,' he said.

42

He jumped off the bus at the end of Musselburgh High Street and walked in the main entrance of Inveresk. He felt like he was trespassing but no one stopped him. It was as if a spotlight was shining on him, he imagined everyone looking at him, but they weren't. This was Saturday afternoon so they were out of uniform, everyone kicking around in hoodies and jeans as if they were real kids and not paying thousands of pounds for the experience. He couldn't believe there wasn't security to keep people like him out.

He kept his head down and walked along the tree-lined path, more cover than if he went straight across the grass. The huge stained-glass wall of the chapel dominated the square, and he remembered sitting in there with Flick, thinking about sanctuary.

He turned left and strode past the back of the chapel and the mustard-coloured science labs to the building in the corner, Eleanora Almond House. He went up and rang the doorbell, shuffled his feet with his hands in his pockets.

A short girl with black curly hair in a fringe and big-framed glasses answered.

'Is Flick around?' he said.

She looked at him and shouted back into the house. 'Flick, your friend's here.'

Then she disappeared.

A moment later Bean appeared carrying the box with the puppies in it, Snook following at her side. She put down the box and hugged Tyler.

'I missed you,' she said.

'I missed you too.'

Flick appeared at the doorway in jeans and a tracksuit top zipped all the way up.

Bean tugged at Tyler's hand. 'Can I let Mario and Luigi out on the grass?'

Tyler looked down for a moment. 'As long as it's just this bit here. And look out for them.'

The puppies were trying to clamber over the side of the box and Bean lifted them out. They spilled onto the lawn, Snook nosing behind.

Tyler turned to Flick.

'Thank you,' he said.

She rolled her eyes. 'Oh my God, everyone loves having her here with the puppies. This is a house full of seventeen-year-old girls, remember. I'm a hero.'

Tyler looked at his feet. 'I meant thanks for everything.'

Flick stepped out of the house and they began walking clockwise round the small quad. More mustard-painted buildings lined the edges, he hadn't noticed them the first time he was here in the darkness.

'I'm sorry,' he said.

'Shush.'

He stopped and looked at her. 'No, I need to say this. OK?'

She nodded at him to continue and they walked on.

'I got you into a load of trouble,' he said. 'And I am so sorry. When I think what could've happened I want to die. I knew I was up shit creek, I shouldn't have dragged you into it. It was selfish and stupid and I'm sorry.'

'You already said that.'

'I know. I'm sorry.'

There was silence for a moment. It was sunny, and light played through the leaves of the trees, a breeze bristling them, peace and quiet away from the world.

'Are you finished?' Flick said.

Tyler chewed on his lip. 'I don't know what else to say.'

'You don't need to say anything. I'm a grown woman and I make my own decisions. You didn't drag me into anything. I thought we were friends, and I wanted to help a friend, got it?'

Tyler didn't speak. They reached the end of the square and turned, walked past an art studio.

'This is a different world,' Tyler said.

Flick tutted under her breath. 'I hope this isn't one of those "we're from different worlds, we'll never understand each other" things. That's such bullshit.'

Tyler laughed. 'I'll shut up.'

They headed back towards Almond House, Bean lying in the middle of the quad and letting the puppies lick her face and flop over her. She was giggling and smiling, and Tyler wondered about everything she'd been through. He thought about that thing he'd read, that the human brain was more impressionable in kids.

'How did it go at the police station?' Flick said.

'They're going to ask you to confirm my story.'

'What is your story?'

'We stayed at your place on Hope Terrace all night.'

'What about Bean?' Flick said.

'They won't ask her.'

Flick had a quizzical look on her face. 'How did you swing that?'

'They're not very interested in finding out how Barry died.'

'And how do you feel about it?'

They stopped walking and stood watching Bean and the puppies.

Tyler thought about his dream last night, being ripped apart by dog versions of his siblings. He felt a tightness in his stomach as he pictured Barry lying in the Holts' kitchen, dead from the bullets Tyler had fired into him. He'd killed his own half-brother, and he was always going to have to live with that. Everyone carries stuff around with them, but this was overwhelming. He wondered how he could go on, but then it came to him, he was looking at the reason, Bean, lying on the grass, tickling Mario.

'I'm trying not to think about it,' Tyler said. Bean was getting Mario to chew on a stick. 'How do you think she's taking it?'

'She's a tough little thing.'

She was, but he had his doubts. Christ, the stuff she'd been through and she was only seven. She seemed fine at the moment but maybe she hadn't processed it yet. Maybe you never did, maybe you just get on with life, because what else is there?

'Do you think she even understands what happened?' Tyler said.

'I don't know. What matters is that you love her and you're here for her.'

That didn't seem enough, but maybe it was.

They were a few yards from Bean, in the shadow of the trees, as a couple of ruddy-cheeked girls walked over to Almond House and in through the door.

'And what about you?' Tyler said.

'What about me?'

'How are you coping?'

'I'm fine.'

'Really?'

'Really.' Flick looked around the quad. 'I've seen plenty of dysfunction in my time, remember? I'm used to it.'

Tyler frowned. 'You shouldn't have to get used to it.'

Flick looked at him. 'Maybe. But you learn to cope. I've learned to cope just like you. Our lives might've been different, but we're not so different from each other.'

Tyler wanted to hug her, but he just stood there watching his little sister.

Flick brushed a hair away from her face. 'You know, you could stay at my house as long as you like.'

Tyler frowned. 'I have to look after Mum.'

'She could stay too.'

Tyler looked her in the eyes. He felt tears welling up inside him, blood rising to his cheeks. He looked at Bean, who was smiling at him from the grass, the pups sniffing around Snook now, feeding time. They would be weaned soon and would have to look after themselves. He looked around at the old buildings, the impeccable lawn, the oak trees throwing shadows across Flick's face.

'No,' he said. 'We need to go home.'

43

'It was a dark and stormy night,' he said, his voice booming. 'A fateful night, when the world's greatest superhero, Bean Girl, was born, a force for good battling the dark, evil powers of Niddrieville.'

Bean smiled as he went on, staring up at him from where she sat on his lap. She was getting too big for this now, the weight of her uncomfortable, but as long as she still wanted her bedtime story, he would do it. She cuddled into him and he felt her relax. Her head became heavy on his chest, and he could sense that her eyes were closing. He kept talking about goodies triumphing over baddies, villains getting their comeuppance, heroes striding off into the night after protecting ordinary people once more.

It was a clear and crisp night and they needed the blanket over them up here on the roof. A few stars were spattered across the sky, but the lights from the city obscured millions more. All that energy out there, stars and supernovae and black holes tearing the fabric of space apart, and him and his little sister down here getting drowsy and sharing a story.

He stopped talking and Bean didn't stir. She was asleep, otherwise she would definitely tell him to keep telling the story. She was more outgoing and confident than he'd ever been at that age and he hoped that continued as she got older, that she didn't get bogged down in anxiety about her looks, boys, all the crap of teenage life. But my God, what a place to start from, with everything she'd been through. Not just over the last few days but the years of seeing appalling behaviour normalised around her. Tyler had tried to protect her but it never felt like enough. But he would continue to look out for her as long as he could.

From here he could see the lights of the hospital grounds glowing amongst the wasteland of Niddrie and Greendykes. The gloomy shadow of Craigmillar Castle on the hill, the spread of newer houses to the right, everyone tucked up inside watching television or on their phones, eating and drinking and laughing with each other. Ordinary lives. He thought about the Holts doing the same over in their house, about all their neighbours doing the same, rich people trying to get by, the same as everyone else. He thought about all the girls and boys at Inveresk, missing their parents maybe, sad and isolated, or maybe loving it, the freedom and friendship and sanctuary of that campus.

Cities had a pulse and he felt Edinburgh's life beneath him through the fifteen floors of concrete and steel that was his home.

He heard a noise behind him, the metal door from the ladder up to the roof.

He turned and saw Flick walking towards him holding two steaming mugs. She handed one to him and he caught the whiff of hot chocolate. She sat down on the seat next to him and blew across the top of her mug. She looked at Bean's face and smiled.

'You were right, it's amazing up here.' Her voice was low.

'You don't have to whisper,' Tyler said. 'Once she's out, you can't wake her.'

They stared at the blackness for a long time. Eventually Tyler felt her hand rest on his.

'How was Mum?' he said.

'She's OK.'

Tyler had talked to Angela about Barry earlier. He hadn't known what to expect but she seemed to be taking it calmly, didn't seem in shock. She knew what Barry was like, had no doubt suspected he might not live a long and happy life, but that didn't make it any easier. And having to identify his burnt body, Jesus. He was her son, despite everything. And now she'd lost two children in the space of a couple of days. Tyler had expected her to go straight out and score after the news of Kelly then Barry, but so far he'd been surprised. As far as he could tell she hadn't injected since the overdose, although she was back to drinking, saying she needed it while she detoxed. But even now she wasn't crashed-out drunk, just bleary-eyed and sad. Maybe in a weird way Barry's death had freed her somehow, freed her from the hold that part of the family had over her. She wasn't sober but she was trying and that would do for now. Tyler wondered about help or support, if there was even anything like that for people like them.

He thought about Monica lying on the floor of her hall, blood seeping out of her. About her persuading Deke to let them go. About Ryan, his own age, ready to step into Deke's world. About the house they had, the cars, the holidays and the rest.

He thought about the feel of the gun going off in his hand, the explosion of blood from Barry's chest. The connection between the two, a thread linking Tyler's life to Barry's death forever. And the dogs, Christ, the dogs.

'I can't stay long,' Flick said.

'I'm just glad you're here.'

'Me too.'

He'd been surprised when she turned up an hour ago. That she wanted anything to do with him after everything that had happened. As he'd ushered Bean away from Inveresk earlier, she kept asking questions about Flick, when they would she see her again, and if she could go to a school like Inveresk. The answer to the last one was easy – not in a million lifetimes. But for the other question he fudged his answer.

Then a few hours later Flick was on the other end of the buzzer asking to come up.

'The view from here is incredible,' Flick said, gazing up at the sky.

Tyler was looking at her. 'It is.'

When she turned and saw him watching her, realised what he meant, she rolled her eyes and nudged him, almost spilling his hot chocolate.

'Oh my God,' she said. 'Shut up.'

He did what he was told.

Acknowledgements

Huge thanks to Karen Sullivan and everyone else on Team Orenda for their love and support. Thanks to Phil Patterson for all his hard work and enthusiasm, and the biggest thanks to Tricia, Aidan and Amber, as always.